Having previously worked as [illegible] pist, Caroline Dunford enjoyed many years helping other people shape their personal life stories before taking the plunge and writing her own stories. She has now published almost thirty books in genres ranging from historical crime to thrillers and romance, including her much-loved Euphemia Martins mysteries and a brand-new series set around WWII featuring Euphemia's perceptive daughter Hope Stapleford. Caroline also teaches creative writing courses part-time at the University of Edinburgh.

Praise for Caroline Dunford:

'A sparkling and witty crime debut with a female protagonist to challenge Miss Marple' Lin Anderson

'Impeccable historical detail with a light touch' Lesley Cookman

'Euphemia Martins is feisty, funny and completely adorable' Colette McCormick

'A rattlingly good dose of Edwardian country house intrigue with plenty of twists and turns and clues to puzzle through' *Booklore.co.uk*

'The sharp dialogue capture(s) the feel of the era . . . an engaging and entertaining read' *Portobello Book Blog*

Also by Caroline Dunford

Euphemia Martins Mysteries:

A Death in the Family
A Death in the Highlands
A Death in the Asylum
A Death in the Wedding Party
The Mistletoe Mystery (a short story)
A Death in the Pavilion
A Death in the Loch
A Death for King and Country
A Death for a Cause
A Death by Arson
A Death Overseas
A Death at Crystal Palace
A Death at a Gentleman's Club
A Death at the Church
A Death at the Races
A Death in the Hospital
A Death on Stage
A Death of a Dead Man

Hope Stapleford Series:

Hope for the Innocent
Hope to Survive
Hope for Tomorrow

Others:

Highland Inheritance
Playing for Love
Burke's Last Witness

A DEATH OF A DEAD MAN

CAROLINE DUNFORD

First published in 2023 by Headline Accent
An imprint of HEADLINE PUBLISHING GROUP

1

Cataloguing in Publication Data is available from the British Library

ISBN 978 1 4722 9537 8

Typeset in 10.5/13pt Bembo Std by Jouve (UK), Milton Keynes

Printed and bound in Great Britain by Clays Ltd, Elcograf S.p.A.

Headline's policy is to use papers that are natural, renewable and recyclable
products and made from wood grown in well-managed forests and other
controlled sources. The logging and manufacturing processes are expected
to conform to the environmental regulations of the country of origin.

HEADLINE PUBLISHING GROUP
An Hachette UK Company
Carmelite House
50 Victoria Embankment
London
EC4Y 0DZ

www.headline.co.uk
www.hachette.co.uk

To the National Health Service, where would we be without them?

Acknowledgements

My thanks to my editor Clare Foss, my amazing agent Amy Collins of the Talcot Notch Literary Agency, my family for both help and hindrance, my writing group The Schism, and all my friends who I haven't seen for ages.

Chapter One

Of Frightened Donkeys and Ruffled Feathers

'Euphemia? I need your help.'

The telephone apparatus had rung in my little office at White Orchards; a room that no one but I ever entered. It was where my secure line was, where I kept, in an excellent safe, any papers I was analysing for the department, and where, on the frequent occasions Fitzroy was staying with us, we made our plans.

'Do you want to meet?' I said.

'You'll have to come up to town.' Fitzroy's voice crackled slightly on the line, either that or he coughed. ''Fraid you'll have to stay up here too. It's bound to take some time.'

'I can do that,' I said. 'Bertram understands there is a war on. You can book me into an hotel.' I said the last part very seriously. After our last somewhat disastrous mission, one that I still had to tell my husband about, or rather the crucial personal parts, I had stayed at Fitzroy's apartment for some time. He had looked after me well, but we both knew that that kind of behaviour, unless under extraordinary circumstances, simply wasn't on. Even if Griffin, his man servant, was technically there to chaperone.

'Actually,' said Fitzroy and then repeated himself, which he never does, 'actually, I've bought you an apartment. Different block to mine, naturally, but walkable distance. It's rather nice. I think you'll like it. I've kitted it out a bit. Told the store what kind of colours you like and that sort of thing. But you'll be able to tweak it to your own tastes. Bring in your own things in time.'

'You've bought me a what?' I said. I tend to answer the

telephone standing up, especially if I think I am about to be given orders, but my legs felt suddenly unsteady, there was a rushing noise in my ears, and the light seemed dimmer. I sat down. 'You've done what?'

'Oh come on, Euphemia, you've always known I was of above average wealth.'

'But this is too much . . . I can't . . .'

'Oh,' said Fitzroy, his voice filled with that annoying knowing tone he can employ, 'you thought I was exaggerating when I told you I was rich. Well, I am. Positively swimming in the stuff. I own a dozen or more properties at the present. Mostly small, mostly sublets. If you like we can say you're renting this from me for now? Does that make you feel better? I'll have to think about the rent, obviously.' I could tell he was beginning to enjoy himself. 'I certainly don't have any need for any money from you, so what should I charge you in? Certainly not cakes, your cooking is atrocious. Maybe compliments? I like it when you say nice things about me. You don't do it often enough.'

'Fitzroy,' I said, trying to get a hold on the conversation. Talking to this man could be like wrestling with an oiled eel. 'What is the mission we have?'

'Oh, no mission. I need your help. Nothing to do with the department. Me. That should be good for a month's rent, don't you think? Besides, you'll feel much more comfortable not lying to Bertram about staying with me. One less lie. A good way to go, don't you think?'

Fitzroy had something of a – well, not love-hate relationship with my husband; more a respect-hate one. For all Fitzroy lived a louche life, he could be extraordinarily proper about how he expected me to behave, and how I should respect my husband. Or, that was, for as long as it suited him.

'It's not a mission,' I said. I had learned to respond only to the parts of this kind of conversation that I really wanted to know about. This was Fitzroy in one of his odder moods.

'No, it's something come out of the past. Bit of a hiccup. If it turns out – well, let's not get ahead of ourselves. I need it sorted out, and you're the only one I can trust.'

I knew he trusted me, but it did make me soften towards the idea. Fitzroy trusting me was rather like a wild wolf laying his head in your lap, and asking you to scratch him under the chin. You were fully aware that at any moment the wolf could take your arm off, but all it did was to give you a gentle lick on the wrist.

I shook my head. Thinking about Fitzroy licking my wrist simply would not do. 'Of course I will help,' I said.

'Good. Catch the usual train tonight and I'll meet you at the station.'

I agreed. There was no point in asking for more time or making allowance for my own plans. I had agreed to go and Fitzroy wanted me there now. In some matters he had no patience at all.

'By the way, Euphemia,' he said. 'Bit sloppy of you not to pick up it wasn't a mission. I didn't use your code name. You're slipping. Buck up, me girl.' Then he hung up before I had time to insult him.

We had barely driven away from the station when Fitzroy took his eyes completely off the road and turned to me, frowning. 'I think the only thing to do is hush things up. I don't like doing it, but there's a war on and our next mission will be upon us any instant. Probably have to break in and steal a few files, I would imagine. There might be a witness or two I'll need to strong-arm, but frankly I think they'll be happy to be paid off, and not have to go through it all again. I realise I'm asking a lot, but you don't object to breaking the law for the greater good, do you, Euphemia?'

I took a deep breath. An omnibus was coming far too close for comfort. Fitzroy corrected his course without turning, presumably seeing things in his peripheral vision. I can't say I felt scared exactly, but this was possibly the most wound-up I had ever seen my spymaster. On our missions together he always presented himself as suave and sophisticated to the rest of the world, but was sometimes a bit shouty with me. I coped with this by ignoring him when he was in a pet, and only discussing matters when he had calmed down. More than anyone I knew, despite the smooth veneer he was a passionate man – passionate about injustice, passionate about fairness and passionate about serving the Crown. His heart was in all the right places, so normally when he broke a sweat I let him rant on. However, this was the first time I could recall that a tirade had been accompanied by an oncoming omnibus. It was not a turn of events I appreciated.

'Eric, dear,' I said in a gentle voice, 'do please pay attention to the road. I won't be able to help you achieve whatever the devil you're going on about if I don't survive the next half-hour.'

The result was much as if I had slapped him. I never called him dear and I never spoke to him in a sweet voice. It was enough of a shock that he faced forward once more and navigated his way through the London traffic. We came rather close to a donkey cart; the poor animal gave the most startled sound. Fitzroy stuck his tongue out at it and drove on. This, if nothing else, convinced me that while the situation might be urgent, it was not serious.

In this I could not have been more wrong.

A short and mildly terrifying time later we pulled up outside the block of apartments where Fitzroy stayed while in London. 'Thought I'd show you your place later,' he said, hopping out of the car and coming to open my door for me. 'Better to get business sorted out first, don't you think?'

I nodded. He was behaving in a calmer fashion, but his eyes still had something of an intensity about them. In anyone else I might have thought they were running a fever; with Fitzroy it generally meant he had mischief in mind.

We went up in the little lift with Fitzroy bouncing on his toes, he was so eager to get inside. I knew even in this small area, and to all intents and purposes alone, he would not discuss anything of import unless we were in his car, where the outside traffic roared, or inside his home, where he considered himself reasonably safe.

Jack, his bull terrier, met us at the door. He immediately recognised me and for once managed to give an actual bark. Generally he is more inclined to whiffle. However I took this as a bark of joy as he jumped repeatedly in the air in a vain attempt to lick my face.

'Calm down, dog,' chided Fitzroy, pushing him into the hall to allow us access. 'Stop that damned bouncing. I know you love Euphemia, but you're not made of gutta-percha you silly thing, you'll break something. Dogs aren't meant to fly!'

As soon as we reached the small drawing room and before I had even taken off my hat, I knelt down to greet Jack. The little dog whiffled in delight and bounced at me some more. However, now he was bouncing at a much lower altitude. He managed to lick my face a couple of times, which I made a great show of disliking, and then pounced on him and gave him a big embrace. Not all animals like to be so caught up in a human's arms, but for Jack, with someone he cared for, it was like heaven on earth. He washed my neck so thoroughly I became convinced I must have crumbs on me from the currant bun I had eaten on the train.

Dinner at home had been impossible, if I was to reach London that night. Bertram, I hardly need add, was not happy. I left him consoling himself with the thought of a whole spotted dick to himself and commanding Giles to bring up one of his best burgundies. It was a challenge to me, as he is not at present in the best of health, but I didn't rise to it in case he entered upon something else even more foolish.

I was finally getting Jack to be calm when I realised I could smell something delicious. 'What is that heavenly smell?' I asked, looking up at Fitzroy, who appeared to have removed my cases and divested himself of his coat while I had been playing with Jack.

'Griffin has made us dinner. It's the least he could do in the circumstances.'

'Wonderful,' I said. 'I'm famished.'

Fitzroy gave a glance down at his shoes, and shuffled slightly. 'I realised you would have missed your dinner in order to catch the train.' This was as close to an apology as I was going to get.

'Indeed,' I said. 'I should go and wash.'

'I should think you need a bath after Jack's lamentable behaviour!'

'I was covered in dirt from the train,' I said, petting Jack on the head. He leaned against my legs and gazed up at me adoringly.

'Remarkable,' said Fitzroy looking down at his dog, 'any other woman he meets he does his damnedest to bite.'

'He has good taste,' I said, looking at Fitzroy from under my eyelashes. It was no secret between us that my partner in espionage was rather fond of female companionship. One might even say overfond.

Fitzroy made a grumbling sound. 'I put your things in the spare room. It's late enough you should probably stay here. We can look at your new place tomorrow.'

I nodded and went off to wash and change. My relationship with Fitzroy was close, but not inappropriate. I had stayed at his home before and had never felt in any danger of amorous advances. Fitzroy only seduces women professionally, foreign ambassadors' wives and the like. In his private life he is only interested in consensual relationships, and I was married to Bertram.

I came back to a beautifully laden table. It even had flowers. Some excellent food and the most anxious Griffin I had ever seen, hopping from foot to foot beside the table.

Chapter Two

At Last the Truth

'You can at least wait until she's finished eating, man,' said Fitzroy to his valet. 'Euphemia has uprooted her whole – what – week at least – for you!'

This was news to me. I looked at Griffin enquiringly. Griffin opened his mouth to speak and then closed it again having glanced at Fitzroy's face.

'For goodness' sake clear off and stop hovering around like Banquo's ghost. I'll shout once we've eaten.'

Griffin, whose relationship with Fitzroy I had never really understood, but which seemed to be founded on a surly subservience, muttered to himself and withdrew to the kitchen.

I lifted the lid from one of the tureens and began to liberally help myself to some particularly nice roast potatoes. We rarely had these at home as Bertram was inclined to make a pig of himself over them.

'Make yourself at home,' said Fitzroy with a chuckle. 'A real lady would help the gentleman first.'

'When I am with you,' I said, 'I am never a lady.' I had the pleasure of seeing his eyebrows rise in shock. He does so like to appear enigmatic and stoic. 'I am your partner in espionage only. So get your own potatoes, partner.'

He laughed again, and reached over to pick up a potato with his fingers. I knew he was about to say something about not being a gentleman ever, or some old quip of his, so I cut him off. 'I hope you washed your hands,' I said. 'There is no excuse when we have the luxury of hot and cold running water here.'

Fitzroy dropped the potato on his plate. 'You are going to make someone a terrible mother.' Then he realised what he had said and impulsively reached a hand across the table to me. He gripped my fingers. 'You know I didn't mean anything by that, my dear. I wasn't thinking.'

I swallowed the sudden lump in my throat and nodded. 'Tell me about Griffin,' I said.

Fitzroy took his hand away and sat back. He talked while I ate. 'You have, of course, realised that the relationship between Griffin and myself is not the usual one of master and servant?'

'H-h-yes,' I said through a soft piece of steak. 'He can be quite rude, but he's totally loyal to you. And he is a doctor of some kind?'

'Consider any questions rhetorical, please, my dear Euphemia. I don't enjoy seeing you masticate.'

I pulled a face at him, but kept my mouth shut.

'In a nutshell, Griffin was once John Griffin MD, a worthy local general practitioner and newly married to the lovely Megan Luckett. He had opened up a surgery in the suburb of Wimbledon. Megan, who was the sister of a university classmate, had been used to living in Scotland. She found the metropolis both exciting and a little overwhelming. So when she told her husband that she had a growing sense of unease, he put it down to the much more populous nature of her new environs.'

'He was wrong,' I said flatly. I could feel my appetite draining away. In all the time I had known Griffin there had been no mention of a Mrs Griffin.

'Sadly, yes. The young couple had had something of a whirlwind romance, and he perhaps didn't know his wife as well as he thought he did. As circumstances would later show, Megan proved to be a young woman of considerable fortitude and courage. Perhaps if she had been of the weaker, more clingy type of female, she might have survived.'

I pushed my plate away from me. By now my appetite had entirely vanished.

'I did suggest we waited until after dinner,' said Fitzroy gently. 'The tale only gets worse, but I think I can spare you the grisly details. Suffice it to say, Megan began to think she was being followed. Her husband gave her a nerve tonic and attempted to soothe her fears. He put aside more time to spend with her, shortening some of his surgeries, and made the effort to take her out and about in the metropolis in the hope she would become more used to the crowds. He felt that in his company she would feel safe. A not unreasonable thing for any ordinary man in ordinary circumstances to think. However, this did mean that Megan was frequently seen outside the home, by his side, looking pale, sometimes frightened, and apparently never willing to engage in conversation with anyone.'

'You mean it looked as if her husband was controlling?' I said.

Fitzroy nodded. 'Then one day, when she was alone in their house, Griffin having gone to visit a wealthy client at their home, she panicked when she thought she heard a noise in the house and fell down the stairs. This left her with a bruise on her face, and considerable bruising on her body.'

'Oh,' I said. 'Are you certain it was the stairs?'

'You are thinking what the police thought,' said Fitzroy. 'Does Griffin strike you as a wife-beater?'

'I wouldn't know,' I said. 'I am aware people can conceal their natures if they wish.'

'Sadly, I have to give you that,' said the spy.

'I take it she was murdered?'

'Yes,' said Fitzroy. 'In a spectacularly unpleasant way.'

'And Griffin was accused?'

Fitzroy nodded. 'No, not exactly. He was considered, of course, being the husband. But then he killed someone else, quite neatly as it happened, and immediately handed himself in. If I hadn't interceded he would have hanged. As it is, he is on a sort of permanent parole – I have custody of him.'

'If I may be direct . . .'

'Are you ever anything else with me?'

'I take it you saw an opportunity to have a servant who would be utterly loyal to you, because betraying you would mean a speedy trip to the gallows. Effectively you have a servant who is as indentured to you as a slave.'

'That is not putting it in its best light,' said Fitzroy. 'But essentially, yes. However . . .'

'However, you would not have taken him on unless you were convinced of his innocence.'

'Oh no, he isn't innocent. At least not of the crime he committed.'

I stared at him bewildered.

'The police considered Griffin for his wife's murder, but they could not prove it. Griffin, it transpired, was smarter than your average police inspector, because he did track down who murdered his wife.'

'Oh, I am glad he got justice,' I said.

'Yes, I suppose you could say that. Griffin murdered the man in cold blood and then gave himself up.'

'Oh,' I said. 'Oh, I see.'

'You know me well enough to know that if someone harmed you . . .'

'You would kill them,' I said. 'The difference is you wouldn't hand yourself in.'

'No, I wouldn't. I also assume you would also kill someone who harmed me and feel no need to hand yourself over to the civilian authorities?'

'Of course,' I said in a matter-of-fact tone that I knew would have shocked Bertram, 'but with either of us it is likely to be a foreign agent who ends our existence. I take it Megan had no such nefarious connections, poor woman, and was the victim of some mentally unsound person.'

'More or less,' said Fitzroy. 'The thing is, how she died was never released to the press. It was, as I said, rather nasty.'

'Oh,' I said.

'Exactly. Another young woman was found two days ago killed in exactly the same way.'

'So Griffin didn't kill the murderer?'

'No, it appears he killed an entirely innocent man, and I'm going to need your help to save him from the noose.'

Chapter Three

Griffin Confesses and Fitzroy has a Bad Plan

'So what I think is we bury Griffin's connection to the case,' said Fitzroy.

'How can we do that?'

'You don't think I didn't do some tidying at the time, do you?' said Fitzroy. 'All we need to do is remove the files that connect him to his original persona. Morley wasn't around then, so I doubt he's ever paid any attention to who works with me.'

'He's been here,' I said. 'He knows Griffin used to be a doctor.'

'Yes, well, I doubt he knows the details,' said Fitzroy, waving his hand. 'I mean our lot won't give two figs about this new case. It's a domestic crime. As long as the regular police force don't come a-knocking it should all be fine.'

'Do you even know where these files are?' I said doubtfully.

'Oh yes,' said Fitzroy. 'You don't think I'd put my name to something I didn't keep track of, do you? There's a couple of places I think we should – er – visit.'

'And no one will notice they are gone?'

Fitzroy sighed. 'Of course we will replace them with forgeries. Decent ones. I'm owed a couple of favours by the right people.'

'Criminals? Can we trust them?'

'No, people in the department. We have some excellent forgers working for us. Think about it. We always have the right papers, don't we?'

'I hadn't really thought . . .'

'So, there you go. I'd ask Griffin to help do the deed, but I don't think it's his forte.'

'Have you told Griffin what you intend?'

'No, I told him I had to speak to you first. We can call him back in and thrash it all out. Well – I mean tell him what we are going to do and that will be it. Should even be able to fit in some time to take you to a show, as well as installing you in the apartment.'

'Eric, I don't think it's going to be as easy as that.'

'Why not?' said Fitzroy.

'Because Griffin will want to know if he did in fact kill an innocent man.'

Fitzroy shrugged. 'I have no doubt he didn't mean to. Kind of thing that could happen to anyone who isn't a professional like us.'

'I don't think he will see it that way.'

'You think he'll feel guilty?' said Fitzroy. 'I expect he will, but he'll get over that.'

'No, you idiot. He will want justice.'

'Justice?'

'Justice for his wife.'

'Bugger,' said Fitzroy. 'Do you really think so? Bugger. Bloody journalists. If they hadn't put the whole thing on the front page we could have dealt with it without him ever knowing.'

From a tactical perspective I could entirely see Fitzroy's point. The last thing we wanted was attention drawn to him, or any of his associates like myself, from the general authorities. We could get Morley to intercede, but whispers spread when civilian forces are concerned. Both Fitzroy and I used our social connections to gain access to events and to people quietly and clandestinely when our country needed us to. Neither of us wanted to shine a spotlight on the espionage side of our lives. However, if I were Griffin I would want to know if I had killed the wrong man, and more to the point I would want to find my wife's real killer and avenge her death, although hopefully this time he would let the civilian authorities do the job.

Fitzroy and I took the dishes through to the kitchen. This was unheard of, although on missions we were both able to fend for ourselves. Griffin was sitting at a kitchen table. He shot to his feet and Jack began barking excitedly. I fed Jack some scraps to quieten him while Fitzroy explained his plan. I saw immediately from the look on Griffin's face that he felt exactly as I had feared. Fitzroy noticed it too, and immediately knocked any other ideas on the head.

'No,' he said. 'None of us will be looking into this new murder. We don't need the attention, and more importantly we have other things to do. I am due in France at the code-breaking station, and Alice will be starting on some critical analysis while I am away. And I absolutely forbid you, Griffin, on pain of being considered in breach of our agreement and thus returned to jail, to investigate this, or cause it to be investigated in any way. The end. No discussion. Euphemia! Brandy!'

Taking this as a summons rather than a command I followed him out of the kitchen and into his snug. This small room contained an open fire, several fine decanters, a small selection of his books and two comfortable armchairs. There was also, of course, a dog bed.

'Well, I think that went as well as can be expected,' said Fitzroy, pouring two large brandies. He passed one to me. 'I'm not an unfeeling chap. But this is not the time to get distracted. We've both had too much time out as it is. And while I wouldn't say we are crucial to the winning of the war, I would say that the pair of us are a damn sight more effective than half the agents Morley has – and I mean that in sum.' He raised his glass. 'To the King and victory for the Empire!'

I echoed his toast. I could hardly do otherwise.

I slept well that night despite my misgivings about Fitzroy's plans. My partner tends to spare no expense nor abstain from any luxury during the short time he spends at home between missions. He continues this extravagance for his guests, and for Jack. My bed had a remarkably comfortable mattress and the sheets were of the best linen – although he had enquired if I would prefer silk. I didn't, and my surmise is he was teasing me about his own usual way of life. Silk sheets might go with his amorously adventurous way of life, but not only was I married, I had no desire to slip off the bed during the night.

In the morning, we had breakfast in the kitchen. I was the last up, although I was by no means a late riser. Griffin was already busying himself about the place. He was moving in a staccato sort of way, and with what I realised was quite a skilled hand, placing crockery away with a force that both gave a disturbing noise, but did not break any items. I surmised that yet again he and Fitzroy were at odds.

'Is it what I think,' I said, quietly sliding into my seat, 'or have you come up with other ways to annoy the poor man?'

Fitzroy gave me a wolfish grin, showing his canines. 'A gentleman has to have a hobby,' he said.

'I still think you're wrong,' I said.

'I know,' said Fitzroy, dipping a bread soldier into his egg. I raised an eyebrow. His cheeks became slightly tinged with pink. 'I cut them myself!'

'I didn't say a word.'

Fitzroy gave a little growl. This reminded me of the warm canine presence against my leg. I took a piece of bacon off his plate and fed it to Jack under the table.

'Madam, I do wish you wouldn't,' said Griffin, breaking his silence. 'I have fed the dog twice today. I believe him to be one of those creatures whose eyes are bigger than his belly. Would you not say he is looking particularly stretched?'

Fitzroy scowled fiercely and opened his mouth. He was always quick in his defence of Jack, so I interjected, 'Do you think I might have an omelette and a cup of fresh coffee, Griffin?' I gave him a friendly smile.

'Of course,' he said and busied himself to the task.

'On your own head be it,' said Fitzroy. 'He makes the most ghastly omelettes.' He wiped his lips on his napkin. 'I'm off to see

Morley. There's a couple of maps in the drawing room for you to look over. I presume despite your misgivings you're still going to help me tonight?'

'Of course,' I said. 'I concede it is a good first step.'

Fitzroy stood up. 'It is the only step,' he said. 'For all I know Morley might want me off to France tomorrow.'

'I thought all the codes were being routed through London?'

'That's the naval exchange,' said Fitzroy with a barely repressed shudder. 'I'm going to meet some of their field johnnies. Sound like a bunch of odd birds, but undoubtedly brilliant.'

'What exactly are you doing?'

'I could say this and that and try to look enigmatic,' said Fitzroy, stroking his moustache.

'But what you mean is you don't know yet,' I said.

'Yes,' said Fitzroy with a sigh. 'You know me too well. All my mystery is spent.'

Chapter Four

In which I Faint

After Fitzroy had gone I unsettled Griffin by helping him collect dishes and tidy the kitchen. Admittedly I didn't offer to help him clean the dishes, a task I hate, having had to do it when Fitzroy and I have been on missions. Fortunately, I found it easy to pretend that a lady like myself had no idea how to do such a chore. Anyway, I flustered him enough that he retreated to his own quarters as soon as was possible. When I was sure he was gone I went to Fitzroy's telephone. For all I knew he had a way of logging the communications that went in and out, but even if he did, it would be far too late by the time he found out.

Hans met me in the foyer of the middle-sized and rather nice hotel I had suggested. We had a cup of tea together, and spoke about Bertram. My brother-in-law had clearly come straight from his London office. Forever one to indulge in the peaks of sartorial elegance he was looking especially smart. His blond hair now held traces of grey at the temples, and there were the faintest lines around his eyes, but considering the attack on his wife (Bertram's sister) and her lingering convalescence, he had been through a hard time. However, I also knew that he was meant, for the duration of the war, to be staying on his estate. Hans is half-German. Although you would never know this except perhaps because he is too much the perfect English gentleman.

I had telephoned him at his financial office, but we both knew the reason he had ventured into the capital was to visit his mistress. I had no idea who was currently enjoying his favours, but Hans has always been partial to petite brunettes. I do believe he is genuinely fond of Richenda, whom he married for her money, and she him for her freedom from her brother, but he has always had a wandering eye.

'So how is she doing?'

'She has good days and bad days,' Hans said. 'I think it will be a time yet before she can no longer be considered an invalid. Although our enforced time in the country has finally convinced her to take up an interest in the estate's tenants. As there is no possibility of her visiting them, they come each Wednesday afternoon, and she receives them like a queen in the drawing room. It has been surprisingly effective. The new school is finally outfitted, and the women's sewing circle is sending socks to the front line.' He raised one elegant eyebrow at me. 'I don't suppose you have any idea how much longer this deplorable state of world affairs will continue?'

I shook my head. 'I don't have a crystal ball.'

'That the Kaiser should turn against his beloved grandmother's people is incomprehensible to me.'

I put down my teacup. 'I think you comprehend very well, Hans.' I gave him a level stare. Financiers always know which way the wind is blowing. Sometimes even before the security services.

Hans shrugged. 'Perhaps. But you have caught me in town, Euphemia. I assume you want something from me.'

'And, in turn, I will not mention your appearance here to either the authorities or your wife.'

Hans's mouth turned up slightly at the corners. 'You have changed a great deal from the beautiful young woman I first met. Although you are still beautiful.' He said the last words in a slightly deepened tone.

I chose a small cheese biscuit off the tiered plates that had accompanied our tea. 'No, thank you,' I said and bit into it.

'No thank you?' echoed Hans, looking slightly surprised. 'You act as if I were offering you a glass of water.'

'I am not interested in embarking on an affair with you.'

'A pity. I think we would be good together. But then again, I like Bertram. My commiserations on his continuing invalidity. I thought perhaps . . .'

'We might console each other over living with an invalid?' I found myself saying.

'Exactly,' said Hans. 'You know if you had been rich I would have asked to marry you, not Richenda. We are – as the French say – *sympathique*. Besides, Bertram has no heir yet, does he?'

'I asked you here, Hans,' I said before I lost complete control of the situation, 'to get you to accompany me to a police station.' I saw him stiffen at this. 'I have no intention of handing you in to the authorities, but I need you in this one instance to act as my husband. I will be giving false names, and asking to see the body of a woman recently murdered. I will suggest I think she may be my sister. After they take us through to the viewing room you will then cause a distraction so I can examine the body more closely.'

'Don't you have people to do this with you?'

'I have no idea what you mean, Hans.'

My brother-in-law opened his mouth to speak again, but I shook my head firmly. I have never confirmed to him what I am and I had no intention of doing so now.

'Of course not. When do we go?'

'As soon as you have finished that cup of tea.' Hans paled slightly but nodded curtly. Whatever I thought of his morals I couldn't help liking my brother-in-law. He had gumption.

The police station where I had ascertained, also thanks to Fitzroy's telephone, that the body was being held was near to St Pancras Station where the poor woman had been found on a platform. Fitzroy has mentioned the similarity between the two killings, but kept the grisly details, as he put it, to himself. I needed to see the full picture.

From reading the paper Griffin had left lying around, and reading between the lines, I saw that there had been something of a tussle between the railway police force and the regular London police as to under whose authority this lay. But it was inevitable that New

Scotland Yard, on the Victoria Embankment, would take over. The Metropolitan Police force had an almost uncanny knack of becoming involved in the grisly murder of women. Indeed, when the new building was being built in 1888 the dismembered torso of a woman was found. Fitzroy had spent one winter evening filling me in on the 'Whitehall Mystery', which was never solved. I could only hope that in this case the truth would be uncovered or rather covered much more easily. We took a cab to the local station.

So far the body had not been moved to whatever mortuary New Scotland Yard was using. I was aware I had a contact inside the force, but I was loath to utilise him unless absolutely necessary.

I pulled a veil out of the small bag I carried, and attached it to my hat. I took Hans's arm, and leaned on it more than was necessary. Holding a tissue to my eyes, I guided us into the police station.

It was of normal appearance, empty this early in the morning, save for a sergeant bent over the desk. I sniffed loudly. The sergeant's head shot up as fast as Jack's when he heard the dinner bell.

'How can I help you?' he said. His voice held the inflection of someone not born far from this part of the city.

I pinched Hans's arm and got him to walk right up to the desk. 'I telephoned the station earlier,' I said in my natural accent (refined). 'I believe the body you have here may be my sister.' I allowed my voice to break over the last words, and made play with my handkerchief. It was hard to tell if I was overdoing it. As an agent of the Crown I had been called upon to play many parts, but rarely a bereaved relative.

The policeman, no doubt surprised to see a lady in his station, scrabbled hastily through his day book to find a record of my call. I used the time to make further play with my handkerchief, and turn to my companion for comfort. 'Put your hand on my arm,' I hissed at Hans under my breath, 'I am distraught!'

This intimate gesture allowed me to shield Hans from the sergeant for a moment, and convince him to stop gaping like a goldfish. Honestly, I am astounded how little imagination most men have! However, he had doubtless heard the tales of how hard

I had stepped on Bertram's foot when he failed to come up to the mark. (My wedding present to my husband had been a pair of steel-toed boots; a gift that had brought misty tears to his eyes.)

'Ah, yes, ma'am,' said the police officer. 'I do see as how you telephoned earlier. I believe my colleague suggested you send a gentleman to look at the cor— your sister. Or possibly your sister.'

I could almost hear Hans's blood running out of his cheeks at this. 'That will not do,' I said, attempting to channel the voice of my fearsome mother. 'If it is my sister I must be the first to know. We have been close ever since we were children. Almost as one in fact. I have brought my husband with me, so you need not fear being troubled by me should I become hysterical.' I gave a little laugh. 'As if that were possible. I am distantly related to Queen Elizabeth the First and I have her stomach!'

This literary allusion was going too far for the sergeant, whose eyebrows rose in a perplexed and bemused manner. 'Goodness man,' I snapped, 'I don't mean that literally. Now take me through.'

I didn't need to ask again. It was clear that the man wanted me out of his station as quickly as possible. Probably so he could have a nice cup of tea and a little lie-down. I can, when channelling my mother, have the same effect that she does on most gentlemen of her acquaintance.

The room where the body was laid was unpleasant. It smelt odd, and I saw Hans swallow hard when he entered. I am no stranger to death, but this was something else. It was a tiled room, and I could glimpse various tools that were employed in examining the dead set out on shelves. I deliberately chose not to look at these. I am no coward, but the indignities we heap upon the dead to persuade their bodies to give up their stories make me most uncomfortable. My father was a vicar, and as far as I am aware he buried his dead intact – none of them ever being a victim of a crime. Again, as far as I knew at the time. He cultivated in me a strong respect and lack of fear for earthly remains.

I understand we must investigate crimes, but this room was

squalid. The body lay under a sheet, quite alone with neither a prayer book nor a candle near it. You might argue that such items do not belong in a police station, but I could not help feeling sorrow for this poor young woman, who had been left alone in this dark and miserable room. Should the dead remain until they are buried, as some believe, I believed her very spirit would be weeping and alone. I suppose it was this that motivated me to approach her side without invitation. I placed my hand on the side, having quickly ascertained it was clean, and looked down at her, my head bowed. Perhaps foolishly, I thought, *I am sorry you are here. I will do my best to avenge you.* In that moment I realised regardless of the war or what Fitzroy wanted, I would ensure justice was done for this poor woman, whoever she was and whoever had killed her.

I pulled the sheet away in one smooth movement. The sergeant gave a cry. I saw the corpse and immediately fainted on the spot.

Chapter Five

Hans and I Strike a Bargain

I awoke to the most atrocious smell beneath my nose. My immediate reaction, before even opening my eyes, was to swat it away. My hand connected with another's. This was quickly followed by the sound of glass smashing. Ha! So they were trying to drug me! I struggled in the arms that held me, opening my eyes and attempting to reorientate myself.

'For goodness' sake, Euphemia!' said a familiar voice.

Hans.

I came to with a rapidity that surprised even myself. I leaned on Hans's shoulder and despite his and the sergeant's protests levered myself to my feet. The sheet was still hanging off the gurney. I kept my face turned away.

'I warned you, miss,' said the sergeant, and I suppressed an impulse to give him a good swat too.

'Yes, you did,' I managed to say. 'Thank you.'

Hans, ever the gentleman, offered me his arm. I took it and leaned on him. 'It's not her,' I said. 'Please take me home.'

Hans hesitated for a moment, and then seemed to remember he was part of a subterfuge. 'Of course,' he said. 'If you will lead the way, Sergeant.'

On the way out the sergeant attempted to get us to sign his book. I feigned dizziness and when that didn't work, threatened nausea, and so we managed to get away without further hindrance.

'Wait here,' Hans commanded, as we stood outside the station. 'I will hire a cab and escort you home.' He stepped away, then turned and came back. 'Where is home, Euphemia?' he asked. There was a look in his eye that I didn't like. 'You were not a guest at the hotel where we met, were you?'

'No,' I said. 'I am staying with a friend.'

'Do I know this friend?' asked Hans, raising an eyebrow.

I knew he would like nothing better than to catch me out in an indiscretion. I had never mentioned his mistresses to Richenda, his wife, but he was constantly aware that I could. An indiscretion on my part would make us equal in his eyes. Normally, I found it easy to deal with Hans, but although I was not about to faint again, I felt far from my best. I leaned back against the wall of the police station and closed my eyes.

'Very well,' said Hans, and hailed a cab. I was still thinking about where I might direct it when Hans gave the cabbie a direction I did not know. I rested back into the seat and closed my eyes. I would deal with things later. I needed time to marshal myself.

I have killed men. I have walked over the corpses of the dead. My stomach is not easily turned, but what I had seen in those few moments before I lost consciousness was imprinted into my mind's eye. I have by no means the anatomical knowledge of a medical person, but I have learned more about the body than most. In part this has been in order to more efficiently direct attacks, but also Fitzroy had taken time to teach me what might be termed 'battlefield' first aid. It went beyond merely bandaging or making slings, into understanding blood flow, where major organs were located, and how to stem bleeding. One look at the corpse and I had immediately known the agony that had been inflicted on the poor woman. But worse, the more I reflected, the more I realised there could be only one reason to inflict such cuts and in such a way. It made no sense. It was a cruelty beyond abomination. Surely, whoever had done this could not be in their right mind.

Hans handed me down from the cab, and we went into a lift. I paid no real heed until we were inside a neat apartment. Hans took my coat and gloves. 'I shall call down for some strong tea,' he said.

'We have a kitchen that serves all the apartments here. It is highly convenient.'

He disappeared into another room, and I took stock of my surroundings. The room was well furnished, but impersonal. It reminded me of a hotel. The colours were pastel and relaxing, but there was nothing personal present. No pictures, books, or ornaments. It only then struck me that Hans had brought me to the place he obviously used to meet his mistress. He reappeared as I realised and sat down opposite me.

'I see from your expression you have realised this is my bachelor abode. It is sometimes good for a family man to have a little break from the business of home. As you are aware I still have connections in the city.'

'I am also aware that you are meant to be remaining in the country at this difficult time.'

He nodded. 'As arranged by your very good friend Fitzroy.'

'My partner,' I said flatly.

'Partner in what?' asked Hans with a slight smile.

'Espionage,' I said flatly.

Hans's face went from smiling to frowning to smiling again.

'It's not a euphemism,' I said. 'You must be aware of what Fitzroy is considering the way he prevented you from being interned as a foreign national?'

'I'm not ungrateful,' said Hans. 'But I have always known he didn't do this for me.'

'No, as much for Bertram as anyone, and myself, of course.'

'You would have me believe you work for some kind of secret service? You, a woman?' He went on quickly. 'I mean no disrespect, Euphemia. Of all the people I have known, I have found you extraordinary in a number of ways. However, I cannot see any secret service employing a woman – other than for the obvious reasons.'

I decided to ignore the slur. 'Bertram is aware of my activities,' I said. 'And approves. So you can remove any impure thoughts from your head. My relationship with Fitzroy is purely professional. I could not give you an address earlier because it was – it is – secret.'

'I am aware I referred to you earlier as having people to help you. The idea that you work for the British Secret Service has I believe become somewhat of a jest in the family, but beyond perhaps thinking you do the occasional piece of clerical work I never truly believed it.'

'And Fitzroy?'

'You appeared to have accidentally chanced on one another during one of his cases, and I thought he had taken a liking to you. White Orchards seemed to me to be a place where he occasionally – er – "hid out" – if you forgive me using the term. I thought there had to be some exchange of favours between you, and assumed the most natural. Seeing you together, you are clearly very fond of each other. I see it in the way the pair of you try not to stand too close or speak for too long whenever you are in company with others. As you have so boldly asserted, that kind of behaviour is not unknown to me.'

A bell rang, and Hans went to the door to retrieve the tea, which came with small yellow cakes on a delicate plate of bone china, adorned with a tasteful floral pattern.

Hans set the tea things down on a table near us. 'Come, Euphemia, have some tea and cake. Truthfully, I do not wish to argue with you. I wish us to be friends. Eat, drink, you still look pale.'

'What kind of friends?' I said, taking a teacup from him.

'Do you really think so little of me?' said Hans, sitting down with his own cup. 'I might betray my wife, but I am not the kind of man who would – who would inflict himself upon a woman. Should you ever be interested in pursuing what I had hoped was a genuine liking for each other, I would be delighted. But I have no interest in blackmailing you.'

'What do you want?' I said.

'That you cease to blackmail me. Please.'

'I was not aware . . .'

'Not in so many words,' said Hans, rising to place a small table by my side, so I could set down my cup and attend to the cake. 'But when I ask you . . .'

'To do anything,' said Hans, 'I hear an "or else".'

'I see how that would make you uncomfortable.'

'It makes me feel like a long-tailed cat in a room full of rocking chairs. Despite my extra-curricular activities I am fond of Richenda and I do not wish to hurt her. It was never a love match, and I am discreet. She is happy to ignore how often I stay overnight in town as I always return home. However, should she be explicitly told . . .'

'I have never said I would do that.'

'Or tell Bertram?'

'Bertram knows exactly what you are.'

'Ouch,' said Hans. 'Yet, you I cannot understand. For example why you fainted clear away today. I did not take you for one who fainted at the sight of blood.'

The cake in my mouth turned to dust. I took a sip of tea and swallowed hard. 'What do you want, Hans. Be clear.'

'Do not blackmail me. Agree never to mention my peccadillos to Richenda, and I will aid you in whatever you and Fitzroy do, whenever you ask. I am aware that he pulled strings for me. I would like to show my loyalty to this country. I understand my background means I could never join whatever organisation Fitzroy works for, but helping him, or you, might help me keep the standing his efforts have afforded me.'

'You are concerned you may still be interned?'

'I read the papers, Euphemia. I am aware this will not be a quick conflict. Many will suffer. I am only glad I do not have a German accent or I would genuinely fear for my family.'

I didn't reassure him. Conflict breeds hate, and I knew that as the war demanded more and more British lives, the government would respond by ensuring the blame, in the eyes of the public, rested firmly on the German people.

'So you will do what I need without question?'

'As long as it does not concern my family.'

'A reasonable request,' I said. 'You are correct I am not at my best, but I see no reason not to agree to your terms. If you want us to go into further details that will need to wait for another time.'

Hans nodded. 'You do not ask for an assurance I refrain from blackmailing you?'

'You have nothing,' I said. 'Bertram is fully cognisant of my work.'

'Then you are either extremely clever,' said Hans, 'or you are being used by an extremely clever man.' He smiled. 'I hope it is the former.'

I shrugged.

'Indulge me in one question?' said Hans. 'Why did you faint?'

'Because they had cut out her womb.'

Chapter Six

Griffin Confuses Me

I arrived back at Fitzroy's flat only to be told by Griffin that Fitzroy had been and gone. 'I believe he wanted to show you the apartment he has purchased for you, Mrs Stapleford. However, he was summoned away. He will be back for dinner.'

I sat down, throwing my hat and gloves on to a chair. Griffin picked them up. Jack bounced on to my lap.

'Would you like me to remove the dog, madam?' said Griffin. 'You look a little pale.'

Jack growled. I fondled his ears gently and he curled up on me.

'He's fine,' I said. 'But I would like to talk with you.'

'Shall I fetch tea?'

'Please no,' I said. 'I shall float away on a tide of it, but do fetch yourself refreshment if you need it.'

'Would you mind if I checked you over first? It's not that long . . .'

'I fainted.'

'Really?'

'Why does everyone seem to find it so hard to believe I fainted? I've done it before.'

'You are hardly one of those women who make a hobby of it.'

'Thank you.'

'What brought it on? Was it an odour?'

I almost snapped and told Griffin he was not my doctor. Except he had been not so long ago, and he'd been bloody decent about it. So I told him the truth. He paled himself. 'I think I will have that tea,' he said.

I did wonder if he might hide until Fitzroy returned, but he came back quickly enough clutching a large mug of tea. The absence of cup and saucer suggested poor middle-class Griffin was very shaken. He stayed standing, sipping at his mug rather like a man on the wrong end of a firing squad, who had requested tea in lieu of the usual cigarette.

'I take it this was some kind of backstreet abortion gone wrong? It's not surprising it upset you.'

'No, it was the girl found at the railway station.'

'But the major said . . .'

He got no further. 'Is that what you call Fitzroy?' I asked. 'The major?'

'I can hardly call him by his first name. I don't know his real name, and he has asked me to stop using his code name. Which given the war I quite understand.'

'Well, no matter what the major said I thought I would look into things a little. And please, Griffin, don't feign ignorance. This is how your wife died, isn't it? How the man killed her?'

'I have been commanded not to discuss this with you.'

'Well, you're not in military service, and I'm not going to tell him. I've got this far by myself. He doesn't need to know we ever spoke.'

'He will assume, madam, and he will release me.'

'No, he won't. He wouldn't do that. Whatever he says.'

'You do understand that with this murder it almost certainly proves I killed the wrong man.'

'It's this bit I'm interested in. Tell me how you worked out you had the right man.'

'But I didn't,' said Griffin. 'I should turn myself in.'

'Oh for heaven's sake, Fitzroy will be back soon.'

'I understand you're trying to help me, madam . . .'

'I have my own reasons,' I snapped, 'and not all of them concern you!' Jack grew restive on my lap. He raised his head and growled at Griffin. Fitzroy's valet took a step back.

'Are you able to control that dog, madam?'

I didn't even bother replying, but stroked Jack until he snuggled back down. 'I regret snapping,' I said, 'but your comments coming on top of recent events were a little . . .'

'Disrespectful?' suggested Griffin.

'Wounding,' I said, looking him level in the eye. I saw him flinch and knew I had the upper hand. 'Sit down,' I said. 'Let's talk this over sensibly.'

Griffin perched nervously on the edge of Fitzroy's favourite chair. I thought about warning him to hang on tight to his tea, but I guessed it would only make him more nervous. I wondered if he had cleaning stuff in the apartment to remove tea stains. I knew this conversation was going to be difficult for both of us.

'Was your wife with child when she died?'

Griffin started slightly at the bluntness of my question. A tiny amount of tea splashed, unnoticed, on to his trousers. 'I had wondered that myself, madam,' he said. 'She had not declared so to me, but as we had previously lost one pregnancy, very early on, she may have been waiting to be sure before she told me.'

'Why do you say that?'

'She had been brighter in the days prior to this. Her skin had seemed less grey, and her eyes had a new lustre. I got the impression she was happier than usual.'

A lover, I wondered, but did not say out loud. 'They could not tell?' I asked.

Griffin swallowed. 'Even before I was suspected, I was not allowed to do the autopsy. It is not usual to do so for a member of the family.'

'What are you saying? That it was done badly?'

'No, not exactly. I would have looked for the telltale signs of pregnancy that are very slight. Being in general practice, it is common to see women who feel something is wrong before they are confirmed pregnant and a midwife takes charge of their community care. You get a sort of sixth sense about it, which is why I wondered about her. But yes, there are also some minor physical changes that can be noted if you know what you are looking for.'

'The changes in the womb?' I suggested.

Griffin shook his head. 'He took that out of her completely. My only consolation being that the wound was so great, and the blood loss so heavy, she would have lost conscious—' He stopped and swallowed, took a deep breath and said, 'In fact she may not have been aware of what was happening at all.'

I felt horror crawling at the back of my mind. What kind of monster does that to a living woman? What could be the motivation for such a travesty? Such inhumanity? It must have shown in my face.

'Quite, madam. I think even the judge who sentenced me felt compassion for my crime. It is perhaps why the major was able to take me into his custody.'

'How long is this custody to last?'

'For life,' said Griffin. 'It suited us both. I am enough of a coward not to want to be hanged, and not to be able to face self-destruction. However, my life was empty and had no purpose. While polishing the major's boots will not change the world, I came to work for him on the understanding that I would be able to do more and more as our relationship grew, and he was able to trust me. I always knew, you see, madam, that he was a spy, and he offered me the possibility of being able to serve my own country when he had sufficiently trained me.'

'I see,' I said.

'It is indeed a long process,' said Griffin, following my thought. 'The major finds it hard to trust anyone. The only exception, madam, being you. If you don't mind me saying.'

I brushed it away with a wave of my hand. 'We're partners,' I said.

'I believe it to be more than that,' said Griffin, quietly.

I chose not to hear. 'You must have been confident you had the right man. How did you kill him?'

'A fatal injection,' said Griffin. 'I told him why he had to die, and he didn't deny the crime. He cursed at me, and said many foul things, but not once did he plead his innocence. It was this that gave me the strength to administer the poison.'

'Did he suffer?' I asked. It was easier to ask it this way than to ask if Griffin had played the sadist in his revenge.

'I had given him a sleeping mixture, so when he awoke and found he was bound, I imagine he was frightened as well as displaying his anger. But if you are asking if I gave him strychnine or some such thing. I did not. I am not a violent man by nature. I had dedicated my life to preserving life, and to come to take it was not easy. But the thought of what he did to her . . .'

'To Megan,' I said.

'Yes,' said Griffin in a low voice, 'to my Megan.' It was the first time he had mentioned her name. 'Even then I could not do more than give him a quick exit from his life. What was the point of making him suffer? It not only increased the chances of my being caught and him rescued, it was – it was, well the thought of inflicting pain makes me nauseous. I did need him to know why he was dying, and to be sure of who I was.'

'But you were able to kill him?'

'I thought of it as a surgeon might. I was removing a cancer from society. No other woman would suffer at his hands.'

I held up my hand to stop him. 'There are two things puzzling me,' I said. 'Firstly, it seems you always thought that this was not a singular crime. And of less importance, how Fitzroy got inolved, but then he does always turn up at the most unlikely places. It is almost a hobby of his.'

'Indeed.'

'So you did not feel that Megan's death was personal. That he wanted to kill her for some especial reason.'

'Oh, no, I didn't say that at all,' said Griffin. 'She was targeted because she was my wife. I have no doubt of that.' He took in the confusion on my face. 'I see I will have to explain it all,' he said. 'If you will forgive me, I think I will exchange this tea for a glass of the major's best brandy.'

Chapter Seven

Griffin Tells All

'I was of the minimal age when I entered medical school. My parents were hard-working folk, who aspired to the middle classes. My father rose to be a senior gardener on the estate where he worked, and my mother ran sewing circles and other such community enterprises, among the women of what she perceived as being her own level. In other words, the wives of other more senior servants on the estate. In many ways they lived above their means. The parlour, kept for guests, was luxury compared to the rest of the house. My parents would regularly eat less and poorer food than they gave to my sister and me. We were the family hope. I earned my place at an excellent grammar school, and was put forward to enter medical school. My parents were beside themselves with joy, and I was full of idealism and naïveté.

'Still, it would have been impossible for me to attend medical school if the owner of the estate where my father worked had not helped the family financially. I am aware that the major and his father are set on a path of enmity, but despite that the major's father, although known as having a fiery temper, took – indeed takes – his noblesse oblige extremely seriously.'

I found myself speechless. After a brief pause, Griffin continued.

'And so I advanced to medical school, which I found as wondrous as I had hoped. The human body, although perhaps I should not say this to a lady . . .'

Again, I waved his concern aside.

'The human body is a marvel, and we have only just begun to understand it. Modern medicine is at the cutting edge of invention . . .'

'I admire your passion but is this pertinent to the tale?'

Griffin paused. I could almost see him shuffling the thoughts in his head. 'We were a small intake, around thirty students. All male of course. It was a most traditional and respected school.'

I made a half-cough, half-growl noise. Griffin's eyes widened and he hastened on. 'We all became, if not the best of friends, at least known to each other. We came from different backgrounds, even different countries in a few cases, but we were united in our devotion to medicine. I say this, so you will understand everyone on the course was truly committed to following an active career in medicine, curing the sick, rather than simply following an interest, or wishing to be an academic of a sort. Indeed several instructors voiced the opinion we were the most inquisitive and ardent lot they had had through the doors. We became a kind of venerated year. Our mutual dedication and desire to push forwards the boundaries of medicine, and our own knowledge and skills, led to a fervent camaraderie.

'I do not mean to imply that we were all gregarious, outgoing fellows.'

I smiled at the thought of Griffin being an 'outgoing fellow'. Or perhaps he had been before his wife's death and I was doing him a great injustice. The man in question did not notice the play of emotions across my face; he was already quite lost in the past.

'We had all types of personality within the year. From the men so loud one could barely consider them gentlemen to the more conventional. All of us, bar two men, were at the very least congenial and interested in some degree in our fellow man as well as the organs that made him up!' He stopped, his eyes blank, obviously deep in his memories.

'The two in question?' I prompted gently.

'Walter Gibbons, a serious man in his late twenties, the type that can be charming to women when they choose. He had something of the elegant gentleman about him, clearly considered himself a man of standing even then. In our first session he was mistaken for one of the lecturers. He had a slow, serious, sombre voice, and had little to no interest in the living. He was considering a career in examining the dead or possibly some kind of cadaver research.'

'And did he go on to do that?'

Griffin shook his head. 'I have no idea. We didn't keep in touch, and he never attended a single one of the class reunions. I don't even know if he is alive or dead.'

Obviously not your victim then, I thought, but I merely said, 'The other?'

'Nathaniel Warburton, the youngest of all of us. Rather immature, he laughed at – inappropriate things, but he had a stronger stomach than the rest of us. He didn't turn a hair at his first autopsy. I felt mildly nauseous, but some of the chaps did vomit. No one fainted. As I recall Nathaniel was always rather keen, trying to edge closer to see the body. Although that may be my making more of it after the event.'

'The event?'

'I had him thrown out of the school. He never qualified. It transpired his eagerness to watch the demonstrations was only the tip of the iceberg. When we were allowed to spend time on our own recognisance down in the anatomy halls, the joke went round that other than attending lectures that was where Nathaniel now lived. I suppose there were signs something was wrong. He had a hesitant, lisping manner, and never looked one in the eye. But that's just the kind of thing, as a medical man, you try not to judge others by. One of his eyes had a slight squint, and he bit his nails. They were always down to the quick.'

'Unhygienic I would have thought?'

'Yes.' Griffin nodded eagerly. 'He'd never have made a good doctor.'

'So what did he do that allowed you to . . .?'

'It's all rather nasty. I don't think I should give you the gory details. Can I condense it down to saying that he was taking parts of the various cadavers home?'

'For what purpose?' I gasped. 'Dear God, not to eat?'

Griffin paled. 'What a mind you have, Mrs Stapleford. I would never have thought of that.' He took a strong pull of his brandy, swallowed and looked down at it sorrowfully. I could almost read the regret in his eyes that he was unlikely to be able to filch another. I waited for him to speak, all the while conjuring more horrific possibilities.

'I thought that he was either selling them – and no, before you ask, I never thought to ask to whom or why. Either that or he was taking them home to study them outside the anatomy hall. Whatever it was it was disrespectful to the dead, and frankly showed he wasn't right in the head.'

'But how did you discover it exactly?'

'I was going in as he was going out, and he was carrying a cotton bag of some kind. He had a parcel within it, and it started leaking blood. I pointed this out and said how unhygienic it was for him to bring his supper into a room full of cadavers even if it was cool enough for the meat. The very idea of someone doing that makes me feel sick to this day.

'He started to ask what the devil I was talking about. He was angry and spoke louder than I had ever heard him speak before. I immediately knew something was up. Then he followed my eyes to the bag, and uttered a cry of dismay. I was about to say if you don't do it again I won't report you, when I saw the expression of utter fear on his face – I mean his eyes widened. Sweat broke out on his brow. He frowned and his eyes darted back and forth more than usual. He even gained slightly in height, and I realised he was preparing himself for flight.'

'Oh, that's jolly well observed,' I said. 'Fitzroy couldn't do better himself.' I was genuinely surprised, but I didn't think a little flattery was going to do any harm. Certainly, Griffin, who had been edging further and further to the edge of his seat, and whose grip on the glass showed whitened knuckles, relaxed slightly. The potential for exploding glassware had been averted.

'Anyway, I grabbed him by the collar; he was a weedy little squirt then, so it was quite easy for me to haul him off to the proctor. He protested all the way. Even burst into tears.'

'What did he say?'

'Nothing that made any sense. More blabbering than anything. I was concentrating on not letting him get away. He wasn't strong, but he twisted and squirmed like an oiled eel. Funny thing was when I got him to the proctor's office it was like they had expected it. They thanked me, and took him inside. I offered to explain why I had brought him in, but the proctor looked at the bag and told me to go.'

'So you never did find out if it was a half-pound of mince or a collection of eyeballs?' I said.

'Eyeballs don't bleed,' said Griffin. He might be more observant than I had realised, but he was as humourless as ever. He and Fitzroy must be such a trial to each other.

'But you never got to find out what was in the bag?'

Griffin shook his head. 'It was serious enough that none of us ever saw him in college again.'

'Could taking raw meat into the area be considered a serious enough offence for dismissal?' I asked. 'Aren't trainee doctors known for their rather macabre sense of humour? Isn't it a way for young people to let off steam? I mean most young men, until this war began, didn't have to think about mortality, and suffering. Or worse yet realise that one day other people's lives would be in their hands.'

I expected Griffin to pooh-pooh this idea, but he didn't.

'I agree to a degree,' he said. 'There was a story even when I was there of someone removing a hand from the anatomy hall, to well, play a rather unseemly joke. The student in question certainly got into trouble for that, but they weren't removed from the course. The pressures you describe are very acute when you first begin to study. There is the wonder of the human body, but for most of us at some point we realise not only are we cutting up someone who might well have been beloved, but that we too are no more than sacks of meat. There is a recognition of both the wonder of life, of animation of the body, and of consciousness itself, but there is also a realisation of what we are not.'

I raised an eyebrow, not wanting to interpret the flow.

'An anatomy hall can look a great deal like your local butcher's at times,' said Griffin. 'Except one hopes for higher levels of hygiene.'

I decided not to make a flippant comment about chops.

'There is no evidence of a soul in a cadaver. That is not unexpected, but to realise that a ham of a pig and the ham of a man are not dissimilar, shakes a man. When I look at a person now I see them not only as person, a personality I know, I look at them as a collection of organs and other such things. It changes you, and for some not for the better.'

'Do you think that is what happened to Nathaniel? You said he was very keen . . .'

Griffin shook his head vigorously. 'No. No. He didn't have any qualms about handing corpses or any part of them from organs to various fluids. He was happiest in the anatomy hall. I expect he would have made a great pathologist. If he hadn't been mad.'

'But the terrible attack on your wife was years later. How did you work out it was him? How did you even set about tracking him down?'

'No,' said Griffin, his voice throbbing with emotion. 'You don't understand. That wasn't how it happened at all.'

I opened my mouth, but the sound of the front door opening caused us both to swivel in our seats. Jack leaped off my lap, barking madly and wagging his tail. Within moments Fitzroy strode through the door. 'I have had the most awful morning,' he said, 'and that drop of soup you served me for a so-called luncheon wouldn't have been enough to keep a flea going. I want a steak sandwich and I want it now. The affairs of the nation rest upon my getting it!'

Chapter Eight

Fitzroy is Suspicious

'And do Euphemia one too. Nice and bloody for both of us. None of your usual carbonised attempts!'

Griffin fled into the kitchen without giving me a backward glance. 'So have you looked over the plans?' Fitzroy asked.

I was in the process of containing my nausea at the thought of eating steak after my recent discussion with Griffin. I knew Fitzroy would think something was up if I refused. I mean, who refuses a steak, especially in these unquiet times? I was off my guard so I answered truthfully, 'I was talking to Griffin about the man who killed his wife.'

Fitzroy shook his head. 'Nasty business. You know I'm not Griffin's greatest admirer, but it seems a little cruel to take him back to those times. Not really like you, Alice.'

'Obviously, I don't want to distress him,' I said, stung. 'But simply removing a few documents isn't going to make this all go away. The killer is still out there . . .'

'But that is exactly what it will do. As far as we, and Griffin, are concerned the problem will go away as if it had never existed.' There was a set to his chin that I knew all too well. On occasion I can talk Fitzroy around to my view of matters. This requires me to be correct in all aspects of my argument for he is not a stupid man by any means. But it also requires him to be in an approachable mood, because when he is so minded my partner can make a pack of mules seem reasonable.

'Did it go well with Morley?'

'No,' said Fitzroy, standing up and starting to pace. 'No, it did not. He blamed me entirely for the injuries you sustained during our last mission.' He glanced back at me. 'And we know he doesn't know the half of it.'

'Well, it's entirely unfair,' I said, my own temper rising. 'None of it was your fault.'

Fitzroy's face softened slightly. 'I am still your superior officer. I have no issue with accepting the blame, nor with Morley giving me a dressing down. I should have looked after you better. I should have . . .'

I got up and walked over to him. 'It's past. We can put it behind us. Forget Morley, you've always said that all you ever need him for is to rubber-stamp missions.'

'Did I say that? It was unfair of me. He's clever in his own way. Still doesn't understand our way of working rarely takes a direct line. But no, we had a flaming row because he doesn't want you to ever go back into the field. At least not while the war's on.'

'What?' I sat down. I could almost feel the blood rushing out of my face. 'I'm never to go back in the field?'

'Well, I agree we don't want you at the front line,' said Fitzroy, 'but other than that he's being ridiculous. I started out making my case most reasonably—'

'Ah,' I said. 'But when you left?'

'I think I stormed out, saying something rather unprofessional.' I couldn't help laughing at this despite my deep fear of being kept working in the office.

'He's never liked us working together,' continued Fitzroy. He ran a hand through his carefully styled hair, a sign he was annoyed with himself. 'First of all he says I take too few risks when you are around, and then he tells me I'm taking too many.'

'It was I taking the risks,' I said. 'Risks you didn't even know about. But is it not possible that as a front-line soldier, albeit invalided out of the trenches, he cannot conceive of a woman doing more than tending to a men's injuries?'

'He doesn't understand espionage at all,' said Fitzroy bitterly. He stomped around for a bit. There was clearly something on his mind that he was working up to say to me.

'You didn't agree to keep me out of the field?'

'I swore at him, and walked out, but not before I'd told him that if the department wouldn't use you in the field I would resign.'

'Goodness,' I said.

'You're my protégée. Everyone knows that. Apart from my desire to allow your ambitions, I would look a fool and it would set women back a decade or more in our profession. This war is a great opportunity for your sex.'

'So what is it that you haven't told me?'

He gave me a grin like a naughty schoolboy with his hand caught in the biscuit jar. 'I might have been offered a position as Morley's deputy.'

'What? Promotion to deputy head of the department. Why on earth didn't you take it?' I paused. 'Please don't tell me it was because of me. I wouldn't ever want to hold you back.'

Fitzroy came over to me and put his hands on my shoulder. 'Don't you realise if I had taken the position I could have given you any mission you wanted? Well, within reason. The thing was, I'm not ready to retire behind a desk yet either. I've been in the game more than a decade. None of my cohort have survived as long in the field. Although a fair number have slid sideways into desk jobs in other departments. No one in their right mind would expect me to last much longer in the field.'

'I take it you don't agree?'

'No, of course not. Where are our bloody steaks?' He walked away to yell in the direction of the kitchen.

'Fitzroy, I think I should tell you—' but the rest of my speech was cut off by Fitzroy's cry of triumph as Griffin brought in two plates.

'About bloody time!' shouted my partner. 'Did you have to butcher the bloody cow yourself, Griffin!'

The opportunity to confess I had been meddling where I shouldn't had passed. Annoying Fitzroy during a good meal was a sure way to arouse his ire. Although my partner is in general a lover of animals, he is exceptionally fond of his meat. I decided to wait until coffee; only to be confounded again.

Fitzroy sent Griffin off on a number of errands and charged me with looking at the plans properly. Then he returned to the departmental office. 'I've fed my stomach, and I shall gird my loins,' he said, striking a heroic pose. 'But I shall not return until Morley is bent to my will.' Then he dropped the melodrama, and gave me a cheeky grin. 'That's what will happen, but I'll make sure he thinks it is all his own idea. I should know better than to go into an argument hungry or try to go head to head with a soldier. Can't use my charm on Morley, but I'm still as slippery as an eel fresh out of the Thames.' Unusually, he gave me a quick peck on the cheek before trotting out whistling. He left Jack with me, and the dog complained vociferously for a full quarter of an hour.

The plans he had left were detailed, and he had annotated them with notes on guards, and other potential personnel on site, at various times after eight p.m. As I went through them I realised that Fitzroy was going to prefer a climbing option. Fortunately I had brought with me my night operational clothes. Griffin was going to be scandalised. I could see his point, but on the other hand I was a good climber when I wasn't hampered by a skirt.

Fitzroy returned looking careworn, the lines on his face more evident than normal. 'Is Griffin back?' were his first words, barely audible over Jack's excited barking.

'No,' I said. 'Your dog acts as if he hasn't seen you for a month.'

'Ah well, for some, my dear, half a day parted from me feels like an eternity.' It was his usual narcissistic joshing, but the laughter didn't reach his eyes.

'What happened?'

'Let me change out of my jacket and sit down. Could you manage to make us some drinkable coffee? I'd rather have something stronger, but if I'm going to be hanging off a roof later I suppose I mustn't?'

'Coffee,' I agreed, and he wandered off to his room looking

rather forlorn. I went into the kitchen. In the cupboard there was a bottle of Camp Coffee. I considered this. It was so much easier to make, but tasted like chicory. Not surprising, really, as this was its main component. In the end I reckoned Fitzroy might just throw it at my head if he'd had a bad day. I made real coffee and managed not to burn the beans. This not only took all my concentration, it stopped me worrying about whatever Fitzroy was worried about.

I placed the coffee tray in the little drawing room. I had even managed to find some biscuits. 'Good Lord,' said Fitzroy, when he entered, 'will wonders never cease.' I poured him a cup of coffee and he made a great play of being surprised it was drinkable. I found myself getting more irritated by the moment. I had only managed a quick visit to the police station, and half a chat with Griffin. If I wanted to solve this before Fitzroy noticed my involvement I needed to act fast. I was also fretting over Hans. He was too much of an unknown for me. I doubted he would ever deliberately cause me harm, but I felt unable to predict how he might act. I kicked myself for recruiting him as a potential asset. An asset was—

'Euphemia, are you paying any attention to me?'

I came out of my thoughts with a shock. 'I'm sorry,' I said. 'I was elsewhere.'

Fitzroy's lip curled slightly in a sneer, not an expression I often saw directed towards me. 'I was saying your career in intelligence is safe. I am unsure when I will be returning from my next mission, and we need to leave in ten minutes for the optimal time for the operation tonight. You should go and change.'

Chapter Nine

Night Work

'I'm not going through the sewers, Fitzroy!'

'But it would be an adventure, Euphemia!'

'Drowning in sewage is not my lifetime's ambition!'

'Pah! You should see it down there. Parts of it are as high as cathedrals. Higher!'

'You've been down there? Tell me that you at least checked water levels and – and – tide times.'

'It's not the sea, Euphemia.'

'No, but it does have times when the er – water rises. And I don't believe for one moment that it is all as high as you suggest everywhere.'

My partner positively pouted.

'I'm sorry to spoil your fun, Eric. I'm happy to risk my life for King and Country.'

'But not for Griffin?'

'I am fond of Griffin, but I am not prepared to take unnecessary risks to save him.'

'But we need you in your climbing costume.'

'Which my coat will easily cover. Why again am I the one doing all the climbing?'

Fitzroy sighed. 'Because if things go sideways a well-dressed gentleman has more chance of talking our way out of things than a lady out on her own at night. While I am doing so, you can skedaddle across the rooftops. Even do a back flip if you want.'

'I can't do a back flip.'

'Really, when I was your age I could flip like crazy.'

'Stop changing the subject. We are not going through the sewers. Honestly, I'm surprised even you would be that reckless. Especially as you're off on a mission straight afterwards. You could get a scrape and develop an infection.'

Fitzroy got up and went and picked up Jack, who was sleeping by the fire. The dog woke with a start, but seeing his master nuzzled his face rather than protested.

'I thought it might be a bit of fun,' said Fitzroy. 'You will look after Jack if I don't make it back, won't you? He loves White Orchards. I know Bertram would protest, but don't let him foist Jack off on some farmer. He wouldn't like that at all. You're his favourite person after me.'

I watched him holding his dog. If a child had held an animal like that you would have no doubt it would be for comfort. However, Fitzroy wasn't the kind of person to show weakness in front of anyone, even me.

'I don't think I've ever seen you pick up Jack like that before,' I said cautiously.

'Oh, I do from time to time. He can't always get up the steps. His personality is much bigger than his size.' He flashed me a smile. 'Whereas I am both large and have a large personality.' Then he winked. His face fell again. 'You would look after him?'

'Of course,' I said. 'I always imagined you'd left him to me in your will. And no matter what Bertram felt I wouldn't turf Jack out. He's family.'

Dog still in his arms, Fitzroy bent over and kissed me on the forehead. The dog tried to join in and lick my face, but was fortunately too far away. (I had already put camouflage make-up on my face.) 'Bless you for that,' he said. He put down his dog and rubbed the back of his hand across his lips. 'I assume you are going to wear a veil? You'll give the average Londoner a hell of a shock looking like that.'

I stood up. 'Right, let's get going.' Usually Fitzroy was excited about a mission. I thought the best thing to do was to get active. He was always happiest when he was working.

'Let's just hope the Germans don't pick tonight to start their bombing raids on London.'

I was halfway into my coat. 'You don't think they will, do you? That would be dastardly.'

'Dropping bombs on civilians and the country's infrastructure?' said Fitzroy. 'Destroying the morale of the country on the home front? Attempting to terrify London's citizens into pushing their prime minster to surrender? No, of course not. Not even the dastardly Germans would do that.'

'The sarcasm is dripping off you like tar,' I said. 'Does that mean you will be relocating to White Orchards between missions?'

'Not bloody likely,' said Fitzroy, locking his front door. Then he turned and faced me. 'I'm not a total idiot. I've had the cellars of this building reinforced. We must see to it that yours are done too. Until then you'll stay with me while you're in town if there's raids. I won't take any risks with you or Jack.'

Fitzroy's tenement block has two rather lovely lifts with wrought-iron gates that are never out of order, but today we took the back stairs. It wouldn't do to encounter anyone. Although I have yet to meet anyone who lives in the same block. Very occasionally I have heard murmured noises from behind another door, or I might well have believed he had bought the whole thing for himself.

We emerged into a crisp London night. The moon was unfortunately bright, but it seemed as if the local authorities must share Fitzroy's belief that German bombers were a possibility as there were no lights on show. I could, however, still see very clearly.

'Damn bright,' muttered Fitzroy. 'Be careful not to be caught out on the skyline.'

I nodded. Normally, I would have said something cutting about how I always do all the climbing anyway, but tonight my partner seemed unusually tense. It wasn't the time for a conversation, so I catalogued the questions that came up in my mind for later. I had a lot.

The first part of the journey was easy enough, and yet the hardest.

We were walking along main streets. Fitzroy wouldn't countenance taking a taxi even part of the way. Nor had he been prepared to bring his own vehicle. The area where he lived was largely residential, and by now most of his neighbours were either settled in their own homes or had left for parties elsewhere. If, that is, people were still having parties. Somehow I had expected the metropolis to carry on as if nothing was happening. The very idea that London could be cowed in any way made me both angry and fearful. For London to change was for the very fabric of British existence to change.

However, Fitzroy, who is as British as they come, was his usual self. He walked along at a pace between slow and brisk, looking every inch the English gent out for a night on the town. He wore evening dress, and was whistling silently. Which is as ridiculous as it sounds.

'You look very odd with your lips like that,' I said.

'Sssh,' said the spy. 'I don't want us to be overheard.' He then adopted a slightly more swaggery walk, with a touch of tipsiness, and stuck his free hand in his pocket. With the other he swung his cane with even more abandon.

Anyone who knew him would have instantly recognised this gait. But then the likelihood of anyone who knew him being out tonight was remote. I kept my own counsel, merely slipping more deeply into the shadows. If he asked later, I would say that I could not countenance walking alongside a man who showed such disrespect for his tailor. I knew he would bluster about being in character, although spoiling the suit would have cost him great pain. I smiled to myself. Then seeing a rather encouraging drainpipe I decided it was time for me to get up aloft. I had the pleasure of seeing Fitzroy glance round and do a lightning-fast double-take before glancing up and giving me a cheeky wink. I was fairly sure he couldn't actually see me. I was crouching low, hiding from the skyline, but the direction of his gaze was uncannily accurate. I decided I wouldn't be telling him this later.

From the rooftop I could see him strutting along like a slightly tipsy gent on a night out. However, from my perspective I could also see how he staggered just enough this way and that to ensure he saw around corners and into shadows. Watching him was something of a masterclass. I decided I wouldn't be telling him that either. My partner was more than aware of how good he was.

My left foot slid on a slimy slate, and I had to quickly correct my balance. No more studying the ground support! We had planned the route I would take together, but what we could not have foreseen was the number of landlords who did not clear their guttering. The result was that moss had grown inside, and spread out over some of the roof. On the tiled roofs this was less of a problem, but on the roofs that were covered with black slate it was barely visible and insidious.

For the third time my feet slid underneath me. It happened fast. I shifted my centre of gravity, but both my feet found no purchase and I slid quickly towards the roof's edge. I dropped lower and threw myself towards a short chimney stack. I grabbed on to it. My feet went from beneath me. I landed flat on the slimy slates, but my grip around the chimney held. My sigh of relief failed to materialise as the roof had knocked all the air out of me. I lay there, gathering my breath. I needed to be able to get up without sending a shower of broken slate below. Those sleeping beneath the roof would be bound to notice, and the last thing I wanted to do was draw attention to us. Fitzroy would never let me live it down if I aborted the mission through what he perceived as my clumsiness.

It never occurred to me that I might fall the three storeys to my demise. Climbing over roofs was neither something I feared nor felt inadequate about. Finally able to take a deep breath, I raised my upper body, still hanging on to the chimney, to have a better look at the state of the slates around me. I had barely managed this, my upper body strength still suffering from my enforced rest after our last disastrous mission, when I saw a pigeon fly straight at me. I ducked. Then it was all noise, and flapping. Motion and aroma. I suppressed the instinct to cover my head with my arms. A wing fluttered at the edge of my face. The bird ejected a trail of guano that miraculously missed me.

Then it was all silence once more. The bird settled not too far away from me. It staggered drunkenly in a circle, bobbing its head and showing no interest in me. I eased myself up slowly again. The thing was clearly demented. I hadn't seen another single pigeon. Only I would find the sole bird in London who was both insane and insomniac. I smiled to myself, thinking this was one part of the night I would tell Fitzroy about, when I caught sight of blood on the pigeon. At almost the same moment, I felt something touch my leg.

The stupid bird tripped over to me. I hissed at it and tried to send it away. I had no idea how close the ceilings of the rooms under the eaves were, and if anyone might hear a cry. Certainly, sound always seems to travel further in the night. The pigeon came closer to my head. At the same time I felt four stealthy paws creeping up my body.

My indignation at the cat calmly using me as a platform for his stalking was only exceeded by a fear that the two animals might choose to have their fight close to, if not on, my head. I pulled my body slightly higher up the roof, securing the grip of my left hand more firmly around the bricks. Then I tensed myself and let my right hand go. I waved at the pigeon, trying to get it to fly away, but the thing was either too stupid or too injured to do so. If anything it moved closer.

'Go! Flee! Run, you stupid thing,' I hissed at it. Then it began to rain. The rain came down in sheets, quickly soaking me, and making the slates glisten in the moonlight. Damn, I thought, maybe I will have to abort, the roofs are going to be impossible now.

The cat on my back had paused midway. For now it was perfectly still. I could twist my body and endeavour to throw it off, but this would either mean it embedded its claws as deeply as possible in the flesh of my back or fell off the roof to its death. Neither of these options appealed to me. Being less of an animal lover than Fitzroy I did seriously consider sending the cat flying.

I felt the cat wiggle on my back. It was preparing to pounce. I waved frantically at the pigeon. Twisted my back in an attempt to throw the cat off on to the roof, but the moment I moved it jumped. There was a moment that the shadow of the feline hung in the air, a shadow above me. Then it landed and all hell broke loose. The pigeon, that I dismissed as helpless, fought like a crazed thing, flapping its wings in the cat's face. It didn't fly, but dodged and weaved, and pecked at the cat. The cat, who had clearly got in an easy blow before, leaped in the air and pushed itself off my face. I felt the claws bite. It came down again, and the fight renewed. The pair of them were backing towards me. I put my head down and waved with my free arm, hoping to drive them away.

It was then I felt the mortar between the bricks under my left hand begin to crumble. I tried to hold on. I hit out blindly at the animals. Then my left hand came free and I was falling.

My stomach lurched. I scrabbled with my hands. I no longer cared about noise. Raising the alarm was the least of my worries. I could not survive the fall from this height. I slid fast across the roof. I felt the empty air under my feet. It was sheer survival instinct rather than skill that allowed me to catch on to the guttering.

I was lucky: whoever saw to this roof had kept the eaves in a good condition. I found myself hanging on to the guttering, dangling like a doll on a washing line. I looked down to see the small figure of Fitzroy beneath me. How the hell was I going to get out of this?

Chapter Ten

Burglary is not for the Faint-hearted

I wasn't precisely panicking, but fighting gravity was harder than fighting your average enemy agent. My arms hurt. They felt as if any moment the bones would pop in my shoulder sockets. If that happened I wouldn't be able to use my arms to pull myself up. Eventually I would lose my grip and fall. I needed to haul myself up now.

When I was in peak condition this would be hard enough, but weeks of bed rest had made me soft. I wasn't going to make it. Faintly I heard a scrabbling noise. Fearing another, and this time fatal, attack from the cat, I managed to glance down. To my astonishment I saw Fitzroy, his coat, hat and scarf cast to the ground, shinning speedily up a drainpipe.

It was the nearest climbing point to me, but I could see at once it wouldn't get him close enough to me to help. I could already feel the muscles in my arms going into spasm. For the first time in all our adventures together I began to seriously think this might be the end of me.

Fitzroy stopped on a level with me. The gap between us included a space between the buildings, and the edges of these offered no clear handholds. Besides, even if he got across to me I couldn't see how without a rope and a belaying point on the roof he would be able to rescue me.

'For goodness' sake, Euphemia,' hissed my partner across the void between us, 'what on earth are you doing hanging around like this. Time is of the essence, old girl!'

'I am not doing this for my own amusement,' I snapped. Then I felt myself flooding with emotion. 'I can't hold on,' I said. 'I'm going to fall!'

'Why on earth would you do a thing like that?' Fitzroy said, looking if anything annoyed. 'I need your cooperation on this mission. Not womanly hysterics. You need to swing up your leg and hook it over the gutter. Once you've got a decent purchase you can push yourself up, using your hands against the wall. Child of three could do it.'

'I'm not as fit as I was after—'

Fitzroy cut me off. 'The longer you hang about feeling sorry for yourself the more likely it is I will have to explain to the local constabulary why pigeons are eating your brains off the pavement. Buck up and get swinging.'

'What if the gutter doesn't hold?' I said.

'Then you'll fall. As that seems to be your current plan I can't see why you don't get on with it. Look sharp. That's an order.'

Then to my utter dismay he began climbing down.

'You're leaving me?' I hissed after him. 'Leaving me here?'

'Can't reach you,' said Fitzroy. 'You have to get yourself out of this. Besides, that's my favourite scarf down there and I don't want a thief getting their hands on it.'

'Oh well, if it's your favourite,' I started to say, but he slid the last bit and was almost at the ground now, and out of earshot.

I found myself blinking back tears. Not so long ago, I had thought the man devoted to me – devoted as a partner and friend. Now he seemed quite content to leave me to die. A slow fury began to burn within me. I'd damn well show him.

I knew my arms had little strength left. My shoulders felt as if they were on fire. I didn't have time to try this more than once. I put my last effort into swinging out to my left. Then as I swung back, I pushed off with my left leg, and threw myself up towards the guttering. For a moment I hung in the air without support. Then my right leg hooked on to the guttering. I hung there, upside down for a minute, savouring being alive, and shook my arms carefully to bring the blood back into my hands. Then like some strange crab I wall-walked my hands up, until I had one handhold at the top. I paused for a moment. Took a deep breath and then hauled my body up on to the edge of the guttering.

An alarming creak came from underneath me. It was giving way. I let go of my handholds and, with the very last of my strength, rolled myself up the roof, praying for a handhold.

I found one, and managed to pull myself up on to a flat part of the roof. I sat down. I hugged my knees into my chest, and with no one to see me gave way to several tears. I allowed myself no more than a few moments' grief. Then I stood up. Shook out my body, and looked at the rest of the climb I had to make.

I was two-thirds of the way to the skylight we had identified as an entry point. I chose a slower route than we had planned. It was still raining. I stayed away from the edge. As the skylight came within sight I thought it would be a long time before I clambered across rooftops again. Although after the words I intended to shower on my partner, and senior officer, it might be I would never work for the Crown again.

The skylight opened easily. Too easily for what was supposed to have been a police station. We were lucky. With so many men away at the war, the police service was much diminished, and many of the stations had been closed. This was one such one.

I dropped down into a reassuringly dusty corridor. Clearly no one had been up here for some time. Fitzroy had observed an officer whose rounds by-passed this place, but he had not observed a night watchman. We had both thought it likely that the shortage of able-bodied men again meant that there was no one to spare.

As I crept through the dark building, it soon became clear that shadows were my only companions. With no one active on the premises, and eating their luncheons here, even the mice had vacated the site. It took me only a few minutes to reach the side entrance and unbolt the door. I'd barely slid the last bolt back before Fitzroy was inside, and already closing the door behind him.

'You took your time,' he said in a low voice.

I had no words to answer him.

'This way,' he said and led me towards the back of the building. What came next was ten or twelve agonising minutes of my watching him pick various locks. The files stored here were as protected as the station could make them. While I had found my way down from the skylight clear and unhampered, Fitzroy faced a number of locks before we reached our prize. This was his part of the mission. I could pick locks to a degree, but even with his damaged fingers Fitzroy still had the lightest touch, and our aim was to leave no trace of our presence.

'There is no way I am going back across the roof,' I whispered. 'It's too wet.'

Fitzroy, midway through wiggling some lock-picks in a door lock, cast me an annoyed sideways glance. 'I'm concentrating,' he said.

When the lock opened with a tiny click he rested back on his heels for a moment. 'I realise that,' he said. 'But we have to re-bolt that door from the inside. All I can think of is that we will have to go out of the front door. I am counting on finding a way to lock that behind us. Not sure how yet. We can't exactly post the key back through the letterbox. If there even is a key. And the chances of being seen are much higher. But it's that or risk you dragging me off a roof to my death.'

His voice was entirely dispassionate. 'Go and see if you can find a spare key to the front door. It's our best shot. I'll keep working here.'

Eventually I found a key that fitted the front-door lock in the top drawer of where the desk sergeant would normally stand. But only after I had searched the offices, thinking the senior officers were most likely to have the keys. Of course not! What was I thinking. Senior officers always left the mundane jobs to their juniors.

I returned to find Fitzroy slipping files into his jacket. 'Got 'em,' he said. He glanced at the key in my hand. 'Let's go.'

Chapter Eleven

Farewells

We were both very quiet on the way back to Fitzroy's apartment. I had to keep to the shadows due to my dress. Fitzroy didn't offer me his coat. I was cold, angry and becoming sadder by the minute. When we finally slipped into his building I found a final spurt of energy to get me quickly up the servants' stair. I went immediately to the guest bathroom and began running the water.

'Not too hot,' Fitzroy yelled at me over the noise of the taps. 'You'll give yourself hypothermia.'

'Much you'd care,' I muttered, but I adjusted the temperature to warm rather than the scalding hot I would have preferred.

When I had dressed, I went into the drawing room. I was hoping he might have gone to bed, and I could sit by the fire and dry my hair. It was still much shorter since our mission to Europe, but I didn't fancy going to bed with it even damp. I still felt cold through to my bones.

I found Fitzroy standing in front of the fire nursing a glass of brandy. As I came forward he thrust it at me. 'Drink this, and don't you dare ever give me such a fright again!'

The words I was about to say died on my tongue. My surprise must have showed on my face.

Fitzroy ran his hand through his own slightly damp hair. He was fully dressed once more, though he had clearly bathed and changed. His neatly combed hair vanished into curls and tufts. I found myself involuntarily smiling. His face softened in response. 'When will you ever realise how much I value you?' he said. He turned away before I could respond, and stood facing the fire, his back towards me. 'I thought you were going to fall. I don't remember the last time I felt such fear. A moment's reflection showed me I could not reach you, and there was nothing near to us I could use to break your fall. It was up to you, and I could see the muscles in your arms already beginning to spasm. You were clearly cold, and possibly wet through. The only thing I could think that would get you out of it was your own stubbornness. After all you can be almost as stubborn as me. So I climbed as high as I could and did my best of annoy you in the hope it would spur you on. And it did. I'm rather hurt that you believed every word I said.'

'If I hadn't I would have fallen,' I said. I found myself shuddering at the thought.

At this Fitzroy turned around. 'Are you telling me I am just too good at what I do?'

'Exactly,' I said, coming forward and giving him a quick kiss, high on the cheek. He flinched as if I had struck him, but as I stepped back he composed himself.

'So we are friends again?' he said.

'I expect we will always be friends,' I said.

Fitzroy shook his head. 'So strange,' he said, 'I never thought to be friends with a woman who wasn't—'

'What next?' I said, interrupting this train of thought.

Fitzroy indicated the brightly burning fire with a nod. 'All the papers will shortly be ash.'

'Was that wise?' I said. 'Are you sure . . .'

'No, I am not certain we might not have needed them again. But as we are hiding them from the service there really isn't any place to put them. At least not that I could arrange tonight. I'm leaving in a few hours.'

'This is the overseas mission? With the code-breakers?'

Fitzroy nodded. 'Won't you enjoy that?' I said. 'You love breaking cyphers. I mean you taught me well, but it's always a chore for me. Whereas you seem to get actual pleasure out of it.'

'Sense of achievement,' said Fitzroy. 'Feeds my competitive

streak.' He strolled over to a chair and hitched his trousers up slightly before sitting down.

'You are looking awfully smart for a man going to France.'

'I am appearing to be a rich, but rather stupid, English gentleman who is attempting to rescue some treasures from his house in Normandy before it is overrun by the Boche. I have arranged for some dubious men to meet me and take me there. Not the best cover story, but it will do, I suppose.'

'You would have done far better,' I said sincerely.

'Either of us would,' said Fitzroy. 'I'm meeting some scouts, who will take me to these code-breakers. Even I don't know where they are, but they're a set of oddities we're currently relying on.'

'What's your brief?'

'See if I can get them moving faster, I suppose. I've been asked to look over the operation. I'm beginning to think that even Morley doesn't know what I will find.'

'Still, you won't be away that long, will you?'

Fitzroy shrugged. 'No one will be able to ask awkward questions about how I acquired Griffin – that is if anyone makes a connection. Hopefully it will all blow over.' He took a breath. 'I know you want to look into the murder, partly for Griffin's sake and his peace of mind, and also partly because of your own damn curiosity . . .'

'And my sense of justice!'

Fitzroy nodded. 'All right, I'll give you that. But even so, Alice, don't. I have honestly thought about this in some depth. It is better to stay well away from this piece of the past. Focus on the analysis Morley will be sending you. There's some interesting stuff in it. You know the form – examining facts and events from the perspective of the Germans rather than ours. I still don't think Morley can manage to put himself in the enemy's shoes. He can't think like them. But you can. What is right and reasonable for one person, or one nation, is anathema to another.'

'Yes, I agree. But you're talking about everything but what's on your mind,' I said. 'I know you better than most and you are extremely worried. I don't believe for a moment that's about Griffin.' Fitzroy didn't answer for so long, I began to think he never would.

'Most things I can avoid,' he said. 'But we had news yesterday that one of the code-breakers had been shot.'

'So the enemy know where they are, and have sent snipers behind enemy lines?' This got me a quick smile.

'So nice to work with a mind that's almost as sharp as my own,' he said, a twinkle in his eye.

I gave him one of the looks that I had learned from my mother. Not the one that had made a duke cry, but a stern be-serious sort of one. He sighed and spoke in quite a different tone.

'Yes, I'm afraid so. Most things I can take into account, but there are some excellent German snipers. As a country they are serious about their hunting, and any man of rank there can hold his own with a hunting rifle. For once being taller than most men of my generation does not seem quite so appealing.'

'You think you will be in real danger?' It was a stupid question to ask. He had already said as much, but I could feel butterflies in my stomach, a lump in my throat and my mouth was going dry. All obvious signs of anxiety, and I suddenly wanted him to take those away. To tell me everything would be all right.

'Usually I can say I will be careful. But though there are a few obvious precautions to take against snipers, the danger cannot be ruled out. Especially in the wasteland our two armies have created over there. But this time there is a chance I will not return. I have to say I blame you entirely.'

'What?' I said, thrown.

'I've always expected that I would die in service. I'd much rather die on a mission than be put out to grass behind a desk. I like taking risks, dammit. There's very little that's as good as the aftermath of dodging death. But now . . . I'm not afraid of death. Not terribly keen on the dying part. Always hoped for that to be swift. Bit cowardly of me really. But now . . .'

I stood waiting, wondering what he was going to say. Suddenly he caught my hand. 'I think it's ridiculous of you, but I rather suspect my death would cause you distress, and I don't want that.'

I struggled to speak for a moment. 'Then don't die,' I said.

'My plan is to come back alive,' said Fitzroy, 'but plans encountering enemies . . . well, you know.'

I had an impulse to throw myself on to him in the chair and put my arms around his neck. I wanted to embrace him tightly. At that moment I never wanted to let him go. But of course, such a display of intimacy was entirely out of place. We might be close as partners, but I was a married woman. I could not embarrass him in such a way.

I pulled my hand away. 'If you die I will be extremely cross with you. I will find a medium and tell you so myself.'

He laughed at that. 'Go to bed, Euphemia. I'll be off shortly, and you know how I hate goodbyes. Besides, you'll need all your strength to deal with Morley in the morning.'

'I'm not following you, am I?'

'Good God, no. Where I am going is no place for any woman, even one as extraordinary as you. To be honest it's no place for any man. Between us, Germany and the British Empire have done their best to create hell on earth.'

'I do know what's going on,' I said gently. 'I have been working with Signals Intelligence.'

'Not the same as being there, my dear,' said Fitzroy, rising from his seat. 'Go to bed. That's an order, but before you do, I wonder might I take the liberty of giving you . . .' and before he said anything more, he pulled me slightly towards him and gave me a kiss on the cheek. It was hardly a full embrace. His hands held on to my arms, and we were near enough for a moment that I could feel the heat of his body. He leaned into me after the kiss, and spoke softly in my ear, 'I will do everything in my power to come back,' he said. Then he pushed me away from him. 'Bed,' he said. 'Take Jack with you. He whines so if he sees me go out.'

He bent down and patted the little dog. 'You be good for Euphemia,' he said. Jack jumped up at him and made his funny little bark. 'Guard,' said Fitzroy. Jack's ears stood up stiffly, and he came to my side.

'I've been teaching him that,' said Fitzroy. 'You might have a bit of trouble leaving him now. Best to take him with you. Morley will love to see him again.'

With that he turned and picked up a book from the shelves. Then he settled himself before the fire. I crept away knowing there was so much more to be said, and nothing more that could be said. Jack followed me and curled up tightly at my side in bed. I stayed awake listening for sounds of him leaving, but I heard nothing. Yet in the morning he was gone.

Chapter Twelve

Moving On

I was awoken by a persistent noise. As I surfaced from the depths of a dream that involved chasing an enemy who only spoke in snorts and threw flames of fire at me, I realised I was hearing a coughing sound. I struggled through layers of dreams and pushed away the blankets that had become entangled around me. In so doing I disturbed Jack, who felt like a fireball at my side. He whinged and rolled over.

'Is something wrong, Griffin?' I called out. My voice sounded strange. My mouth was incredibly dry. That would teach me to let a dog into my bed.

'I just wanted to say I will have breakfast ready in twenty minutes, if that would suit, madam?'

'Perfectly,' I said.

'I shall serve in the small parlour.'

I sat up, pushing my hair out of my eyes. It was finally beginning to grow back to a more lady-like length. I acknowledged it looked feminine, but I hated it. Having had short hair I never wanted to go back to my long heavy locks. I wondered how many other women would feel the same if they had the chance of just once wearing their hair short like a man's.

Jack licked my other hand, making me start. He was now sitting up with his ears pricked. I knew I shouldn't be surprised that he knew the word 'breakfast'.

'Oh, in the kitchen is fine,' I said. 'No need to lay a proper table for me.'

'I would prefer it, madam,' said Griffin.

'Griffin, you cannot be worried about the two of us being alone in the flat. For goodness' sake, you're my doctor. You probably know more about my body than my husband.' The moment the words were out of my mouth I regretted it. There was a strong silence. Griffin was the only person I knew who could make not speaking painful. Fitzroy bellowed. Bertram argued and Morley scolded. Griffin did painful, white-hot silences.

I scrambled out of bed, and pulled on a dressing gown. I intended to apologise but I heard the sound of footsteps receding before I managed to open the door. Jack lolloped past me, tail erect and heading to the kitchen.

'Damn!' I said. One of Jack's ears twitched, but nothing would divert him from his pursuit of sausages. I went off to brave Fitzroy's showering apparatus. I preferred baths, but I had to agree with him that these stand-up facilities took much less time, and did tend to freshen one up in the morning.

Breakfast was served in the kitchen, but Griffin was absent. It was laid out in dishes as if for the parlour, but along the kitchen side. Without either Griffin or Fitzroy present if felt rather odd. This became even stranger as I helped myself to some scrambled egg and no Jack appeared at my side. I realised Griffin had taken his master's dog for a walk, rather than be left alone with a visitor in the servants' area. If Fitzroy realised that Griffin saw him as my chaperone when we ate informally in the kitchen, he would have laughed himself sick. However, sensitive to Griffin's tender feelings, by the time he returned with a rather muddy Jack, I was seated in the parlour drinking coffee.

'Good heavens, I would have made that for you!' exclaimed Griffin.

'What happened to the dog, Griffin?'

'Swans, madam, swans. Although I am happy to say I managed to prevent him catching any.'

'Jack, honestly, don't you know they can lock you up in the tower for attacking the King's swans.'

Jack gave a defiant whiffle.

'Indeed, we did leave rather sooner than I had intended,' said Griffin. 'There were two park attendants paying rather too much attention to Jack's exploits. Would it be a police matter if the dog caught a bird?'

'I'm not entirely sure,' I said. 'It's technically treason for someone to poach a swan. I don't know what happens if your animal savages a bird. Do you think he is actually trying to catch them?'

'Oh yes,' said Griffin, looking down at Jack with a singular lack of affection. 'He wants to eat one. In truth there is little this small animal does not want to eat.' He sighed. 'I shall have to bathe him now. Please ignore any sounds of distress you may hear.'

'Does Jack hate his bath that much?'

'The sounds of distress, madam, will be coming from me. He bites.'

When Jack had had all the mud removed from his fur, and I had rebandaged Griffin's hand, having firmly reminded him of my nursing training, he told me Fitzroy had charged him with showing me the apartment he had acquired for me. 'I did overhear you discussing the arrangement,' said Griffin, tactfully referring to our row, 'and whether or not you decide to accept his request, I do feel it would be more proper for you not to stay under the same roof as myself.'

'Let's not forget Jack,' I said with a twinkle in my eye.

'It is possible I may also be arrested for murder shortly,' said Griffin, 'and it would not at all be the thing for you to be present.'

'Yes, well, we're going to sort that out,' I said. 'Fitzroy has already got rid of the circumstances that connect you to your current position.'

'I do not have the major's confidence that the documents would not be replicated elsewhere. I believe it will only be a matter of time before the civilian police contact me. Thus, it is most important that we establish you elsewhere. I am afraid I will have to ask you to take the animal. He cannot be trusted to be left alone in any building, or he will attempt to eat the furnishings.'

I frowned. 'I do not remember Jack being such a problem previously.'

'His behaviour tends to degrade when his master is away,' said Griffin. 'I have ordered a taxi to take us to the new place. I trust your bags are repacked?'

'Almost,' I said, and went away to hurriedly pack. While I didn't share Griffin's fear of impropriety, the thought of him packing up my intimate apparel made me unexpectedly uncomfortable. Fortunately, Fitzroy had taught me to pack by rolling clothes, which was not only speedy, but surprisingly effective. Griffin, I imagined, like the maids at home, folded things in ounces of tissue paper.

Not many minutes later, Griffin, Jack, I and all my luggage were transported a short distance to the new flat. I would not, of course, accept it as a gift, but to please everyone I would stay in it for the duration of my time in London. I recalled hazily that I was meant to see Morley today, but as I had had no direct communication I decided to take a very Fitzroy attitude to the timing.

The flat was smaller than Fitzroy's, which was really a double apartment, with a section designated for servants. I had a room for a maid, should I require one, two bedrooms, a sitting room, with a desk that looked out over a park, a dining room, a well-fitted kitchen and bathing facilities. The flat was completely furnished, and while it lacked the obvious opulence of Fitzroy's taste – the sheets were a fine linen, not silk – everything was of exceptionally good quality. There was no art work, but the flat was well decorated in smart shades: a deep blue with gold touches for the bedrooms, wooden panels in the dining room, the sitting room a delicate ivory, and a shiny black telephone, which sat on an elegant desk. The furniture throughout was more modern than I was used to at White Orchards, but it was all tasteful. It was clear no expense had been spared, and this hardened my resolve not to accept the flat as a gift – as if I ever would. Griffin led me around explaining how various systems worked. 'Although I would advise you to hire a maid if you are spending an extended time in town. You have seen the accommodation, and I believe your department can supply a list of available vetted staff.'

I was only half listening. I had stopped before the kitchen stove. 'Ah, yes,' said Griffin, 'the major wanted you to have the best and safest cooking facilities. This is right up to the minute.' He stroked one finger along the edge of the hob plate. 'Quite a spectacular piece of machinery.'

I inwardly speculated where the nearest decent restaurants might be. 'I expect I would normally end up dining at the m— at Fitzroy's if I was in town,' I said.

'Possibly,' said Griffin noncommittally. 'And as you see we have a dog basket for Jack here. It already has the type of rug he is so fond of, and several dog toys. I am sure he will feel quite at home.'

As if he understood Jack hopped into the basket, turned around three times, and flopped down with a contented sigh.

'I shall now leave you to unpack,' said Griffin.

'But we have much about the situation to discuss!' I said.

'The flat? I thought I had been quite thorough.'

'No, your situation, Griffin,' I said.

'I will telephone you this evening to discuss matters,' said Griffin. 'The major has left me with a number of tasks that I must perform today. I anticipate being free after the dinner hour, and it would not be appropriate for either of us to call on the other. Your line and the major's are, I believe, what you call secure.' He paused. 'I also understand you have an appointment with Morley this afternoon. May I remind you it would not do to leave the animal alone?'

'I thought Jack was not a favourite with the colonel.'

'I believe not, madam. But I have strict instructions to leave the animal with you.'

Jack, lying in his basket, parted his jaws in a doggy grin. 'We'll be fine,' I said.

'He always lies down before a lit fire by seven o'clock each night,' said Griffin. 'He is a creature of habit. Eggs in the morning, a small piece of steak after his luncheon walk and three sausages in the evening.'

'Are we talking about Jack or Fitzroy?'

'The quantities for the major are larger, but similar,' said Griffin with an entirely straight face. 'I have left some fish in the cold cupboard for your luncheon along with a few other necessary provisions. I will talk to you this evening. Have a good day, madam.' He placed the keys on the kitchen table and left with an alacrity that took me by surprise. Jack gave a short bark in farewell.

Chapter Thirteen

Fitzroy Explains his Present

I saw Morley, who was horrified to see I had been left with Jack, and allocated me a serious amount of material to analyse. So much that he had arranged for most of it to be delivered to the flat after my return. He was clear I was to keep it in the safe provided.

I then made my way back to the flat as I needed to find the safe. I chose not to share this information with Morley. Griffin hadn't mentioned it, and I realised he probably didn't know where it was.

I stood in the middle of the living area, confused. There were no pictures in the flat. Safes are generally hidden behind pictures as any career burglar will tell you. I could not imagine where Fitzroy had hidden a safe in this neat and well-decorated apartment. There was no clutter. Everything might be elegant, but it was functional too without any hidden drawers or compartments. I found myself checking everything. I even checked the complicated stove.

It must have been around seven o'clock, as Jack was making gruffling noises in front of the unlit fire, when I remembered that Fitzroy had always laughed at how I had had to climb on a chair to reach the safe fitted in my operations room at White Orchards. It occurred to me that being alone here he would not want to put me at risk of the usual home accidents, which included falling off a chair.

In the bedroom there was a particularly lovely Persian rug by the side of the bed. It was covered in roses and not the style I would have normally have associated with '*things Fitzroy might choose*', but then the man could still surprise me. I started to roll up the rug, hindered a great deal by Jack.

'You are as bad as your master,' I said, quite unfairly, and stopped searching for a moment to put some sausages in the oven for him. I expected he liked them fried, but staying with me would be a different experience from being waited on hand and foot by Griffin, and the sooner he got used to it the better. I added some extra sausages for myself, chopped up some potatoes and set them boiling. The stove was surprisingly easy to use. At this rate I might even consider using three ingredients tomorrow, if I had the time. Unlike my partner I am not a natural cook, and consider it something that takes time I could always use more wisely. Fitzroy always claims cooking makes him think, and that while creating elaborate meals he solves many analytical and cypher problems. But even he has Griffin to cook for him on busy days.

I left Jack sitting in front of the fire, now lit, and not smoking in the least. He sat with his nose in the air, clearly torn between the hearthside, a station in front of the stove, and getting in my way in the bedroom.

I finished rolling up the rug, and after some careful fingertip inspection I found some pressure points that lifted the cover plate by the fingerhole. There was the safe, very cleverly installed to be completely flush with the floor. I opened it using the original combination that had been set at White Orchards. One I would change almost immediately.

Inside the safe there were a letter and a sealed envelope. The envelope had written on it 'Only to be opened after my confirmed demise'. The word 'confirmed' was underlined. I felt myself smiling at this. Some years back, before I became an agent, I had been Fitzroy's executor. Only when I went through the list of tasks assigned to me I discovered he was not dead, but had been captured. I always felt bad that I had not reached him before he was subjected to torture, but he claimed that I was his saviour, as no one else had worked out he was still alive. He retained somewhat of a grudge against the department to this day. If I was to be coldly logical I might think that one of the great imperatives for making me an agent of the Crown was because he had a severely diminished trust in his colleagues. Not, that is to say, that they were double agents, such a suspicion is constant among spies, and surprisingly doesn't seem to worry them as much as it does me. No, he was afraid of incompetence. Something he despised.

The other envelope contained a letter.

Dearest Alice,

Well done on finding the safe. I do wonder how long it took you. I have no doubt Morley will call you to London more and more. Telephone conversations are really not as useful as having someone present to analyse information.

I am also very glad you have accepted the flat. No doubt you are still thinking about it as a loan. Let me explain. You cannot go to the front lines, and I expect that as this war continues I may be called upon more and more to go into the battlefield. I don't particularly relish leaving you alone with Griffin. It is not simply that it might damage your reputation if it became known, but also the man is a complete bore, and ultimately a depressing companion. You may, of course, summon him whenever you need anything. Do try to do this at the most inconvenient times, won't you?

Jack will probably want to be with you, and I know you love him. However, if it becomes difficult to look after him due to your duties, do not hesitate to get Griffin to look after him at my flat. The man needs a good biting every now and then to remember his good fortune.

I also wanted to give you the flat – and this is the part I wasn't courageous enough to say to your face – and I might add that after you have read this we need never discuss it. Perhaps you should get a glass of the nice brandy I left you before reading this? It might encourage you to think more fondly of me.

Ready?

Well, my mother was married to a horrible man (my father). I have no idea if she loved him. I was far too young to understand their relationship, and then she died. I have always felt that women do not have enough standing in our Empire. You know I believe you deserve the vote, but this will not come for some time. Etc. etc. However, I have always felt that should a woman need to leave her marriage that she should have an escape. Now, Bertram is nothing like my father. I might not like him, but he is mostly a good man. However, though it pains me to say so, there are some events of a recent nature that have made me worry about your situation. I hope these are completely groundless and you will have a long-lasting and happy marriage. But being a spy and being in a relationship is not easy. I wanted you to have somewhere you could go – other than to me – for I am as difficult a male as any, and it would only make things worse with your own husband. I wanted you to have a bolt-hole of your own. Owned outright, with nothing beholden to anyone. And I hope you will come to see this flat as that.

I am disgustingly wealthy, and the cost of your flat is truly insignificant to me. I do not run a larger establishment because I am a bachelor. But I could if I wanted. You have saved my life on more than one occasion, and this flat is a thank-you for that. It is entirely yours. You can even sell it if you wish. Although I may sulk about that for a while. But it is yours to do with as you wish. You could even invest the money in that money-sink of Bertram's White Orchards.

Don't be cross, Alice. I'm entering into a dangerous stage of my career, and I worry about you. I might not always be around to protect you.

Your best, and ever affectionate friend, F.
P.S. As well as Jack, you will also inherit Griffin. Sorry about that.

I sat back on my heels and stared at the letter for quite some time. It was a lot to think about. I was aware I should be angry, but the thought that kept running through my mind was how much danger was Fitzroy in? And what could I do about that? I knew I should be furious that he had cast aspersions on my marriage, but then he and Bertram had never liked each other much. Respected, perhaps, but there was no friendship. I had accepted that. I was confident and secure in my relationship with my husband. Nothing Fitzroy said could shake that. It occurred to me that he might be obliquely referring to the invalid status my husband had, and that he might simply think I needed a break from that. It would be just like him to suggest my marriage had problems, rather than say he thought I needed a break from the sickroom. He knew my duty to my husband would not allow it. But he might think if he couched it another way I might accept? My brain whirled with thoughts. Usually I was good at seeing through my partner's intents. This time all I could come up with was that he was providing a haven for me, for whatever reason, because he feared he would no longer be in a position to have me visit his home. And the only reason he would ever deny me access to it, I knew without doubt, would be if he was dead.

My heart was in my throat, and I found myself digging my nails into my palms. I could not imagine my life at the department without him. Indeed, my life without him at all would be a colourless and empty affair.

I – my macabre thoughts – were cut through by a howl from Jack. Jack never howls, so I was on my feet and running before I knew it. I found him in front of the stove, his eyes begging me for assistance. The sausages were cooked, and smelled as if they were about to burn. I opened the stove door, and took them out. Jack bounced. At least one of us was happy.

Chapter Fourteen

A Telephone Call that Changes Everything

The files were delivered by two particularly stoic and unremarkable men, so at least the department had my address registered. I had hidden the papers away as soon as they left. My mind was in too much turmoil to think clearly. I had been given a date for my report, and I felt I could spare the evening settling in.

Despite Jack's fears supper proved to be edible for us both. I sat with my meal on a small table in front of the fire, something I would never have done at home. Jack, now full of sausages, curled up contentedly on the rug and snored softly. At least I presume he was snoring. It sounded awfully like a purr.

Although not far from Fitzroy's own apartment, this part of London did not have the restaurants and elite clubs that were close to his. There was little coming and going outside. All respectable people were doubtless in bed. In fact it was remarkably quiet. I heard the soft ticking of a clock, a small tasteful timepiece on the mantelpiece that I hadn't even noticed before. The loudest noise was the sound of my knife and fork. This gave me a funny feeling. I examined it. Things felt odd. I have never been afraid of being alone. Indeed, as a child I would happily walk through the graveyard of my father's church to fetch him home for dinner, without the slightest qualm. I had spent hours alone, climbing trees, and sitting by the side of the river, or riding bareback around the countryside. If anything I had sought out time to be alone, away from my parents' difficult marriage.

But when I entered service, and later when I married Bertram, I had gone through a period when I was never alone. I had been surrounded by more people than felt comfortable. The truth was I had never been alone since that time as a child.

Not that I was properly alone with Jack at my feet. But the silence remained unsettling. I was by now a well-trained spy, and more than capable of defending myself. It was not a fear of intruders or any such threat that was discomposing me.

My husband has a dicky heart, and I've always known he would likely predecease me. Now Fitzroy was away on a mission that for the first time I could recall he thought might prove a threat to his life. For the first time I realised it was possible that one day I would be without them both. Both of the men who were so dear to me. Of course, I would always have 'Little Joe', my brother who was now much taller than me, but he would be starting out on his own path in a few years. My mother was doing well, and was happy with her new husband, the bishop. But they were growing older. For the first time in my life I envisaged a time when, if fortune did not favour me, I might end up alone. I found I did not greatly like the idea.

I had allowed myself to become isolated at White Orchards. Merry spent less and less time with me. She felt it was not appropriate with her husband having been our chauffeur before he enlisted. No protests from me seemed to impress upon her that I valued our friendship highly. Fitzroy spent a great deal of time around me and at White Orchards, but this only deepened the isolation. I knew our own people there looked strangely at this man who visited so frequently. Bertram loved the isolation of the country. He spent much of his time in the library, and now wrote for a number of publications. Not for him the round of country dining with the neighbours. I did my duty by our people with visits and the like. But other than Dr Butcher, and the vicar, both decent men, but hardly suitable friends for a married woman, who already received far too many visits from a handsome man-about-town. My world had become Bertram and Fitzroy. Both of whom were not people destined for old age.

If only I had not lost our baby, I thought. At least then I would have something to remember Bertram by, and I would not be so terribly alone. A single tear ran down my cheek.

This really would not do. I gave myself a mental shake. If the worst happened I would deal with it, as I had dealt with other misfortunes that had come my way.

'I am being self-centred and melancholy,' I told Jack. 'It is ridiculous. I am one of the luckiest women alive.'

Jack opened one eye, and gave a slight whiffle. 'Exactly,' I said. 'Of course he will return. The man is like a bad penny.'

Jack closed his eye and snuggled further down in the rug, rubbing his face into the pile. 'I know,' I said, rising, 'I shall phone Hans. I've left him hanging as it is. The operator is sure to be able to find the number.'

It wasn't quite that straightforward, but in a short while I was listening to the sound of Hans's telephone ringing. It was only as I heard him curtly answer that I suddenly thought he might not be alone. After all, he had admitted to me more than once that he didn't come to the city only for business.

'It's Euphemia,' I said.

The tone changed immediately to one of concern. 'Are you in danger? Unwell? How can I help, my dear?'

I glanced over at the clock, and recoiled slightly at the time. Without the usual evening rituals of White Orchards, or even those at Fitzroy's flat, I had quite lost track of the time. 'I am sorry to intrude so late,' I said. 'I wanted to let you know that I have thought over what you said about being of help to me in my work.'

'So you are—'

I cut him off. 'I think at this stage we should leave it on an informal basis. If we can prove that you are of help then we can see about getting you official permission to be in London.'

'Yes,' said Hans. I could hear the embarrassment in his voice. 'I am aware the terms of my non-internment were set such that I must remain in the countryside, but—'

'I don't know all the details,' I said, 'but I suspect that

technically I should report you. I need you to give me your word as a gentleman that you are not working against the Empire.'

'Good God, Euphemia. I am shocked you even have to ask.'

'Your word.'

'I give you my word that I am a loyal subject of the King. Do you think I would bring danger down upon my wife, and my children?'

'Working with me might do exactly that.'

'Perhaps, but I would like the opportunity to prove to your – er – people that I am not a threat. That can only be a good thing for my family. Besides, you are well aware how much I enjoy your company.'

'Stop there,' I said. 'I have made it clear on numerous occasions that you and I will never be more than brother-in-law and sister-in-law.'

'Never is a very long time, Euphemia. You strike me as a woman who enjoys company, and as one who is frequently without it.'

'If you make one more remark along these lines, I will rescind any arrangement and report you,' I snapped. Trust Hans to hit upon my raw nerves. Despite my annoyance, it made me remember just how charming and manipulative he could be. I could use that. He would make a good asset if I could keep him under control.

'Very well, Euphemia. I apologise. I will make no more such remarks.'

'Good,' I said. 'I will be continuing to investigate the death of the poor woman we saw at the police station.'

'You haven't heard?' said Hans. 'They have caught the murderer. The last editions of the newspapers all carried the story.'

'No, I haven't seen tonight's newspaper. Are you sure? Did they name him?'

'No, it is a very discreet article, but it allays the fears of the populace neatly.'

'I will look into it in the morning,' I said. 'I am sure there will be work for us both. I will contact you.'

I put down the telephone receiver without saying goodnight. I was shaken by the conversation for more than one reason. However, I strongly doubted an arrest had been made. The last thing London needed at this time was a butchering murderer on the loose. I suspected this was mere propaganda. I would call the department tomorrow and see what I could discover.

I took myself off to bed, and allowed Jack to accompany me. I knew Fitzroy never let him in his bedroom, and that by starting out like this I would be unlikely ever to get him to sleep in his basket, but I wanted the company.

I found I was surprisingly tired, and fell quickly into a deep sleep.

Then at four o'clock in the morning my telephone rang.

I leaped out of bed and ran to the living room. I could only imagine the direst of emergencies. My heart was in my mouth. I feared most for Bertram. Any news of Fitzroy would take far longer to reach me, and he had barely left the country.

I snatched up the receiver. 'Yes, this is Alice.'

'Thank God,' came Griffin's voice, 'They've arrested me for murder.'

Chapter Fifteen

Things Take a Turn Very Much for the Worse

Matters became clearer in the morning. I had risen early. After Griffin's panicked telephone call from a department-associated detention centre I had not been able to attain any quality of sleep. When I had dropped into dreaming I had been haunted by a series of bad dreams. None of which I cared to dwell on in daylight.

Jack, as ever, was only interested in his breakfast – six well-scrambled eggs, after which he wolfed down several slices of dry toast. I was beginning to share Griffin's astonishment at how much this small animal could ingest.

The telephone rang again at seven a.m. with a request from Morley's secretary to attend the office at my earliest convenience. It was barely eight a.m. when I clipped Jack's leash to his collar and headed out to catch a taxi. It was drizzling, with a blurry grey morning light that sucked all the energy and hope out of one. The cloud cover was low and thick enough that there was no sign of the sun, and the world smelled of wet leaves and mulch.

All the while the dog gave me dark looks. I thought at first he was blaming me for the weather. Then I recalled Fitzroy never put him on a leash, but I was yet to trust him to behave with me.

In the taxi, where I had to pick him up, I discovered Jack was not only damp, but shivering. I held the little dog close. I didn't recall seeing a coat for him at the flat. I thought I should apply to Griffin to purchase one, and then I recalled that I couldn't.

I tried to put the scant information I had in some kind of order in my head. Griffin had, he said, been arrested on his return to

Fitzroy's flat. This has taken place on the doorstep of the main door. Whoever had made the arrest had not had the gumption, or perhaps the permission, to enter Fitzroy's flat. Currently, Griffin had said he was being pressured to sign a permission to access. I wasn't clear what he meant, but only that he was currently refusing. In fact, all in all, I was woefully unaware of what was happening. It was not the way I would have chosen to stand in front of Morley, who could be short at the best of times.

When I arrived, Dotty, who was guarding Morley's office like a veritable guardian to the gates of hell, took one look at Jack, came out from behind her desk, and swooped down to pick him up. He immediately licked her powdered and painted face. She surprised me by in return kissing him firmly on the nose.

'I've always wanted to do that,' she said. 'He's such a lovely dog. Just look into his eyes. You can tell he's a sweetie!'

Jack snuggled into her ample chest, clearly seeking warmth. I decided this must be why he hadn't bitten her. Fitzroy might pick him up occasionally, but he was a medium-sized animal and not a lapdog.

'Always thought the major might have something to say about my doing this. You won't tell him, will you?'

'If anything can endear someone to Fitzroy it's liking his dog,' I said, 'and the dog liking them. You couldn't have a better endorsement.'

'Oh, how could anyone not like little Jackie? You go in and see the colonel. I'll take care of him. We must have a towel somewhere. Shall we look in the colonel's bathroom?' The last statement was delivered to Jack as she wandered off still carrying him. I heard Jack whiffle in an appealing sort of way. He was quite as manipulative as his master.

I knocked on Morley's door. He answered at once and I went in. Morley was standing behind his desk with a frown on his face. Considering he had a prosthetic replacing the lower part of one of his legs, it showed that he was extremely concerned.

'So what are you going to do?' he demanded.

I sat down in one of the chairs opposite his desk. 'Good morning, Colonel,' I said calmly.

'Morning, Stapleford,' said Morley. Instantly his cheeks reddened. I could tell what an effort it had been not to call me 'Mrs'. The question of my rank or not-rank bothered the department a great deal. Fitzroy had decided he was my superior and that was enough for him. The colonel continued, 'Thought you'd like to know, the major is on the ground safe and sound. Despite his ridiculous schemes. I have no idea why you couldn't have taken him rather than involve a female outside the department. Still, it's useful you're here and can deal with this Griffin business. Didn't know it was going to blow up in our faces, did he?'

As Fitzroy had believed our late-night burglary had put any difficulties to bed, I could truthfully answer, 'No, I don't have any reason to believe that.'

'Humpf! Be just like him to leave us to sort out his mess.'

'I'm not aware of the major ever doing anything like that, sir.'

'You're not in London all the time. The scrapes I've had to work with. I just hope he doesn't get this girl killed. Daughter of someone we don't want to annoy.'

'Girl?'

'His lady friend that drove him down the side of no man's land. That's what they're calling that godawful mess in the middle. Quickest way to get him to where he was going was to cut across it.'

'That must have been frightfully dangerous,' I said, digging my nails into my palms. I was determined not to ask who the woman was, but I also very much wanted to know.

'Oh, these women are driving about all over no man's land. Germans have said if they wear a bright green headscarf their snipers will leave 'em alone. Seems so far they have. Rather sporting of them, I suppose.'

'You mean being able to pick up all their injured players at half-time?' I said without thinking.

Morley stopped pacing and gave me a long look. 'I can see how the nature of war would be difficult for a woman to understand.

Females don't generally tend to have an honour code, do they, Stapleford?'

'It depends on the female, sir. But in general, no.'

'It's pretty brutal out there. Wouldn't want a daughter of mine nursing the men out there. Not so much nursing as butchery – cutting off the bad bits to try and save the good. Take a stronger stomach than a lot of men have.'

'So the driver was a nurse?'

'Oh, yes. A viscount's daughter, if you can believe it. Wanting to do her bit. Fitzroy knew her before she signed on. Been in contact with her since she got to the front apparently. They write to each other.' He gave me another long, stern look.

'He's never mentioned her to me,' I said. 'But the major often has many assets in play. As you say I'm not in town all the time, and I can't know everyone.'

'Hmpf! Strange partnership you two have. If he's not letting you in on what's going on, what are you? You did that hospital training. You might be more use on the front line. Ever thought about it?'

I tried hard not to notice the hopeful gleam in his eye. 'The major's opinion was that my talents were best utilised elsewhere.'

'Obviously,' said Morley. 'Otherwise he'd have taken you with him.'

I needed to change the subject to conceal my discomfort that Fitzroy had not only gone without me, but made it clear that I would never be near the front lines. Until this moment I had thought the triage centres and medical facilities at the front line were solely staffed with male medics.

'I understand Griffin was arrested last night outside Fitzroy's flat by a member of—'

'Very well, on to business. Yes, he was taken up by our own police. Thank God it wasn't the London police. We should be able to keep the execution quiet.'

'Execution,' I said. 'Has it come to that already?'

'Man owned up to the murder, didn't he?'

'Did he?' I said, surprised. 'He didn't mention that to me.'

'Why should he?' barked the colonel. 'And where are all the files relating to Fitzroy's part in all this? That's what I want to know! All vanished. Overnight if I can believe the archivist.'

I mentally sorted through the questions in my head. 'Griffin rang me at four a.m. to ask for my help. If he had killed this girl, I think it would have been an important fact for him to mention.'

'Did he by God? But that's not the murder I meant. The first one. The one he did.'

'Isn't that old news? I thought that had all been dealt with.'

'It was based on the assumption that the man he killed had killed his wife. Obviously that was wrong.'

'I don't see that,' I answered quickly. 'This could be a copycat killing by someone who knew the original murderer. Or someone else who witnessed the body of his wife.'

'Like the coroner?' said Morley with strong sarcasm.

'Like the ambulance men who removed the body. Like someone the murderer boasted to before Griffin killed him. Like someone who was passing in the street and saw the body. There are a hundred and one possibilities.'

Morley stopped pacing. 'Possibly. Possibly. But the man in charge of the case is keen on closing it down. Almost as keen as I am. You may not know this, Mrs Stapleford, but there are a number of separate departments working on our sort of thing. All of us need financing. It's an ongoing competition. Of course, our contributions to the war effort and the country speak for themselves, but that doesn't stop the bean-counters trying to thin us down.'

'Yes, but you can't weigh Griffin's life against that!' I gripped my hands together to stop myself jumping up in anger. This was ridiculous.

'I can assure you, my dear, that during a war men's lives have counted for far less. We save lives. Many lives. If I have to sacrifice Fitzroy's butler to keep us going I won't think twice.'

'If you have already decided why call me in?' I snapped.

'Kindly remember we are a military organisation, and you will address me with respect.'

'I'm sorry. I must have forgotten the situation when you called me my dear.'

The edges of Morley's moustache twitched. He could be curmudgeonly, but he was generally fair.

'Yes, well, what do we do about it?' He sat down on the chair behind his desk and leaned back, bending his swagger-stick between his hands. 'It's almost as if the man in charge has a vendetta against Griffin. Do you know if they ever met? Did the major steal his girl or some such?'

'I don't know who he is,' I said. 'I was elsewhere when he was arrested. I have my own flat in London.'

Morley's eyebrows rose slightly. 'Quite right. I should never have assumed you were staying at Fitzroy's place. Even with him away at the time. Didn't trust you with Griffin, was that it? But if he had doubts about the man why did he ever take on the arrangement?'

'I don't believe he had doubts. I do know why he took Griffin on. Total loyalty. That's what he wanted.'

'Yes, sounds like the kind of thing the major would do,' said Morley. 'So he had no doubts over Griffin. You're sure?'

I nodded. 'Neither do I.'

'It's Rory McLeod.'

'What?' I said. 'I thought he had moved to the civilian police?'

'By way of the front line,' said Morley. 'Seems like a good man.'

'I know him,' I said. My voice sounded rough. My mouth had gone dry.

'Really? I hope he's not an old flame. Doubt your husband would like that? Haha!'

'We were in service together,' I said. 'And I came across him during two previous missions. I am certain you recall this in my reports, sir?'

'Oh, that man! I do recall now. The name . . . but yes, he was helpful in both, wasn't he? Very keen to do his duty, as I recall?'

I had not, naturally, put any of my true feelings towards Rory McLeod in my reports. I had been fair, and kept my comments short. Of course, this was before I knew there was any chance of running across him again.

'All the better if you know him. You'd better go down and have a quick word.'

'You mean try to get Griffin released, sir?'

Morley turned away and appeared to inspect his view from the window. 'Not sure that's on the cards to be honest.' He tapped his swagger stick against his leg. 'Need you to get the lie of the land. I mean, if you can get the man out, no fuss and all that, I daresay Fitzroy would be delighted. But with him being away not sure there is going to be much we can do.'

'You mean I'm not up to the task?' Realising how rude I was sounding I added, 'sir'.

Morley didn't react with displeasure as I had expected. 'No, not that, my dear. Thing is the man should never have been left unsupervised.'

'But you ordered Fitzroy on a mission.'

'That's his job,' said Morley bluntly. 'But as McLeod tells it it's a condition of his parole or whatever it is that Fitzroy keeps him under his eye.'

'But he was when the killing in the station happened.'

'Not sure that doesn't make it worse,' said my commanding officer, looking down at his boot. ''Fraid they rather have us over a barrel here. Seems some documents went missing recently too. The whole agreement if you can believe. McLeod managed to dig up a copy from somewhere, but . . . he's got it into his head that Griffin stole the papers – that the man was about to make a break for it and go on a killing spree.'

'But that would be madness!'

'That's what he's claiming. He believes Griffin is criminally insane.'

'You've spoken to him then?'

Morley shook his head. 'Sent me a nice little report. All correct and proper. Doesn't even openly blame me for letting this fiasco continue. Implies it heavily, of course.'

'How unjust! How rude!' I blurted out.

'Nice of you to say so,' said Morley. 'But if he's right and this Griffin is some kind of insane maniac . . .' He went over to his desk and picked up a file. He read, 'It is my belief that the individual known as John Griffin was driven to the edge of insanity and is unaware of the actions he performs when not in his right mind. He claims to have no memory of stealing the files, but they have been removed. From observing him I posit that he is one of these rare individuals who is able to separate his mind into two halves . . .' Morley paused and looked up. 'Have you ever heard of such a thing, Mrs Stapleford?'

I shook my head, speechless.

'Anyway, he goes on to say if he is found to be criminally insane, they won't hang him but incarcerate him. Personally, I'd prefer a quiet death rather than being shut up in one of those asylums.'

'Does it not strike you as nonsense, sir?'

'You tell me,' said Morley. 'I never met Griffin.'

'But is this the kind of report a policeman would generally write?'

'Apparently, he's back being one of our lot again. Spy police. What-do-you-call-them? Anyway, no odder I'd say than the people they police.'

'But this whole thing is riddled with inconsistencies,' I objected. 'I don't believe Griffin could climb over a wall to save his life.'

'So you're familiar with where the files were being held,' said Morley looking at me sternly from beneath his eyebrows.

'I presume it has walls, sir.'

'Humph! If I discover that you or Fitzroy had any part in—'

'In what, sir? Killing young women?'

'Enough!' barked Morley, so loudly I gave a tiny jump of surprise. 'I am aware of your outstanding loyalty to the major, but there is a chain of command here, Stapleford, and you will be conscious of that, and give it respect.'

'Yes, sir,' I said.

'Now get over there and see what you can do to keep this mess quiet.'

I was leaving when I heard the colonel mutter, 'In service?' I heard the intake of his breath, but I was on the other side of the closed door before he could question me further.

Chapter Sixteen

The Ex-flame Burns Hot

Morley hadn't actually told me where 'over there' was. However, I asked Dotty when she presented me with a very happy Jack, who was now wearing a tartan dog coat with matching bow tie on his collar. 'Doesn't he look smart!' she said. 'Fitzroy should get him one of those little Scottish bonnets. It would keep his little ears warm.'

'A tam-o'-shanter?'

'That's the ticket. I think he looks very up to the minute, don't you?'

'He seems very pleased with himself,' I said diplomatically.

'Ah, that'll be the chop and the gravy.'

I almost asked how, where and whose, but I had the sense to realise I might not like the answers.

'You've been very kind, Dotty. Thank you. The colonel is sending me across to our branch of the police.'

'Oh, to see the limping man?' said Dotty. 'Terribly handsome. Wonderful green eyes. Almost glowed, they did.'

'But the colonel said—'

'No, he didn't see him. Said he was too busy to be interrupted. The limping man took that rather hard. I don't think he was at all happy, but he left a report. I think the colonel still has it. Do you want me to go and fetch it?'

I shook my head. 'I know what's in it. Did he say where he would be?'

Dotty gave me a precise description of how to get there. 'But it won't look anything much. You know what those types are like. Even more in the shadows than us. Have you got your pass with you?'

'All relevant paperwork,' I said with a smile. 'I'm so terrified of losing it I take it everywhere.'

'Very wise,' said Dotty. 'You know Jack has eaten Major Fitzroy's twice. Ever such a fuss there was.' She bent down to pet the dog, who looked up at her adoringly.

'Thank you. I had better get going.'

'Do you want to leave the little lamb with me?'

'Little lamb? Oh, Jack! No thank you. I don't know where I'll be heading next or when. It's best I keep him with me.'

Dotty looked a bit crestfallen. 'Just thought I'd offer.' She opened her desk drawer and passed me a paper bag. 'Just some bits of chicken in case the poor little thing gets hungry. You should have seen what he put away earlier. I'm not sure the major is feeding him enough.'

'I'll bear that in mind,' I said. I looked down at Jack. His mouth lolled open, and his pink tongue showed. A slightly more fanciful mind than mine might have thought he was laughing.

Once we were outside I caught an omnibus like any ordinary citizen and took a roundabout way to Rory's new office. I needed time to think.

The building was as unprepossessing as Dotty had suggested. It looked like the office of an accountant. Its grey walls and heavy beige curtains certainly belonged to a dull and respectable business. A young woman sat at the reception desk.

'I'm terribly sorry,' she said in a very faux upper-crust voice. 'Madam cannot bring the canine in here.'

'Madam,' I said, showing her my pass and using my natural accent, 'is here to see Rory McLeod.'

The woman looked at my pass, and raised one perfectly plucked eyebrow. 'I was unaware that Commander McLeod had any appointments this morning.'

'He does now,' I said coldly. 'Morley sent me across.'

'A moment.' She picked up a telephone and turned away so she could speak quietly without me reading her lips. She had clearly learned something from dealing with spies. In a moment she turned back, having replaced the telephone handset. 'Go through and take the lift to the third floor. He will be waiting for you. You'll need to tie the dog up outside.' She went back to checking through the enormous diary in front of her. I didn't bother offering my thanks and I took Jack with me.

The lift must once have been very plush. There were signs of where the cushioned seat for passengers had once been. Before its adoption by this odd branch of the SIS this must have been an important building. I'd ask Fitzroy. He was something of an encyclopaedia when it came to old London buildings. Jack found many interesting smells in the corners.

The door creaked open and standing before me, in a suit far more expensive than I had ever seen him wear before, was Rory McLeod, leaning on an ebony cane. Rory, who I had once been engaged to, and whose hatred of me for jilting him had only dulled to a raw dislike after our recent encounters.

'You're looking well,' I said.

'I see your hair is beginning to grow back in. Whatever did you cut it for? Surely not nursing?'

I shook my head. 'Another mission.'

Rory turned and led the way back to his office. 'Don't tell me you were masquerading as a man.' He chuckled drily at his own joke. I said nothing. He opened the door to a well-appointed office. It looked out on to a park, and sunlight flooded in through the window. A cushion lay in the pool of warm light. The receptionist must have warned him about Jack. The dog took one look at it and looked pitifully up at me. I let go of his leash, and he trotted over and curled up. Within moments he had begun to snore softly. I found it reassuring. This had all happened without Rory and me exchanging another word, and it gave me a chance to take in his new environment. In comparison to Morley's office this was an example of ultra-modern furnishing. The lines of the desk, coffee table and shelves had a crispness, and the chairs by the desk were a strange S-shaped design. I sat down in one gingerly while Rory took the one behind the sleek pale oak desk. Neither of us considered sitting on the small sofa with its emblematic sunrise bursts on each end. This was a confrontation.

'So?' he said.

'Colonel Morley sent me over to discuss the situation with Griffin.'

'Do you have his authority to move the situation on?'

'I think you'll need to clarify that,' I said. Morley, as ever, had not given me precise instructions, but by now I had a good sense of how far I could go. And how much further I could push things and still expect Fitzroy to tow me out of trouble. Only he wasn't here. He was in France with his pen-friend.

'Can you sign off on his institutionalisation?'

I blinked at that. 'You have doctors who will attest to his madness?'

'I can get them,' said Rory. His eyes were cold and flat like jade. I wondered when they had lost their glow. Only Dotty claimed to have seen it. Perhaps it was only with me that he was so cold.

'I may not be a medical practitioner . . .'

'You were a nurse long enough to see that some men lose their minds as well as their limbs in war.'

I nodded slowly in agreement, 'But Griffin hasn't been to war.'

'Any act of extreme violence may cause a mental storm,' said Rory. 'That is what was originally assumed happened to Griffin when he found his dead wife. That the grief and loss of a dear one in such violent circumstances, and being a doctor knowing the agony she would have endured . . .'

'It was done while she was alive?' I gasped.

Rory paused. 'You didn't know.'

'I knew nothing about Griffin's background until this week,' I said. I remembered Rory had always been uncannily good at spotting a lie, so I determined to stick as close to the truth as I could. Even if I applied the spy's old favourite, lying by omission.

'This week?'

'The discovery of the woman at the station brought it all out.'

'Well, clearly not all,' said Rory. 'If you—'

'I've known Griffin on and off for a year, or is it two? Shuttling between missions, dealing with the fallout from the war, and still maintaining a semblance of my home life, tends to skew my awareness of the passage of time,' I said. 'I'm not asking for sympathy. I'm merely saying that I can be a bit hazy about everyday details.'

'How convenient.'

I ignored him and carried on. 'So I have known Griffin for some time and not observed anything of particular note about him other than the slightly fractious relationship between himself and Fitzroy. He has been nothing but courteous to me. I knew he had once been a medical man, and that he no longer practised.'

'Fractious relationship?'

'They were clearly never friends. Fitzroy was in charge, but Griffin might debate matters with him in a manner that he would never have suffered from a junior officer.'

'So what did you think he was?'

'Beyond a curiously loyal asset? I had no idea.'

'You never asked?'

'Of course I asked,' I snapped. 'I was simply never told.'

'I think it would be fair to assume that you don't know this man well. You don't know his plans or his state of mind.'

'As much as one ever knows another's,' I said, unsure if he was talking about Griffin or Fitzroy.

Rory frowned and shifted in his seat. 'Does it still trouble you?' I asked.

'I was told it would always be a hindrance,' he said, 'but then you know full well that one can't let circumstances hold one back.'

'I can't agree to Griffin being institutionalised,' I said bluntly.

'Your department will disagree. The last thing they will want is for him to be put on public trial.'

'That is the alternative you are offering?' I said. 'What do you want?'

'Spoken like your master,' said Rory without bothering to disguise his sarcasm. He leaned forward on his desk. 'I want no more young women to die. That's it. I have no agenda here, but to keep the likes of you and Fitzroy in check and keep the public safe.'

'You make it sound as if we would act against the public interest,' I said.

Rory opened his mouth. I put up my hand. 'No, don't bother answering that. You have never liked this world. You always saw Fitzroy as arrogant and reckless, and now you put me in the same category. No wonder you sought—'

'He accused me of being a traitor and a murderer,' said Rory, 'when he knew full well I was neither. He used me as a pawn to draw the murderer out. But if it hadn't worked . . .'

'You think he would have gone through with it? Seen you hanged?'

'Rather than lose face, yes. I believe he is that kind of a man, and from what I can tell you have thrown in your lot with him. I cannot understand why your husband allows you to run around unchecked. If you were my wife—'

'Which happily I am not,' I interjected, 'but this is all old history. Why should Griffin pay the price of our – our encounters?'

'He isn't,' said Rory. 'I want to stop him murdering anyone else. He is a convicted killer, Euphemia, and Fitzroy had him set free.'

'I believe he handed himself in,' I said. 'I haven't heard a word of proof that he is guilty. This is all circumstantial, isn't it? Don't tell me you don't have an agenda here. I think you do. I think all of this comes out of spite. You're no better than any of us.' I could feel myself breathing heavily. I knew what I was saying was unwise, but I couldn't strike a crippled man. Could I?

'Think what you like,' he said, sitting back in his chair. 'You have the options available to you. If you aren't authorised to make the choice then crawl back to Morley and get his approval.'

I stood up. 'I suppose you forget that when you were locked up and everyone thought you were guilty, I was the one who stood up for you. I was the one who worked to get you free.'

Rory flushed. 'No . . .'

I slammed my hands down on the desk. 'And do you know why I did that? Went against what seemed overwhelmingly powerful people when I was nothing to them?'

Rory swallowed and looked away. 'No, not really. I thought it was because—'

'Because I believed you innocent. As innocent as I believe Griffin to be now.' I straightened. 'What's the point. You've made up your mind.'

'You'll agree to him being sent to the asylum.'

'Will I hell!' I said. 'I'll prove him innocent even if I have to go over your head to do so, Rory McLeod. You may think you have the upper hand, but by God I'll not let an innocent man's life be ruined because of your quarrel with Fitzroy and me. I thought you better than this, Rory!'

Chapter Seventeen

A Pact of Convenience

Rory was on his feet. His face was contorted with rage, when suddenly quite another expression crossed it and he slumped. He managed to catch himself on the chair, but his face had gone grey. I shot round to the other side of his desk and began opening the nearest drawer. I found the pills and I shook one into his hand. There was a jug of water on the coffee table, but by the time I had poured him a glass he had already swallowed it without water.

'Does this happen often?' I asked.

Rory, sweat beading on his forehead, shook his head slowly. 'Rarely,' he said with effort. 'I've been busy.'

'Overdoing it,' I said. I looked at him collapsed in his chair. 'Holding the SIS to account is as important as fighting in the front lines,' I said. 'It can be hard to find the line when you're working in the field, when so much is at stake. We do need to have someone to hold us to account. Whatever you think of Fitzroy or myself, there is a line neither of us ever crosses.' I deliberately didn't attempt to spell out this line, as I was unsure where my own was. I knew Fitzroy had his own code of honour but I suspected his was far closer to the horizon than mine. Spelling any of this out would do neither of us any favours.

'You really think he is innocent?' said Rory.

'Yes.'

'I can give you a fortnight. No more,' said Rory. 'If by that time you haven't provided evidence of his innocence he will be sent to an asylum. Or worse. Morley will never let him go on trial. That's the best I can do.'

Back at Fitzroy's flat Jack was enjoying a late, but enormous luncheon of eggs and bacon. The bacon was my apology for the lateness. I could hear him slurping away as I turned over Griffin's things. I have, on occasion, had to pry into other people's personal effects. Although not as often as Bertram imagines. He thinks all sorts of awful things about spying. In reality, my missions have always been targeted and precise. I did far more snooping when Bertram and I had our short play at solving the various catastrophes that came our way. In short I don't like prying. I disliked it even more because I quite like Griffin.

He's not a person I have ever truly warmed to. He's reserved, and deliberately keeps himself apart from Fitzroy and me when we are at Fitzroy's flat. It's as if he makes a deliberate point that he is the servant, although I now knew he was initially far from working in service. I didn't know who his parents were beyond that they lived and worked on Fitzroy's family estate. Griffin's possessions were solidly middle class. He had a large selection of handkerchiefs. White, large, linen and lined. The kind that have a space for a monogram although he had not added one. His tallboy was filled with round balls of cedar to keep the moths away. He had the usual underwear, which I tried very hard to forget I ever saw. His socks were divided into two sections. One lot were woollen and the other cotton. He had one of those wardrobes that combine functions. His shirts were neatly laid out on sliding trays, and his suits hung with creases so fine I could practically cut my fingers on them. At the bottom of the wardrobe were two pairs of shoes, highly polished. Everything was black, grey or, in the case of the shirts, white. There was no colour and no sense of who he was. There were no hats. He must only have had the one.

I found a black umbrella tightly furled and neatly propped in a corner. Eventually I unearthed a bottle of cologne. I opened the bottle, and a very masculine, musky scent emerged. There was a faint undercurrent of spices. It was most distinctive, and I could only think that Griffin never wore it. I had certainly never smelled it in the flat before.

Jack wandered into the room. He walked with a slight stagger, scrabbled at the edge of Griffin's bed and with some difficulty pulled himself up on to it. He then turned round and round, rucking up the blankets to make a nest for himself. He huffled to himself and closed his eyes. I eyed his form with concern.

'Jack, I didn't feed you too much, did I?' The dog opened one lazy eye and closed it again without comment. I had visions of him bursting, as Griffin had always foretold, and on his bed too. For some reason Jack intensely disliked Griffin. That gave me pause for thought. Fitzroy was the kind of man who had an almost preternatural relationship with animals. I'd once come across him at White Orchards with a squirrel on his arm, feeding it nuts. He said it was because animals sensed he meant them no harm. But it was odd to see him whispering to the grumpiest horse in the stable, and watch her became placid. If Jack was anything to go by animals hated Griffin. Did they sense something from him? Something wrong?

I gave myself an inward shake. In analysis of intelligence it is important to be aware of your personal bias. To understand that the enemy is not you, and will not think or act like you. Understanding this had been imperative in my work looking at supply lines, and troop movement possibilities. I had to take into account what the enemy might do both to sabotage our supply lines and to protect their own. So many people forget that fighting a war is not simply about the movement of military assets to attack. It all depends on planning the background support.

If Griffin were to have killed this girl at the station, for example, he would have needed an airtight alibi. That would have taken planning. It was not something that could be done on a whim. The wounds on the victim would have taken time. In all likelihood they had been committed elsewhere, and the body brought to the station. The only reason to do that was to attract attention. Possibly to send a message? To whom?

This was Griffin, a man who if he had had a vendetta against women had had more than ample chance to harm me when I was injured or asleep. I had been taught to consider all sides of the equation. I told myself I was attempting to overcompensate for my positive bias towards believing Griffin innocent. Yet at the back of my mind I could feel a faint sense of foreboding. This room of Griffin's was too perfect, too impersonal. I understood he might have wanted to leave his past life behind, but there was nothing personal here. Would he not even have kept a photograph of his wife if he loved her so much? I continued to search the room.

I came up empty-handed. I went back through to the living area and put a call through to the department. Usually I got someone I didn't know, but this time it was Dotty.

'Hello,' she said. 'I hope the little fellow is liking his jacket?'

I thought for a moment. 'Oh yes, Jack loves it. It's hanging up to dry now, but he's still wearing the bow tie. He's currently sleeping off a late luncheon.'

She chuckled. 'Don't suppose this is what you called for, is it?'

'No, it's about Fitzroy's man, Griffin.'

'Nasty business,' said Dotty.

'Do you think you could see if you could get me an appointment to see him? I know the head of the investigation and I'm fairly sure a request from me would meet with a flat denial. But I thought if the department asked . . .'

'Personal issue between you and him, is there?'

'A past history certainly.'

'I can ask, but the colonel has already been denied, so I don't hold out much hope.'

'Can they do that? Keep him isolated?'

'Honey, you should know. The SIS always plays by its own rules.' She lowered her voice, 'Something the poor colonel hates. Very straight-up army man.'

'Do you have files on Griffin?'

'This was Fitzroy's pigeon. If anyone had any files it would be him.'

'He must have lodged paperwork somewhere?' I said. It sometimes even surprised me how well I can lie. I had helped destroy all the paperwork Fitzroy knew about; it was a long shot that there might be anything in the colonel's files that he had forgotten.

'Does the colonel not keep his own notes about things?'

'He does, but I couldn't let you see those. Tell you what, I'll pop out and get him one of those cakes he likes and take it in with a cup of tea. Then I'll ask him if he's got any information he can share with you about Fitzroy's man.'

'That's really kind of you,' I said, somewhat taken aback.

'Oh, he's a lovely man if you know how to handle him,' said Dotty and hung up.

Images chased themselves through my head of Dotty handling the colonel. I rather thought the man had no chance.

As I was sitting at the desk I picked up the phone again and called Hans.

'Hans, I have a case I need your help on. Will you be free to help me over the next couple of weeks?'

'Will you need me to be in town?' I heard the hopeful note in his voice.

'Yes,' I said. 'But you can't tell Richenda you're helping me.'

'Why not? She is aware that you are – that you sometimes work for the government, is she not?'

'I need to keep things on the quiet for now,' I said. 'Nothing outside the circle.' The last phrase came to me as something that a spy might say in a novel. I hoped it would intrigue the romantic Hans.

'No, of course not,' he said, and I could tell from his tone he had no idea what I was talking about. 'The thing is Richenda gets a bit concerned when I stay up in town for a while. I mean not only am I not meant to leave the estate – does anyone in your department understand how business runs? It's not only that but she worries I might be tempted into – er – misbehaviour.'

'Why the sudden coyness? You were frank enough earlier.'

'There is no need to be ungentlemanly about such matters,' said Hans, in an annoyingly reproving tone.

'I'm afraid you will have to make your own excuses with your wife. As for being off the estate, you are acting as my asset. You'll still have to keep a low profile, of course.'

'Of course,' said Hans, sounding relieved. 'I, for the most part, stay out of the public eye. We have a lovely restaurant at this apartment. They send supper up on request. You should come over and try it one night.'

To another man I might have said I know self-defence, but Hans, as he said, was not the kind of man to lay a finger on an unwilling woman. No, he was much more of a charmer, the kind of man who would befriend one when things were difficult, and to give him his due, probably do his best to help you. But then, he would do his very best to talk you into bed.

'I'll be in touch,' I said and hung up. If I was honest I was all too aware of his charm. In another lifetime I could have accepted an offer of marriage from him. He almost asked me, but at the time he very much needed to marry a wealthy bride. We would never have been in love as Bertram and I were, but he would have been a delightful, charming, intelligent companion. I doubt he would have been faithful, but he would always have been kind. Which is a lot more than most women get when they marry. I fully understood the pull he had over women, and yet, for all my harsh words, I did like him. What was it about me and my affection for amoral men? Fitzroy had never walked the path of the straight and narrow. Were my morals slipping by association?

Association? An idea burst through my thoughts like the sun on a cloudy day. What if Griffin had been contaminated by his association with Fitzroy? What if he had started to think like a spy?

I ran into his room awakening Jack, who woofed in annoyance.

'Sorry,' I said. I tried to gently push him off the pillows, so I could check the cases, and under the sheets and mattress. Jack wasn't budging, so I ended up pushing him firmly. He whiffled at me, but didn't snap or growl. This further reinforced my concerns at the dog's dislike of Griffin. There was nothing in the bed. I apologised to the bull terrier, who I swear gave me a nod of gracious acceptance and went back to building a nest on the bed.

I then checked inside pairs of socks. I looked for a makeshift secret compartment that Griffin might have created in his furniture. I even got down and rolled up the rugs to check the floorboards. Nothing.

Finally, without much hope, I went back to the wardrobe. I picked up a jacket and checked the lining. Clean. I didn't know what I was expecting to find. Something, anything. Then I looked down at the shoes. Three pairs? Presumably he had one set on his feet. I picked them up, and one set had extremely smooth soles. So smooth I wondered if they had ever been worn. But they were perfectly ordinary shoes. Not the kind of thing he might have saved for best. I checked the toes of both pairs. Nothing. Then, looking again at the barely worn shoes, I thought: either he has too many shoes, and never needs to wear them, or this is a sign of an amateur.

I twisted the heel of the left shoe and it opened. Inside was a photograph of a young woman. I would not have been able to recognise his wife, but I recognised this woman.

She was the victim I had seen laid out in the police station.

Chapter Eighteen

Musings on Griffin's Guilt

Why would Griffin have a picture of the dead girl hidden in his room? I sat down on the bed feeling rather sick. It's all very well to consider all circumstances, it's entirely another thing to have them arouse your darkest fears. I sat down on the bed. Jack crawled up next to me either sensing my distress or seeking a snack. He stuck his head under my arm and laid it on my lap.

'What does this mean?' I asked him. 'Why would he have a picture of this woman? Who is she?'

I sighed. 'Time to see if Hans can earn his status,' I said to Jack.

Outside it was a lovely afternoon, and I knew Jack would want a run in the park soon. However, I had a number of telephone calls to make before I could think of going out, and in all of them I was going to have to lie through my teeth.

An hour later I was walking through the park with Jack on a lead. He tugged every now and then, clearly wanting to be let off it. However, I had heard Fitzroy tell more than one after-dinner story of Jack's pursuit of swans. He always made it sound extremely amusing, but I rather thought that chasing Jack through bushes and possibly even into the edge of the river would not, in reality, be such a joy.

I thought over what I had learned. The truth was it wasn't much. By pretending to be a reporter from a magazine – it was highly unlikely anyone would believe a female was a newspaper reporter – I had managed to discover that the body remained unclaimed, and that no one had yet come forward in response to the newspapers' appeal to identify the girl. As far as the ordinary police were concerned she had taken a train from East Sussex to London and died. Before the train journey there was no trace of her, and there were no identifying papers or personal items. It was presumed the killer had taken them as trophies.

I had put the photograph back in the shoe. Plausible deniability. The ordinary citizen in me said I should hand the evidence over to the police, or even Rory. The spy in me said leave it well alone, focus on your own mission and keep to the shadows. Except the fact of Griffin having the girl's picture in his shoe meant it was my mission, didn't it? Coincidences do happen, but not like this. Either we were mistaken about Griffin, or his past was more complicated than either Fitzroy or I had realised. However arrogant my partner can be, he is generally an excellent judge of character. He may take slightly longer to believe the worst of a member of my sex than his own, but this seems more to do with his belief that women, on the whole, make better human beings than their male counterparts. With only a few exceptions I am inclined to agree with him.

I had a further series of handicaps. I couldn't go around asking questions like the regular police. Going to the police station in the light of what had transpired had been a step too far. It had laid me open to recrimination from Rory or, worse, Fitzroy. Fitzroy might pull dangerous and blatant stunts abroad, but he'd have something firm to say about me doing that on our home turf. He still didn't entirely trust my judgement after our last mission and the hideous fallout. If I wasn't careful he'd pull me out of the field for the foreseeable future. I knew his intention was to protect me, but the thought of sitting behind a desk for as long as the Empire and Germany took to battle things out would drive me to hysterics. With an invalid, though beloved, husband, an office to work from in the depths of the countryside, and no more stirring company than the local vicar, whose conversation revolved almost entirely around his church roof, it would be I, not Griffin, who would be ready to be put in an asylum within weeks. I needed to uncover the truth and do it fast.

And then even that was complicated. Did I want to find the truth or did I want to prove Griffin innocent of any new crime? My father's daughter believed in absolute truth, always. The woman I had become, especially since the outbreak of the war, no longer saw truth in absolutes.

I was so lost in thought it was after a full ten minutes in the park that I realised I was being followed. I noticed because Jack stopped tugging. Instead of trying to get me to let him off the lead, he suddenly changed to staying close to heel. This was so unlike him I actually stopped and bent down to check he hadn't hurt his paw or some such thing. The quick movement behind me alerted me to my shadow, and the fact he was an amateur. A professional would more often than not brazen it out if a mark turned round unexpectedly. Of course, this only works if your face is unknown to whoever you are following. All I saw was a tall, thin figure, in outline male, darting behind a tree. Now, unless I knew him or he was remarkably recognisable for some reason, the best thing he could have done was continue to amble on. Best of all, he could have wandered past me, and if I was an ordinary woman I would think no more about it. His knee-jerk reaction to hide meant that he was in all likelihood unskilled at following people, but also had no idea of my actual profession.

There are times in situations like this when I have chosen to tackle matters head-on. I was confident I could march up to his hiding place, and that between Jack and me, we could subdue him. If he was a total amateur possibly Jack wouldn't even need my help.

But I had this odd feeling. I did not want to go back and beard this man. Even in the warm afternoon sun, I felt cold at the thought. I don't listen to my intuition as much as I should – or so Fitzroy keeps telling me, but I had a strong foreboding that even the bright light of day could not shift. I was not going to turn back and face my stalker.

Instead, I headed towards the nearest exit, Jack for once trotting obediently at my side Every now and then he gave a little growl deep in his throat, but he kept moving. It was only as he left the park without complaint that I realised he had gone into 'guard' mode. I took him to a nearby café in the hope that my follower might be reflected in a window along the way. Behind me, from the park, I saw a uniformed nanny with a pram, an extremely chic young woman whose skirt was so tight she was forced to use tiny steps, an older man walking a terrier whose tail positively quivered in delight, and a middle-aged woman with a large basket that was clearly heavy. None of them gave any sign of looking for anyone nor gave me a feeling that they were up to anything nefarious. Such a feeling came, I explained quietly to Jack, from watching their gait, their movements and whether there was any hesitation. Jack looked back up at me expectantly. I ordered him his own iced bun, and told him I was sure he would have bitten the bad man, and he was a very good dog. Jack looked at me and looked at the bun on the saucer, which I had asked to be placed on the floor. He gave a small woof, and I remembered the time he had taken down someone in front of me. I added extra praise, but said until he did the actual job, it was only a one-bun day.

Then I sat back in my seat and wondered if I was going mad. I reflected I had often heard Fitzroy talk to Jack, and maybe he was the kind of dog that encouraged conversation. Looking over the edge of the table all I could see was a frantically wagging tail accompanied by the kind of scoffing sounds I had always imagined Beowulf to have made. Or maybe, I thought, Fitzroy was lonelier than I had realised.

I finished my tea, and the saucer was removed from under Jack by a formidable matron. Jack growled fiercely, but being told to be 'a good little doggy' he gave up the crockery with a somewhat startled air, and pricked ears.

I needed to be careful, but I thought it was time for me to return to my flat. I had locked Fitzroy's when I left, and there was no good reason I could not pick up my phone messages elsewhere. Besides, if I had been followed it would have been because I had come out of Griffin's (and Fitzroy's) flat. If my tail had given up then I could return home and lessen the likelihood of the stalker finding me. To all intents and purposes as far as I knew it could be any one of Fitz-roy's enemies following me simply because I had exited his apartment. Recently, I had spent some time in town with him, but generally I did not, and I was not fully party to whatever he got up to in the city. Enemy agents often beset him, but then from what he said there was a number of angry husbands that would like to have a cosy chat with him. But then I knew that Fitzroy, like most gentlemen, embroidered his affairs, and that in his case the tall stories he told to me and others were a cover for truths he had no intention of sharing. I respected that. I knew he did on occasion seek out information from the wives of men of importance or those who were suspected of crimes against the Crown. However, these missions he did not share with me, and for once I was grateful not to know the truth. The thought of what he was prepared to do for the Crown frequently made me uncomfortable. Although strangely when I had seen him execute someone it hadn't bothered me in the slightest. It was the women . . .

The lead slipped entirely out of my hand. Fortunately we had gained the park, which I had been crossing to a different gate to reach my new apartment. Jack was off like a rocket, the lead trail-ing behind him. I had never seen him move so fast. I didn't lunge for the lead. There was no way I could catch it without falling flat on my face. Instead I watched in horror as Jack made for the river – and the swans . . .

Chapter Nineteen

On the Hunt

I was dressed as a respectable lady, so as well as lacking in pockets I also had yards of skirt material to contend with. I gathered my skirts into one hand and ran as fast as I could after the dog. Usually the little bull terrier had a loping gait, but right now his paws seemed to barely touch the grass he was going so fast. It was beginning to look like that iced bun had been a very grave mistake. 'Wretch,' I muttered from between closed teeth as I sped after him.

We rounded a small curve in the river, Jack still streaking ahead, and there, magnificent in their plumage, were two swans coasting elegantly along the water. Jack gave a rare bark of delight and headed straight for them. The swans turned as one in his direction and then, to my surprise, turned to look at each other, before rising up, their wings aloft, and honking loudly. They looked both magnificent with their bristling snowy feathers and large wingspan, and also more than capable of taking down a small dog. I wondered if Jack could swim. The faint hope I had that the dog would back down in face of such ferocity faded as Jack ploughed on. I was still too far away to intercede.

I hurried on, fearing the worst. The encounter would not pass without loss of blood on one side or possibly both. Either was a disaster. Fitzroy would be furious if his pet was harmed, and the Queen's courtiers would take a dim view of an uncontrolled dog killing a swan in the royal park. Just as a mutual massacre seemed inevitable a gentleman, appearing out of nowhere rather like a magician, stepped in and caught Jack's now rather damp and unpleasant lead. He gave a series of short sharp tugs, and Jack, recognising a greater strength than his own, not only stopped but dropped to the ground and rolled on to his back.

I rushed to thank our rescuer. He bowed to me and passed over the lead. 'Barnabas Willoughby at your service, ma'am,' said the gentleman in refined accents. Curiously, he was dressed in a loudly checked suit like a member of the lower middle class, but his manners and voice clearly displayed his breeding.

'Thank you, sir,' I said. 'This was pure carelessness on my behalf. I let my thoughts distract me. If you hadn't . . .'

'Your dog would be locked up in the Tower,' said Mr Willoughby. 'I know small canines can be swift, but you have a veritable missile with paws.' He smiled, and bowed slightly. 'I am glad to have been of service. He seems to be quieter now. Would you like me to escort you to the edge of the park in case there is any reoccurrence?' He looked down at the dog at his feet. 'Not that he seems that inclined to race now.'

'Indeed, he is generally a well – or fairly well- – behaved animal,' I said. 'I rather think I shouldn't have given him an iced bun.'

'I do not believe it is in the general way considered healthy sustenance for a dog,' said Willoughby. At this point I noticed the twinkle in his blue eyes. In fact as we spoke Mr Willoughby seemed to become more and more visible. At first I had only noticed the garish outfit, but as we spoke I became more aware of the man himself. He was, I judged, around my age. His dark hair was slightly longer than was fashionable, and he had a neat moustache. He was not an unattractive man, but the laughter that shone in his eyes, and quivered around the edge of his lips, was verging on the charismatic.

'I must not take you out of your way,' I said. He seemed a gentleman, but for all I knew he was my stalker, who had waited for me to return through the park. Only I could not quite believe that. I felt no malice from him.

'It would be nothing for me to walk along the river until the swans are out of sight,' he said. 'I am recovering from . . . The walking is meant to do me good.'

He offered me his arm. 'If you will not think me as bold as my suit?'

I laughed. 'Very well,' I said, 'but you must be prepared for me to suddenly disappear should my pet pull me along!'

'Why do I not hold his lead until we reach the exit?' said Willoughby, expertly removing the lead from my fingers before I could protest.

I smiled, and fell into step beside him. I quickly saw he walked with an odd gait. He tried to mask it, but his left hip troubled him. I assumed he had come by the wound at the front. The awful suit made more sense now. He might have been given it when he was discharged from the army.

'You do not have a dog, yourself?' I asked.

He shook his head. 'No, but I grew up with them. I don't believe we ever had less than four. Of course, we had the land for it. But I think dogs are happier when they have a pack, don't you? They aren't solitary animals by nature.'

'I've never really thought about it,' I said. 'Growing up I had a horse and a cat, but my mother disliked dogs.'

We were almost at the park gate. Jack was behaving perfectly. Occasionally he glanced up at the man holding his lead, but after a quick check over at me, he trotted on unconcerned.

'Ah,' said Willoughby, 'so you had no idea that sugary snacks were not appropriate.'

I thought back to how Fitzroy constantly fed his dog titbits, and realised that it had been generally meat that formed the main part of these, and the occasional late-night crumpet toasted on the open fire.

'It didn't occur to me,' I said. 'Will it make him sick?'

'I doubt it. So whose dog is he?'

'A friend's,' I said. 'She had to go down to the country. Her aunt is ill and needed her. I said I would look after him.' I gestured to Jack. 'I see now he is more of a responsibility than I had realised.'

'Aren't most males,' said Willoughby with a charming smile.

We had reached the gate now. He bowed and handed over the lead. 'I am afraid to say this is still largely disgusting.'

'I am extremely grateful for your help, Mr Willoughby. I wish you an excellent afternoon.'

He raised his hat to me. 'Goodbye ma'am,' he said. 'Goodbye, Jack.' He turned on his heel and walked away as swiftly as his injury would allow him.

I grasped Jack's lead tightly and exited the park. I then took a very circuitous route to my flat. As far as I could tell I was not being followed. However, I had never told Willoughby Jack's name. I only knew that when he mentioned Jack's name he was confirming what I suspected. A man whose clothing did not match his accent, who could appear as if from nowhere, who was able to allow his personality to appear by degrees, could only be one thing. I had no idea who he was working for. I only knew that he wanted me to know that he was the same as myself: a spy.

Chapter Twenty

Heading North

Finally back at my flat or at the flat lent to me by Fitzroy, I took Jack into the bathroom and washed him. He made no protest other than one slight whiffle. At which point I let him know exactly what I thought of his behaviour. He then capitulated. I lit the fire and left him drying in front of it.

It was now very late in the afternoon. I telephoned Dotty, hoping I would be able to catch her before she left her desk.

'Righty-ho,' said the cheerful blonde. 'I didn't manage to get you much, I'm afraid. It's not so much that the files we have on this man Griffin are sealed, as that what we do have is pretty threadbare. Apparently there were more detailed ones, but they seem to have gone missing.'

'Oh dear,' I said.

'Indeed,' said Dotty in an uncomfortably knowing sort of a way. 'This is the tiny bit your partner wrote. "Griffin, MD, ex-local practice GP, thirty-seven, five foot ten, grey eyes, left-handed, sandy-brown hair, stoic by nature, finicky (annoyingly so on occasion), confessed to murder of the man who killed his wife (Megan), conservative in habits, avoids risk generally, but can be motivated by anger (and revenge), dislike of animals (ha!), hates mess (haha!). Practice was a family one in Wimbledon. Originally from Devon. Trained in medicine at the University of Edinburgh. Will consider basic training in observation and disruption should he pass probation."' She paused. 'I'm not entirely sure what the "ha's" are about, but I think we can guess. Doesn't sound as if he liked the man much, does it?'

'I don't think that was a necessary criterion.'

'I think if I was going to invite a man into my home I'd want to like him,' said Dotty.

'They weren't friends,' I said. 'It was a master and servant relationship, and it's a large flat with staff quarters.'

'I wouldn't know,' said Dotty; again I heard a meaningful undercurrent in her voice.

'Well, thank you,' I said. 'It's more than I knew.'

'I hope you know what you're doing.'

'I hope so too,' I said trying to sound puzzled rather than offended.

'Cheery-pip then,' she said and cut the line.

I sat by the desk for a while as the light faded. Jack snored by the fire. Eventually I got up to close the curtains and got myself a small brandy. I sat by the hearth with only the firelight glowing and thought about my next steps.

I had no leads other than the man who had followed me in the park. I could go back, attempt to see if he followed me again and then turn the tables on him. But I hadn't actually seen anyone. It had been a feeling. It could also have been nothing to do with Griffin, or even espionage in general. I had lived a sheltered life, but I now knew there were men who followed women for their own nefarious reasons. This made the prospect of luring this man much more appealing, and if I had had nothing else on my mind I would have been strongly tempted. Morley would have me up on the carpet for using my skills on a member of the public, but Fitzroy would sort it out. He had no time for such men either.

And then there was Barnabas Willoughby. An innocent member of the public? My stalker? My stalker's accomplice. The thought of there being two men involved made me wary. I still doubted they could overpower me, unless they were trained street fighters, but it would be unlikely I would come away without injury.

I also knew after the last disastrous mission I was looking for a way to prove myself. I ruled out going back to the park. The evidence was too flimsy, and it was potentially too dangerous. I could ask Dotty if she knew who Barnabas was, but she had already done me a favour. I was getting the impression from her that she had doubts about my ability. Although I had no idea why. Morley had likely said something cutting about me when he was in a bad mood.

No, there was really nothing else I could do. I could only see one way forward. I telephoned Hans, and without letting him get a word in edgeways I told him to get us two first-class tickets to Edinburgh tomorrow on the early train. He was also to book two separate rooms for us at a decent Edinburgh hotel. I assumed as a man of business he would know how to go about it, or at least have a secretary somewhere who could do it for him. He certainly had more than enough of his wife Richenda's money to pay for it. I went through to the bedroom and repacked my bag. Jack followed me through and climbed up on to the bed.

'Oh goodness,' I said. 'I'm going to have to take you with me. I wonder if the hotel allows dogs?'

Jack wiggled an ear in his version of a canine shrug and settled down to sleep. In a fairly short time I climbed into bed beside him, and joined him in slumbering.

Both Jack and I felt it was far too early to be at the railway station. I was regretting last night's brandy, which must have been larger than I had thought, and Jack was regretting not being able to finish his plate of sausages. There had been no way he was prepared to leave without them, and so now I had three congealing tepid sausages wrapped in wax paper in my coat pocket. At least it was assuring Jack kept close to my side. I had taken a taxi to the station, and had the taxi driver procure me a porter, so that I at least didn't have to manage both my bag (of medium size) and the dog on the crowded platform.

'I need to find my travelling companion,' I told the porter. 'He has our tickets.' I found myself crossing my fingers. I knew Hans to be repeatedly unfaithful in marriage, but whether he was dependable in other matters I had not had a chance to ascertain.

But then I saw him. Indeed, I could hardly miss him. He too

had found himself a porter, but his luggage cart was overflowing with valises and even a trunk. Hans stood, looking around the platform, dressed suitably, but in clothing that had plainly cost a pretty penny. I don't believe the King could have looked smarter.

He kissed me briefly on both cheeks, as befitted a brother-in-law, wearing an expression of relief. 'I had a terrible fear this could all have been a practical joke.'

I gestured wordlessly at the mound of luggage. Hans blinked. 'But you didn't say how long we would be away,' he said. 'Besides, the weather is notoriously changeable in Scotland.'

'Fine,' I said. 'Let's get aboard. It is clearly going to take some time.'

Hans's porter led the way to our first-class carriage. He allowed me to climb in first. I had to pick Jack up. The gap was too large for him to jump – although he wriggled enough to try and convince me otherwise. We had a private compartment off a small corridor. I sat down on the window seat and allowed Jack to climb up, with some difficulty, on to the seat beside me. I then distracted his attention from the open door by feeding him bits of sausage. Meanwhile, Hans oversaw the loading of the baggage.

Finally it was done, and the door to the compartment and the outer door to the carriage were closed. I sat back in my seat, and breathed a sigh of relief.

'Was I meant to get a ticket for the dog?' asked Hans.

'Do dogs need tickets?' I asked.

Hans shook his head. 'I have no idea.' He gestured up at a wicker basket that was over his head in the luggage rail. 'I took the precaution of getting a hamper from Fortnum's, but I doubt it contains dog food.'

'Oh, he'll eat anything,' I said, attempting to rub the grease off my hands on to the outer side of the paper.

'I can believe that,' said Hans, eyeing Jack. 'My issue is that although there are,' he coughed, 'facilities for ladies and gentlemen, I do not believe there is anything like that for our canine companion.'

'Oh,' I said, and more loudly, 'Oh!' as I realised what he meant.

'Does the train run straight through? I assumed we must stop on the way.'

'Only at York,' said Hans. 'Half an hour for luncheon. I enquired. The entire journey will take ten and a half hours.'

'He is very well trained,' I said.

'We must hope so,' said Hans. 'Now, Euphemia, how shall we occupy ourselves for the next several hours? I have ensured we have a compartment to ourselves.'

Jack, on the seat beside me, began to growl softly.

Chapter Twenty-one

The Swan Hat

I am most happy to report Jack did not disgrace himself. It is true he fairly cantered to the door at York, and was most relieved to find the grass by the station. I spent the journey to York briefing Hans on all I knew about Griffin. I saw no point in withholding any details that concerned Fitzroy's manservant. I did not mention why Fitzroy wasn't doing this himself nor where he was, and Hans had the sense not to ask.

Luncheon was given at the railway hotel, and was acceptable. Goodness knows I have had to eat far worse when on missions abroad. Hans, however, was not impressed and ate very little. Jack lay quietly at my feet and I fed him sparingly under the table. All was going well until a lady arrived late for luncheon. She was older than myself, but not yet entered upon middle age. Clearly flustered, she asked the waiter for something quickly as she would be joining the train. I eyed her with deep misgiving. On her head sat an ostentatious feathered hat. The brash whiteness of it showed it to be new, but it was of a much older design. It was more like something my mother might have worn, and sat oddly above the young face. However, this new passenger's sartorial sense bothered me less than the fact the hat looked, as much as anything, as if a pair of swans were sitting on her head. I hooked the empty chair in next to me with my ankle, doing my best to shield her from Jack's sight.

I managed to keep him from seeing the lady and the hat by leaving the dining room before her, and keeping myself between her and Jack. Hans looked at me strangely, but didn't ask me about my odd gait until we reached the train.

'The hat of that woman near to us.'

'The dead swans?'

'Jack loathes swans,' I said, keeping my voice low.

'What did you think he would do?' asked Hans, smiling. 'Grab it off her head? He's a small dog.' So saying he lifted Jack into the carriage. We had barely closed the compartment door behind us when we heard others entering the carriage. Jack, who was again sitting on the seat, as he had discovered he liked watching out of the window, now turned round to look at the commotion. The swan lady moved past the compartment and at that very moment Jack flew off his seat, launching himself at the compartment's inner window and barking like a dog possessed. The swan lady screamed as the full weight of Jack came crashing down against the glass.

In front of my eyes Jack slid in slow motion down the glass leaving a trail of dog slobber behind him. I rushed over to see if he was hurt, picking him up and hugging him to me. Hans stepped outsde to console the lady.

I took Jack over to the window. I could feel him breathing. He sprawled on my lap. I stroked his ears. He whimpered, opened his eyes and looked up at me with regret. Then he nuzzled my pocket looking for more sausages.

By the time Hans returned, which was a considerable while later, Jack had perked up and was watching out of the window. Torn between the need to scold him and the relief that Fitzroy's pet had come to no harm, I was feeding him some ham from Hans's picnic basket.

Hans swept in. 'Oh good, you have it open.' He reached in and took out a very pretty tin. 'I shall just take these biscuits for Esmeralda. She's being a good sport about the whole thing. Considering the poor lady is having to travel alone, it seems the least I can do. You don't mind, do you? I could hardly ask her to join us.' He nodded at Jack.

I did rather mind about the biscuits. We still had a considerable way to go, and I felt the lady should have provided her own nourishment for the journey. On the other hand, I had told Hans all he needed to know about Griffin, which was essentially all I knew, and the thought of not having to make conversation with him for the next several hours was a blessing.

I closed the lid of the basket to prevent further pilfering, and shook my head. Hans gave me a charming smile and disappeared back into the corridor. There was a light in his eyes, and I guessed he was on the hunt. I wondered if I should warn this Esmeralda, but decided it wasn't any of my business. I reopened the basket and after a rummage came up triumphant with a box of toffees.

It was a long journey, and when we arrived in Glasgow we then had to make our way to Edinburgh. As I had left the arrangements to Hans I had no idea how precisely we were doing this. With Jack by my side, I leaned my head back to close my eyes for a few minutes. I wondered where in France Fitzroy was and how his mission was going. There had been no mention of how long it would take. I wondered if the aristocratic nurse was still with him, and why he had no qualms about her being near a battlefront, when he had refused point-blank to let me go anywhere near one. I had assumed all the medical staff there would be men. I was better trained than any VAD . . . my thoughts disappeared down an alley where if we failed to prove Griffin innocent, it might be permitted for him to take his chances working as a doctor at the front lines. This made a lot of sense to me. To waste his skills on the scaffold when . . .

When I opened my eyes it was growing dark outside. Hans was sitting opposite me, his coat thrown open, legs crossed and reading a book.

'You're awake,' he said.

'I am aware.' I have always felt that is a peculiarly stupid statement to make.

'Good. Good,' said Hans. 'I have persuaded the guard to bring us a cup of tea. I am not entirely sure how he is managing it, but we are to ask no questions and tell no one else. It is to be a highly secret round of refreshment.' He grinned at me much like a small boy who has returned from a successful fishing trip.

I peered out of the window. 'Do you know where we are?'

'Twenty minutes from Glasgow. I did not get the chance to explain with all our discussions on more serious matters earlier, but I have arranged to stay at the railway hotel there. It has an excellent reputation. We will be able to catch a further train tomorrow after a good dinner and a refreshing night's sleep.'

I smiled. 'Excellent.'

Hans's grin widened. 'By the purest chance Esmeralda is also staying there tonight. I have invited her to be our guest for dinner.' He frowned momentarily. 'I presume you are not intending taking the dog down to dinner?'

'Under the circumstances,' I said, 'I think not.'

Glasgow Station proved to be much more impressive than I had thought. My previous experience of Scotland had entailed being a servant in a hunting lodge that was in the middle of nowhere. We had travelled up by road and then horse and cart. I had not enjoyed any of it. Although my best friend Merry had found both views to admire, and swains to admire them with. I, on the other hand, had only discovered bodies.

The station was smart, modern and had an exceptionally well-appointed hotel. I had no idea if they accepted dogs, so I did as Fitzroy would have done. I took Jack off his leash, a major risk, called him to heel, and then calmly walked into the hotel. As I signed the register I remarked, 'I will be dining with my cousin and his friend in your dining room tonight. I take it someone can take some steak and a bowl of water to my room for my dog. He prefers fillet, cut into strips.'

'Certainly, madam,' said the man behind the desk. 'Would you also like a member of staff to take him for an airing while you dine? I am afraid there will be a small charge added to your bill.'

'Yes, that would be excellent,' I said. 'My cousin will see to all the renumeration.' I waved my hand as if money was no matter to me like any well-bred woman.

I went upstairs to have a bath and change. A maid came and unpacked for me. She also left me some tea, and a bowl of water for Jack. I put on an expensive, but demure dress I knew suited me well, and went down to dinner.

Hans, who had wilted a little on the train journey, had brushed himself up to perfection, and positively shone when he stood up to greet me in the cocktail bar. He wore a dark evening suit that made his blond hair even more intense. Behind him, already seated, and without her swan hat, was our guest. Pretty, and diminutive with large brown eyes, I could see how she had captured Hans's attention. We went in to dinner.

Esmeralda told us, in the sweetest most melodious voice, she had been recently widowed. He had been a captain with the army, and fallen heroically in combat. At this point Hans made discreet reference to a medical condition that prevented him from joining up. He glanced as me askance when he did so. I didn't react to the lie, but when Esmeralda called him 'Frank' my eyebrows shot up, and I had to cover my surprise by coughing into my napkin. A moment's reflection allowed me to see that when at war with Germany, and moreover attempting to ingratiate oneself with a British war widow, using an overtly German name would not be helpful. However, I did feel he could have warned me.

When our guest excused herself for a moment between the fish course and the entrée, Hans apologised for launching his new persona. 'Fitzroy warned me some time ago I should change my name,' he said. 'I thought he was being pessimistic then about the prospects of war. I should have listened. My intention now is that I will become Frank Miller. Muller is also far too foreign-sounding.'

'It is a good plan,' I said. 'How does Richenda feel about it?'

Hans had the grace to blush slightly at the mention of his wife. 'She never liked Muller and feels Miller is very common. I have promised, after the war, to work towards being knighted for services to industry.'

My expression clearly showed what I thought of this. 'It's not impossible, Euphemia,' he said. 'I am good at what I do.'

I had never paid much attention to Hans's career. Instead I asked, 'How am I called around your new friend?'

'My cousin, Euphemia Martins, as we previously decided.'

I was about to say something sarcastic about sticking to one part of the plan when two things happened to severely unbalance me.

Firstly, Hans said, 'Esmeralda was to travel north to be a companion to a maiden aunt. Such a waste of a young life.'

'She's thirty if she is a day,' I said.

Hans ignored me. 'I have persuaded her to accompany us to Edinburgh. With luck she may meet a respectable Scottish doctor or lawyer, who is not involved in the war. It would be a crime to let such beauty be hidden from the world among the damp heather and windy mountains of the Highlands!'

Many thoughts rushed through my head. These included how difficult it would be to have a civilian dogging our footsteps. Also Esmeralda was not in widow's weeds, so had clearly been single for some time. Whether she did not wish a new husband, or whether she had some other reason for hiding herself in Scotland, it made no sense that failing to find a husband in London she should find one in the tiny city of Edinburgh. Could she be a foreign agent of some kind? She seemed harmless, helpless and extremely biddable. She was either exactly what she seemed, and therefore morally I should do my best to separate her and Hans, or she was lying to us. I attempted to find the words to express all of this to Hans without infuriating him, when I got my second shock.

Exiting the dining room on the far side, and crossing the path of the returning Esmeralda, was a man I recognised even without his checked suit.

Why on earth was Barnabas Willoughby in Glasgow?

Chapter Twenty-two

Auld Reekie

Awkward though it was I excused myself from the table the moment Esmeralda reached us. I hurried towards the exit. Checking right and left I could see a number of people milling around the hotel passageway. One direction led towards the main entrance and the other to the accommodation. I headed to the main lobby.

This large area was thinner of people. It was late enough that few people were checking in. There were several large cushioned seats of the kind that have four positions placed in a cardinal arrangement with tall cushioned partitions between them. I followed my hunch and swept around the room. I did not find Willoughby.

I was cursing under my breath that I had gone the wrong way, and I was about to go off towards the accommodation when I heard a loud 'Woof!'. Jack entered the lobby with his walker, a bellboy, and made straight for me, dragging the poor youth behind him. I had no choice but to greet the dog and thank the servant. As the bellboy praised Jack, clearly hoping for a tip, I felt the chances of me catching Willoughby draining away. I finally got rid of them both by tipping the bellboy and getting him to take Jack up to the room. Then I had no choice but to return to the pleasure of the company of Frank and his war widow.

We set off bright and early after breakfasting in our rooms, on the Edinburgh train. Esmeralda was all astonishment. Apparently she had never been to Scotland before and found it delightful. Hans was all solicitous charm in a manner I felt should not be observed so soon after breakfast. However, I was thankful she was not wearing her swan hat. After giving her a sniff, Jack had ignored her and gone back to his new habit of watching out of the window.

The journey to Edinburgh took only a short time, compared to our marathon of yesterday. Hans, it transpired, had already arranged rooms for Esmeralda at our hotel. Thus we all headed off in a taxi together, and went the very short distance to the Balmoral Hotel, a large, red stone building standing on the exposed and windy corner of the city's main street, Princes Street.

I was astonished to find myself already fatigued, and accepted Hans's suggestion that we retire to our rooms to meet again at luncheon. Although how we were to discuss anything with Esmeralda dogging our footsteps I had no idea. I had never felt so like slapping Hans.

Jack didn't seem the least bit bothered by our perpetually changing circumstances, and immediately climbed on to the foot of my new bed. He settled down and was soon snoring. I decided to bathe and refresh myself. The journey may have been short, but one always acquires a degree of dirt from travelling by train. Then I would rest and make a plan of action.

My bath was run, and I was in my dressing gown, when there was a tap at my door. For some ridiculous reason I had the sudden hope that Fitzroy had returned early from France and caught up with us. I hurried to open the door and found Hans standing there.

'Oh, it's you,' I said.

Hans raised an eyebrow, and swept his gaze over my attire. 'Expecting someone else, cousin?'

'No, of course not,' I snapped. I grabbed him by the wrist and drew him quickly into the room, closing the door behind him. 'You do rather keep springing things on me,' I said. 'This woman, your name change and even our cousinly relationship. This isn't some kind of parlour game, Hans – Frank, a man's life is at stake.'

'I understand that. Which is why I arranged to have Esmeralda have a rest so we could talk. I didn't imagine you were the kind of woman to retire to her bed in the hours of daylight.'

'I was going to bathe,' I said, conscious of gritting my teeth.

'Don't let me stop you. I can wait in the bedroom. We can speak through the door.'

'No, thank you,' I said, sitting down. 'I need to approach the medical school here and see if I can persuade them to let me look at Griffin's work record here.'

'What are you looking for?'

'The man he killed was a member of his cohort when he trained as a doctor. I want to look into both of their histories.'

'Ah,' said Hans, 'the one he got removed from the course.'

'So you have been listening.'

'But why would they tell you?'

'I have been considering that. You are probably unaware that there has been an increase in female private detectives since the start of the war.'

'Good heavens,' said Hans. 'That doesn't sound very feminine.'

'I shall pose as one. I have yet to decide on the full story.'

'Won't you need a licence?'

'I'll deal with that,' I said, my heart sinking. 'Perhaps you could spend the afternoon escorting your playmate around the sights of the town, and start to get to know the city. I have never been here before.'

'I visited once, but it was a long time ago.'

'We can meet for a late luncheon. You will announce your offer to escort us around the city, but unfortunately I will be found to have a previous engagement.'

'What?'

'Visiting my old nanny, who has returned to her native land.'

'Are you making this up as you go along or did you have it all arranged?' asked Hans.

'I don't intend to discuss my methods,' I said. 'You're still on probation as an asset. Now, leave me to my ablutions.'

With only a little more coercion, and a sly, but gentle comment on the attractiveness of my nightgown, I managed to get Hans to leave. I did not feel in any way threatened by him, but he was already becoming tiresome. Although, to give him his due, he had reminded me that I needed a licence. I called down to the front desk, and sent a coded telegram. It was a fairly simple acrostic alerting Morley to where I was, and asking if there were agents on the ground who could provide me with civilian paperwork.

Luncheon proved to be every bit as dull as I had feared. Hans opted for the Cullen skink soup to open his meal, and the smell was grotesque to put it mildly. It completely put me off my own food, so that by the end of the meal I was both hungry and bored. If Esmeralda was truly a foreign agent who had wormed her way into our party, then I gave her full marks for embodying a dullness that previously I had thought only a dead plant pot could assume. However, Hans followed my instructions and departed with her for a tour of the city.

My plans did not fare as well. I received a telegram back from London to tell me that my request would be processed in due course. I marvelled that even in a coded message Morley or one of his minions could have managed to write large between the lines that the mission I was on was not significant to the war, and that I must wait while they undertook more important matters.

There was no point gnashing my teeth. Although I may have thrown a couple of pillows across the room. I determined I would take a cab to look around the medical school and get a feel for the place where Griffin had trained.

Before I left the room I picked up the pillows, plumped them and placed them back on the bed. I do not have it in me to be as angry as my partner.

Chapter Twenty-three

A Discovery in a Library

As the doorman hailed me a cab, it occurred to me how very little I knew about Griffin's case. Fitzroy seemed to have successfully burned all the notes I might have had access to, and Morley or McLeod were blocking the rest. But perhaps the arrest of an old graduate from the city's medical school might have awoken the interest of the city's main newspaper *The Scotsman*.

Once I was seated inside the cab, and the doorman had audibly given the direction, I waited a few moments before directing the driver to change course for the nearest large local library. I had hoped in doing this to throw any would-be followers off the trail. However, as the driver chipperly announced, it was on the way. He also called me 'hen' for no reason I could account for. As I paid my fare and alighted I spotted no sign of being tailed, and felt a combination of relief and disappointment.

The Central Library turned out to be voluminous and elegant. It was oddly situated with its main entrance across a small bridgeway that led from a road that was itself a bridge. The library rose three storeys up and descended three storeys down from this mid-point.

Apparently it is one of the first Carnegie Libraries, as the first librarian I met was eager to tell me; it had circular turrets, Doric colonettes sprouting in every corner, and the place blossomed with heraldic designs. There was also a superfluity of oak panelling. All in all I felt the building was trying too hard to impress. However, there was a newspaper room.

I told the gentleman in charge of the room, a middle-aged

individual with a checked waistcoat, neatly brilliantined hair, and an aroma of old tobacco, that I was an historian. I was writing a book about medical men who had turned out bad, and I had heard that there had been a case within the last few years of a medical man, trained in Edinburgh, who had murdered someone before turning himself in.

The librarian showed his disapproval of my topic by producing a small pair of spectacles from his jacket pocket and regarding me over their thin wire frames. 'If madam will take a seat I will endeavour to find relevant articles. You understand that nothing can be removed from the reading room, madam?'

I nodded.

'I may be some time. I have no recollection of an Edinburgh medical man committing any breach of the law.'

This seemed unlikely to me, and when the librarian further informed me that by some time he might mean more than an hour, I inferred that he remembered the case well, and did not wish any further bad publicity for his home city. I had hoped that giving me some of the facts would have inspired him to search. Now, I realised there was no reason to hold back.

'His name was John Griffin,' I said. 'It is believed he murdered the man who murdered his wife, Megan Luckett. Upon doing so, he immediately gave himself up.'

'You seem to have all the pertinent facts.'

'But not the details. I would prefer to be as accurate as possible.'

The man made a grunting noise and went off. I took out my notebook and began to make my own notes. When making notes I use a code that I have agreed with Fitzroy. My notes would make no sense to anyone but the two of us as it relies on knowing an agreed phrase. (Which I have no intention of sharing here.) I was recording my thoughts on spying Barnabas Willoughby at the hotel in Glasgow when I realised I had left something behind at my current hotel – Jack!

I had half risen in alarm when the librarian returned bristling with newspapers. Unless I particularly wished to draw attention to myself I needed to calm myself and take my notes as any amateur historian might. I thanked the man and set to work. I pushed to the back of my mind visions of Jack climbing out of a window in pursuit of a Scottish swan.

The first piece the librarian had marked was a piece on Dr John Griffin being sent for trial for murder on 17th June 1912. A little further searching found a longer opinion piece by an Edinburgh worthy by the name of Professor James McIvory in a smaller city-wide publication, who recorded:

> It is with lamentable regret that I discovered from an article in *The Times* that one of our own graduates, Dr John Griffin (MD Edinburgh 1910), has, after a full confession, been arrested for murder. The editor of this most respectable publication has asked me, as one of the professors teaching at that time, to pen a response to this heinous crime. Above all, we doctors swear to do no harm, so for one of our own to callously take a life, brings the whole practice into disrepute. In this instance it also sullies the name of our prodigious university. I will not write in his defence, but I will write to alleviate any fears that may have awakened in the public breast. This is an extraordinary case, and I doubt its like will ever be seen again. What has emerged in the court proceedings is but a sliver of the truth suspected by a well-renowned medical family. After long and deep soul-searching discussions with the Luckett family, I have been emboldened to write this piece, offering an insight into what is believed to have occurred by those who knew the persons involved. This is not the story that the reader will have previously read. It is darker, and more full of shadows than any decent person might have suspected. I beg only that my reader keeps an open mind until the end of the article. I have been a professor of medicine for ten years, and a practitioner for thirty. I can honestly say that never in all my time in medicine did I come across so complex and so tragic a case. I regret to fully explain

the series of events I will even have to trespass into the querulous realms of Dr S. Freud, of whose debatable and unpalatably sensual theories much is being written in medical journals today.

Griffin, who had moved to England to open a family practice in London, was one of the best and brightest of his year. Shortly before he left our country, he married the sister of one of his fellow students. A pretty, demure young woman called Megan Luckett. Suitably educated by her father, who was himself a doctor. Megan, whom I had also met, was a right-minded young woman, eager to become a good wife and start her own family. She was in so many ways a model wife for a doctor. Bright enough to be a strong support in his practice, capable enough to run a small household and entirely free of any of the sensibilities and protestations of the suffragette set. I say all this to allow you to understand she was in terms of a wife for Griffin a perfect diamond. Their wedding took place in the Highlands where Megan's familial home was, and by all accounts a good time was had by all.

But from this happy start, almost from the very words 'I do' crossing her pretty lips, things began to go wrong. From speaking to her brother I understand that Megan did not like London. She found it constraining, too busy and bustling. While Griffin was building a flourishing practice, as might have been suspected of one with his skills, his poor wife was left feeling isolated and overwhelmed. It was not long before she became prey, according to her brother, to moods of hysteria.

This caused much discussion among the medical men of the Luckett family. Megan wrote regularly to her mother, as any good daughter should, and it became clear to them all she was no longer of sound mind. In particular she wrote of the other man.

Her brother is convinced to this day that 'the other man' was a second side to Griffin's nature. He believes that Megan, unable as she was to fully process the fact that the husband she loved had a darker side to his nature, created the character of 'the other man'. This aligns with Dr Freud's ideas. However, we can go deeper. Megan, after a full year of marriage, had yet to produce a child. The cause of this failure is unknown. However, Megan's letters attest to her disappointment and her husband's regret. In using the word 'regret' I am copying directly from Mrs Griffin's correspondence. Her family feared that she was writing, elliptically, of her husband's regret at marrying a barren and increasingly hysterical wife.

The family offered to host a holiday for the couple back in the peaceful Highlands. If Griffin was unable to leave work they offered to take Megan alone, her brother even suggesting himself as her chaperone on the journey there and back. This offer, an ideal pause you might have thought, dear reader, for Megan to regain her health and her perspective, was declined. Griffin wrote himself in response saying that Megan was making progress in adjusting to the metropolitan life, and he feared her return to the Highlands would set back all her improvements. It was a reasoned argument, but the family, reading her letters, saw no improvement. Yet, she was his wife. There was little they could do but pray.

Then came the hideous news that rang out in papers across the nation and indeed the Continent that Megan Luckett had been murdered in the most barbarous way. I pray the gentlest of my readers looks away at this point. The details not then announced in the press, but known to the family, were that her female organs of reproduction had been removed after or during her death.

Followers of Freud will immediately see the significance of the removal of a womb from a barren wife. The 'other man', the darker side of her husband, might well have inflicted this as a punishment for not bearing him a child. It also at the same time as inflicting punishment removed the obstacle of his finding himself a fertile wife.

I write this as a possibility not as a fact. It is what her family believe, but it contravenes the accusation and arrest for murder of Griffin. The police do not accuse him of his wife's murder. Neither does he admit it himself.

No, Griffin appeared at a London police station covered in blood and confessing the murder of his wife's murderer, David Bloom.

The article continued on, but at this point I decided that it was necessary for me to remove it from the archives. The theory it upheld was injurious to Griffin, but more important than this odd professor's rambling defence (if he ever got to that point) of his profession were the details of Megan's murder that my department and the London police believed had never been released. Here it was in black and white. I had no idea how many readers would have ploughed through this turgid and fantastical prose, but the fact remained that the details that the authorities were so convinced had been kept from the press, and were one of the main reasons Griffin had been arrested, had been published in a Scottish paper.

However, this wasn't the biggest shock by a long way. Who on earth was David Bloom? Griffin had not been able to finish telling me his story, but of all the people he had mentioned Bloom wasn't amongst them. I had jumped to the conclusion that Nathaniel had been the killer, but Griffin had said I had got it all wrong. How on earth did anyone expect me to prove anything when I didn't even have the right name of the man Griffin had killed? And why had he bothered to tell me about the other two? What else had he wanted to tell me?

During a coughing fit – less than original I know – I removed the page from the paper. I folded it neatly and placed it in my reticule. I placed this particular journal at the bottom of the pile. While this piece might be something of a double-edged sword, with its psychological evaluation of Griffin as a split personality, it also removed McLeod's main reason for holding Griffin. The

Empire, even in our department, does not allow for the imprisonment and holding of an individual on a suspicion or hunch. With luck I would be able to get Griffin released by the end of tomorrow. Then, perhaps, he would start telling me what was really going on.

I walked out, nodding my thanks to the librarian. A part of me wanted to see his face when he found his precious archive disfigured, but as I had left a false name and address in the readers' book I doubted I would ever see him again.

I found a cab to take me to the hotel. Things were finally going in the right direction. Now, if only Jack had behaved himself.

Chapter Twenty-four

The Bad Penny and the Bad Dog

I arrived at the hotel to find an aftermath of chaos. My room smelled strongly of cleaning products, and the two pillows I had vented my anger upon were missing. There was no sign of Jack. Even his food bowl and chew toy were missing.

For the first time ever I felt my blood turn cold. It's an old saying, but I swear at that moment I understood it. I felt as if I had been thrown into an icy lake. If anything had happened to Jack I knew Fitzroy would be distraught. I hurried to Hans's room. If he had returned before me perhaps the animal was with him.

Hans opened the door on the echo of my knock. He remained as sartorially impeccable as ever, but his hair was slightly messed. 'Thank God you are back,' he said. He grabbed me by the wrist and pulled me into his room.

I saw at once Hans had spared no expense and allocated himself a large suite. We were in the lounging area, and fast asleep by a raging fire was Jack. I sank into a chair. 'Oh thank goodness,' I said. 'You have him.'

'Yes,' said Hans, 'but it was a close-run thing.'

'Did he get out?'

'No, he started biting people.'

I collapsed in a chair. Hans came and sat opposite me.

'Then he rather disgraced himself.'

'Oh dear,' I said.

'Esmeralda is with the doctor.'

'What was Esmeralda doing in my room?' I asked, suddenly alert and suspicious.

'She was with me, Euphemia, when the staff, who knew we had booked rooms together, asked for my help.' He gently tried to rearrange his fringe. I didn't have the heart to tell him he had an enormous cowlick. 'I admit,' he continued, 'that she was unwise to approach the animal directly. Jack had been howling for you. She went down on one knee to comfort him. She tells me she generally has a good success rate with animals.'

'But not in this case. Was it a bad bite?'

'Personally I would have called it a nip, but there was a tiny amount of blood. She went into hysterics. All most unfortunate.'

'The shine has come off the gem?' I said.

Hans gave me a hard stare. 'She is a delicate and refined young lady.'

'Unlike myself.' I found myself grinning. 'But really, Hans, you did insist on bringing her with you.'

'Leaving aside the fact that you forgot entirely about the dog, I should have thought it was obvious why I wanted her presence.'

'Oh it was!'

'For your reputation, Euphemia! You can't go running around the countryside with a man – especially one who is known for his fondness of the weaker sex – without damaging your reputation! That, and causing Bertram any distress, is the last thing I want! Really, I am surprised at you!'

'But you're always trying to convince me to become your mistress,' I said. 'Or do I have that wrong?'

Hans sat back in his chair, and calmed a little at this. 'No, I'd be delighted if you were interested in an arrangement with me. But I am discreet! I would ensure that no one ever knew to protect both your reputation and the feelings of our spouses.'

I could have replied that I was perfectly used to running around the country, even the world, with a man with a far more prodigious reputation for womanising than Hans, but instead I said, 'Bertram trusts me. Completely. He never doubts me.'

Hans raised an eyebrow. 'How convenient for you. Or perhaps for us. But you must see my point.'

'Frankly, it never occurred to me that anyone would think I had run off with you. Not least because we are meant to be being discreet.'

'Then don't use your real name, and don't leave an animal to savage staff!'

'How did you get him to behave?'

'Steak.'

'Anyway, I do bring good news. I have found that contrary to what I was told the details of the original killing were released in the press. I will send a formal message to London tonight asking them to release Griffin on my cognisance. There are aspects of this case that confuse me.'

'Well, that does sound like good news,' said Hans. 'When Griffin joins us he can act as chaperone, and I can put Esmeralda on a train.'

'So you are eager to be rid of her?'

'I have her address, and we have agreed to meet again under less straining circumstances. A month or so alone with her aged aunt will realign her ideas of the romantic Highlands.'

'And see what you are offering is far more romantic?'

'You were born much higher in the system than myself,' said Hans, 'but sometimes I wonder if you understand how the world works at all.'

I shrugged and made my way to the door. 'I'll see you at dinner.'

'The dog!'

'Have you never heard the adage let sleeping dogs lie?'

Hans made a strangled noise that I cut off by closing the door behind me. In reality, I had every intention of coming back for Jack. I now knew that Hans was perfectly capable of taking care of him for a short while. Or rather I knew that Jack didn't particularly take exception to Hans. I imagined there was a whiff of his master about Hans. He might well see Hans as a sort of pale imitation of Fitzroy.

I made my way to the front desk, where I gave the concierge a reasonable bribe for smoothing over the events of the afternoon. I also arranged for private access to a telephone.

Of course it wasn't a secure line, but until London cleared my introduction to whoever ran an office on site, and surely in the Scottish capital there had to be an office, then I didn't have access to one. A call to London, I hoped, would drive this point home.

Dotty answered. 'Goodness, back in touch so soon. I thought you would be enjoying your little holiday. Have you had haggis yet? Made from the innards of a sheep, but the locals swear by it, I hear.'

'Not yet,' I said. 'Are you able to put me in touch with—?'

'Soon,' said Dotty, interrupting me. 'If you intend staying up there.'

'Soon please,' I said and hung up. It was already far too much to say on an open line. Hopefully that would get them moving.

I went back and picked up Jack. He grumbled at being woken up, but then became ridiculously excited to see me and disgraced himself on Hans's rug. I decided to take him for a walk. I knew Fitzroy took him everywhere and I was beginning to see why. It was a great deal easier than trying to carve out time for walks when you were on a mission.

Jack and I headed out. We enjoyed a ramble through Princes Street Gardens. Jack met a few other dogs and behaved impeccably. Fortunately, the gardens did not contain a waterway nor any swans. Jack did stop and bark at the Walter Scott memorial. But this was a very ugly thing and I quite agreed with him.

All in all it would have been a pleasant afternoon, except for the man who followed us around the gardens. The walks around the grass ways and trees are lovely, but not of any great size. Indeed the whole plot is small compared to the Royal Parks of London. So while my tail was quite adept at using newspaper, trees and even shadows to conceal himself, I still spotted him.

It was within twenty minutes of entering the park that I felt uncomfortable. This is not an unusual feeling for an unaccompanied female to have even in these enlightened times. But this was something more. Those males of the more lecherous dispositions are rarely able to conceal their interest let alone their often-corpulent physiques. But while I felt the hairs on the back of my neck rise I could not immediately see who was observing me.

I therefore considered if I were watching me in the park which place would give me the greatest scope of vision. There were some benches set on the upper slope. Some of these were recessed, presumably to give shelter from Scotland's supposedly typical weather. I say this, as this day was most bright and warm. But if I were watching I would have chosen an outside bench. I had to assume I had been tailed into the park from the hotel. The main street, Princes Street, had been so busy with tourists, shoppers and others that I would not have spotted a tail. Especially as, I confess, I was not looking for one. I had been running through events so far in my head, and exactly what I needed to say to get Griffin released at once. Rory McLeod was a difficult man, who clearly still held a grudge against me.

So having ascertained my watcher would likely be on one of these benches, I deliberately took a route that would take me out of their sight. Midway along this I spotted a flower that I pretended to study with intense interest. Jack, who I had on a leash, was very quickly bored. There were squirrels here, and I suspected squirrels were less appealing than swans, but more interesting than flowers. He whiffled a few times to try and get my interest in moving. I stayed resolute. In fact it was only when he had snapped off the head of said flower, and thankfully spat it straight back out, that I espied a gentleman coming down the path cautiously, and with his hat partly obscuring his face.

It was not enough. I recognised him as none other than Barnabas Willoughby. I had half convinced myself that I had imagined him in Glasgow, but now in the bright light of an Edinburgh day I had no doubt that he had followed me all the way from London to Scotland. The question was why?

Chapter Twenty-five

Meeting the Locals

Sometimes when you have a serious question the best thing to do is simply ask it. I waited until Willoughby's path took him to the nearest point to me, and then set off at a brisk pace. I did not look at him directly. I focused my gaze elsewhere, but kept him within my peripheral vision. The problem with following someone you don't know well, and I hoped this was true here, is that their actions can be unpredictable. Depending on who Willoughby really was he might or might not expect me to spot him. What I strongly doubted was that he would anticipate a female agent would confront him. Besides, if he wasn't an agent, he would be even less likely to think I would confront him.

So as I strode in his direction, Willoughby, as I had predicted, did not swerve in his course. The professional thing to do was to continue on, and swing around at a further point out of my sight. He had to believe in himself and his craft. Otherwise he was in great danger of giving himself away.

The distance between us was not large. My path turned slightly and now I was walking directly towards him. As we grew closer I could see that his breathing was faster than would be expected for this incline, and his skin a shade redder than was normal. His hat was now tilted most oddly down to conceal his face. I was surprised he could see where he was going. He was flustered. Good!

But to give the man his due he was continuing on, and it looked as if he meant to pass me. I scanned him again for any sign of weapons, and saw nothing. Although he walked with a fairly light step,

I saw rigidity in his shoulders rather than the deliberately relaxed looseness of a man preparing to fight.

It was highly unlikely he would attack me in broad daylight, but I still didn't know why he was following me. It was possible he thought he could kidnap me or Jack and make away with us across the park. I saw no sign of uniformed officers. If this was his intention then it would be a bad mistake.

But more than anything I found it difficult to believe that this man honestly thought that a tilted hat was enough to obscure his identity. We had spoken face to face! But then he might be relying on the concept that when one sees someone where one doesn't expect to see them it is all too easy to misidentify them. Ha! Not for someone as well trained as myself.

I tightened my hold on Jack's lead. I took a deep breath to expel any tension in my body, and readied myself for the confrontation. I would not land an opening strike, but I could hail him while standing directly in his path.

I moved to do so, and as I did I felt a firm hand grasp my elbow. I hesitated on whether to drop Jack's lead, and this was all it took for the man touching me to turn me aside from Willoughby. I was turned around and furious. I looked up to my right and saw a well-dressed gentleman.

'My dear Alice,' he said a smooth tone. 'How fortunate it is that I have come across you in the park. Allow me to lead us to a quiet bench where we can converse.'

'I am following someone,' I said through gritted teeth. By addressing me by my code name the man was signalling he was from my department.

'You rather looked as if you were about to confront that poor man,' said my new companion. 'We do hate to create a scene in the city. Please come with me.'

'That man has followed me all the way from London,' I said quietly, but with anger throbbing in my voice.

'Then I think it likely he will not give up. Unless, of course, he is easily scared.'

The grip on my elbow had grown vice-like and more than a little painful. I stopped. My stance was solid and clearly ready to engage. The man holding me looked down – he was rather tall – and loosened his grip. 'I really would rather we didn't create a scene. Besides, I had been led to believe you were eager to talk to me.'

'I take it you're from the local office?' I said. 'I hadn't expected contact today.'

'Indeed, I had a call from a Colonel M requesting that we expedite a private investigator licence for you. Do you have any training in that area?'

'I am a full member of the London department,' I said.

'Clerical? I suppose you'll have picked up some things.'

I had had enough. I pinned his arm closer to my right side by putting my hand on my own stomach. I extended my right foot as if to take a step and turned sharply. Mr Patronising barely maintained his balance. 'You are still standing only because I have allowed it,' I said coldly. 'I agree with not making a scene in a public place, but I am open to proving my credentials. I have never worked in a clerical department, nor do I owe my self-defence to being a suffragette. While I am personally supportive of their cause, as a government employee I remain apolitical.'

The man withdrew his arm, stepped away and extended his hand. 'May we start again? Ernest Sutherland at your service. I apologise profusely. You rather caught me on the hop. We're having rather a busy time of it at the moment. Can you inform me as to the extent of your investigations?'

I shook his hand, and took my first proper look at the man. He was older than Fitzroy. I could see grey flecks in his dark, tightly curled hair. His eyes were a cool gun-metal grey, and unusually he was as tall as my partner. Of medium build, he carried himself with a looseness of limb, and wore a good, but not form-fitting suit. All in all it suggested that he was trained in street fighting. Doubtless hard and vicious. I would not like to fight him, but I suspected his incipient underrating of women was his Achilles' heel. It would be much easier if we were friends.

'It is need to know.'

'Why are you in my city, then?'

'It obliquely involves the medical school,' I said. 'I am hoping to speak to current professors and possibly former students who still work in the area.'

'The Royal Edinburgh Infirmary is of long standing, and our medical school is held in good esteem. Yet, before the war there had been rumours . . .' He tailed off. 'However, we have a new focus. But you should bear in mind that this is an old city, with old families, and deep interconnected roots. It is much smaller than London, and if anything that makes feelings run deeper. We Scots are a stoic lot, but you don't want to stir up a hornet's nest.'

'I cannot see how I might,' I said.

'Very well. Your permit is in your pocket, and it looks as if your dog is about to eat a squirrel or attempt to.'

I found myself checking my coat pocket and the leash at the same time. Jack had quietly escaped, and was indeed now stalking a squirrel that was sitting calmly eating part of a stolen sandwich. 'Damn it,' I swore. 'I presume these are not royal squirrels?'

'I beg your pardon?'

'He tries to chase swans in London's Royal Parks.'

'Perhaps you should take him to dog-training classes?'

I was standing still watching Jack. 'He isn't mine. I'm watching him for a friend. But I agree. He has already bitten a woman at our hotel, and misbehaved in a variety of ways I prefer not to describe.'

At this moment Jack launched himself at the squirrel, which without even turning its head to look at him flew up into the tree as if propelled by some unseen force. Jack jumped up, but in vain. He continued with his whiffling barking and jumping. The squirrel carried on eating its sandwich, and watched from its superior position.

'Well, if that is all?'

'Actually, I do need to send some messages back to my – er – office. Is it possible to send them from yours?'

Sutherland sighed. 'I will send a cab this evening. We do tend to keep our premises – well, you know.'

I nodded. 'After dinner? Around eight p.m.? You keep almost country hours in this city.'

'Thereabouts. By the way, I shouldn't worry about that mannie who was following you. After your purse, I expect. Very amateurish. I doubt he is the same man you saw in London. Some people have common faces. However, I would go and collect your – or rather your friend's – dog. He has begun to gather admirers.'

I looked over and saw a group of children, ahead of their nanny, who was slowed by the huge pram she was wheeling, bearing down on Jack. One of them was a boy who had a rolling hoop and a stick. 'Dammit!' I said again, and hurried forward. I wanted to ask Sutherland more about the medical school, but I doubted Jack would resist that hoop, or indeed the stick.

By the time I had retrieved Jack, and procured an ice cream for him as a bribe not to bite anyone else that afternoon, Sutherland had vanished. At least it gave me some time to formulate what details of local knowledge I needed to probe him for.

Jack dawdled on the way back to the hotel, getting slower and slower. I began to hope that he might fall into a deep sleep, and not require walking until long after dinner. Hopefully, I could find a bellboy in need of an extra penny or two.

We finally made it back to the hotel, where halfway across the mosaic-laden floor Jack paused, coughed, and was copiously sick. Apparently ice cream and dogs don't mix well.

Chapter Twenty-six

Into the Shadows

For their own reasons it was tonight that the hotel served a particularly elegant dinner. I chose a light cheese soufflé, followed by the poached local salmon, followed by fillet steak in a sumptuous sauce (alas for my inability to understand French), and ending with a collection of ices, the cheeseboard and some petits fours. It is not like me to eat so much, but I had found today trying, and I seemed to have acquired Fitzroy's annoying manner of eating more while on a mission. Not of course that I ate large portions of each course, but Hans, who had happily been pairing wines with each new dish, looked at me in amazement. Esmeralda languished over soup and tiny lamp chops. She had a morsel of queen of puddings when Hans pressed her to eat more.

Esmeralda excused herself before coffee. 'I feel I need a little lie-down before this evening's entertainment,' she said cryptically.

When she had left I raised an eyebrow at Hans, who was helping himself to more Stilton and water biscuits. 'Oh, I've arranged to join a select little party this evening to play whist. I would have preferred bridge, which is more exciting, but I thought she should see what life with her aunt is liable to be like.'

'You need four for bridge,' I said. 'Her aunt may have no friends?'

'Excellent point! No living peers is highly likely.' He grinned in a most ungentlemanly way. 'She will be in raptures to receive my little billet-doux.'

'It's good you are entertaining her. I have another meeting tonight. I shall say no more than that things are looking positive.'

'Excellent. If you could possibly give a day's notice before we return south so I can warn Esmeralda? I should also send Richenda a note, so she doesn't worry.'

'Oh what a tangled web we weave.'

Hans sneered slightly. It looked odd on his handsome features. 'Euphemia, you are if not conspiring with me, certainly not warning the fair Esmeralda of my intentions. Something I rather think you would have leaped to do when we first met.' He tilted his head slightly, considering me. 'You have become a very different person. You inhabit a world of secrets now and it has changed you. I have no doubt you could lie to my face, to Bertram's, or anyone else's you wished, and we would be inclined to believe you. Fitzroy has changed you in many ways, and not all for the better – in the moral sense. However as a plotter and schemer, unlikely as it would have once seemed to me, you strike me as a natural. I speak as someone who has had to keep his own fair share of secrets.'

'The secrets I keep are for the sake of the Crown, not the perfidy of adultery,' I snapped.

Hans, who I now saw was more drunk than I had realised, lolled back in his chair, holding his glass loosely. He raised it to me, as if in salute. 'If you say so, Euphemia. If you say so.'

I finished my coffee and left without further comment. There is no point in trying to reason with a man afflicted with alcohol. Not unless you are prepared to pour cold water over him and then threaten him with a broom. I had never reacted so badly to Hans. At this moment I would have very much liked to slap him in the face. What annoyed me further was I had no idea how he might react. Hans was right in one thing: he was a consummate actor when he needed to be. He would make me an excellent asset if I didn't murder him first.

I stopped at reception to arrange a walk for Jack, but when I went to my room I found a very sad and sorry Jack. If he had been a child I might have arranged warm milk, but I had no idea what one did for a dog. I also knew that my ride was due any moment. I stacked the fire higher, made sure he had fresh water, and hoped that he needed nothing more to get over his intestinal issues.

The department I was taken to was off the centre of the city in the Royal Mile. The cab turned up and dropped me by a narrow opening between two buildings. The driver, who had been taciturn since he established my name, told me, 'Head down the vennel!' He departed before I could ask further questions.

I assumed the vennel was how he described what I would have called an extremely narrow alley. The buildings on either side rose to more than six storeys and were some of the oldest parts of Edinburgh. Narrow enough that two people would be unable to enter it side by side, it was unlit and descended steeply. Looking up and down the street I could see other such openings. Some of them were labelled with names that had 'Close' appended to them, and sported iron gates. Clearly these narrow entrances were as much about security as convenience. I marvelled that whoever had originally built these old buildings had thought to arrange matters so cleverly. Unlike York city where the old wattle and daub buildings have sunk drunkenly together over the years to make the narrow walkways called The Shambles, here the buildings were solid stone and had not moved an inch for centuries.

All this went through my mind while I hesitated at the entrance. My overriding reflection was this would be an excellent place to kidnap or murder someone. I doubted Sutherland, as long as he was who he said he was, would seek to harm me, but I still had not solved the mystery of Willoughby.

I entered the passageway cautiously, with my back to the wall, ready to defend myself. After some twenty steps it opened out, to my great surprise, into a small neat garden. Standing at the back as if dropped there by some passing giant was a small two-windowed cottage. I knocked on the door and Sutherland answered.

'So you found our wee house, all right?'

'Your city never fails to surprise.'

He smiled at that, and stood aside to usher me inside. The door opened directly into an office with a small fire blazing at the back.

'As far as anyone else is concerned we are a rent collection agency,' said Sutherland. 'During the day we have a secretary, and our agents come and go to pick up their job allocations. It works well as a cover. With the war I'm thinking about employing some women as collection agents. We do the real thing as part of the cover. One of the reasons I came to meet you myself. I'm still deciding how I might feel about having women doing anything active in my department.'

He took me over to the fire, and gestured to a couple of seats. 'If I find us a wee dram maybe we could have a fair and frank discussion? Might be able to help each other?'

I sat down. 'I have no objection to a discussion, Mr Sutherland, but I do need to contact my department.'

He pointed back to the desk. 'Use that telephone while I go and dig up the bottle. The one I have in mind is well hidden.' He rose, and opening a door I hadn't noticed, descended some stairs, closing the door behind him.

I went to the telephone, and called my department. I didn't know the voice of the person who answered, and after exchanging code words I was told that no one in my department was currently reachable. In desperation I asked about Rory, and was told Inspector McLeod was on duty.

'McLeod.' Rory's voice sounded stern and unfriendly. Completely unlike the days when we had worked in service together. I took a deep breath, pushing all the memories away.

'Good evening, this is Alice,' I said. 'I tried my department, but no one was reachable. I wanted to draw your attention to,' and I gave the name of the newspaper, the date and the author. 'It details, graphically, what happened to Megan. I believe your primary reason for taking the subject into custody was that this material was never released.'

'It wasn't in London,' said Rory. 'But this is a Scottish periodical.'

'I think the whole issue is tied up with students who attended the medical school. I'm going to see the school tomorrow, and see if I can learn more.'

'Hmm,' said Rory. 'I'll have your information verified and take appropriate action if required.'

'Thank you,' I said, and ended the call.

There was so much more we both could have said on either side. It struck me that Rory hadn't told me not to interfere, or to be careful, or challenged my future plans. Could it be that after the mission I had undertaken at the hospital a kind of peace was genuinely beginning to evolve between us? I had once thought I wanted to be Rory's wife, but Fitzroy had dissuaded me. From early on, he had seen the darker side of Rory's nature. But I still remembered him as my affectionate friend, and missed him. Mutual respect between us would go a long way to healing my wounds – and possibly his.

Sutherland must have seen the thoughtful expression on my face. 'So you are getting somewhere? Tell me about it, lass.'

Chapter Twenty-seven

A Wee Dram and a Wee Chat

The whisky, a viscous amber, was much stronger than anything I was used to. I took a tiny sip, and was rewarded with warmth and the flavour of honey. So smooth, it didn't make me cough; I knew that if I finished this glass I would be asleep in my chair.

I smiled at Sutherland. 'I can't tell you more than you already know,' I said. 'I've not been cleared to do so.'

'Heavens, lass, I'm the section chief up here!'

'With respect, sir, that doesn't change anything.'

Sutherland smiled. 'Fair enough. No need to call me sir. You're not one of mine. Besides, I find it odd coming from a woman.'

'As I said, I will be visiting the medical school tomorrow and asking some questions. I will be discreet.'

'You've not yet found out who your follower is?'

'I have a name,' I said. 'But it may be an alias.'

'Am I permitted to know that?'

I had a feeling I shouldn't tell him, but logically I could see no reason not to. 'Barnabas Willoughby.'

'I don't know it. It's a name hard to forget though.'

'Isn't it?' I said, feeling rather like a mouse in the presence of a big cat.

'Would you like a top-up?' He reached the bottle towards me. I covered my glass with my hand. 'Thank you, no. This is excellent and I am enjoying it, but I am not used to strong spirits.' I took another tiny sip to prove the point.

'The man travelling with you, Hans Muller. Of German descent.'

'An asset,' I said curtly.

'Indeed, you won't mind that I am having him watched while he is in my city?'

'Understandable,' I said, wondering how long, and who he had been watching. 'So, I got the impression you had more you could tell me about the medical school?'

'Aye, it's a grand place, but has a dark history. The actions of Burke and Hare made it what it is today. You ken who they are?'

I shook my head.

'A pair of killers who undertook to supply fresh bodies to the school for dissection. Caused such a fuss when they were caught that the laws on supplying cadavers to the school were changed. Having the real things to work on gave our students a leg-up in the medical world.'

'When was this?' I asked, shocked.

'Eighteen twenty-two, but the city has a long memory. Who are you hoping to speak with?'

'Professor James McIvory would be my first choice, but I think he is retired?'

'Dead. Thankfully. Who else?'

'I was going to enquire about David Bloom.'

'Never heard of him. Who else?'

'Walter Gibbons.'

'Unpleasant fellow. Charms the ladies though. Professor there now. I'd advise you to steer clear of him unless absolutely necessary. And if you do intend to talk to him it might be wise to notify me.'

'Good heavens, why?' I asked, astonished. 'I presume if he is a professor he is a respected member of the medical community? And why are you thankful that McIvory is dead?'

Sutherland reached forward and refilled his glass. He offered me a further drink, but I shook my head. The Scottish agent settled back in his seat nursing his glass. I wondered how long he would play this odd game with me. The day had been a long one, and with the travelling I hadn't rested well since Fitzroy set off on his mission. The malt whisky was making me sleepy. I knew I wasn't at my sharpest, and very much wished the conversation was done and I was back in my bed. I wondered how Jack was doing. Eventually Sutherland spoke.

'You're a rare woman who doesn't fill a silence,' he said. 'I suppose that came through your training.'

I waited for an apology. It didn't arrive.

'So McIvory, big name, famous medicine man. In with the city council. Dined with the best families. Untouchable. Never smelled right to me. He was too close to a number of strange things that happened.'

'But never arrested?'

'No.' He took a pull at his whisky. 'Gibbons is a brilliant man at the anatomy by all accounts. Helps the local constabulary with murders and assaults – and the like. They say what he knows about a dead body Death himself doesn't know. Won't be easy to get an appointment to see him. He's very much in demand.'

'Is he well spoken of?'

'Aye, I've heard nothing to the contrary. We've never had a need to keep an eye on him.'

'But you did with Professor McIvory?'

'How did they brief you when you were coming here, Mrs Stapleford? Or is it Lady? Didn't your husband inherit a title?'

'Yes, but he chooses not to use it. It brought nothing but unhappiness to his family. His father was killed because of it, and his elder brother – well, he was not a good man.'

'Very candid of you,' said Sutherland.

'I have no doubt the details are on my file.'

'Which I have been refused access to. It seems your commanding officer managed to get them sealed. There's very little available except for the directive of the limitation of your work.'

'That I'm not to be sent to a battlefield?'

Sutherland's eyebrows shot into his hairline, and he sat back. 'I wouldn't have thought that would ever be an issue. No, the directive makes clear you are a lady and should be treated as such.'

'But I don't use . . . Oh, I see,' I said, as the truth sank in.

'I looked you up in Debrett's. Your brother, I believe, is in line for an earldom?'

'Is any of this relevant?'

'It's useful for me to know what kind of calibre of woman can do this work. But, no, it is not relevant to your investigation. It's a give-and-take situation.'

'I am competent in observation, sabotage, hand-to-hand combat, evasion, intelligence analysis, driving and horse riding. I am an average cook. I have basic field medical training.'

'Who trained you?'

'Mostly my partner. Occasionally he had others' help.'

'And by partner?'

'I mean my partner in espionage.'

'Who isn't with you?'

'He is at the front line,' I said.

Sutherland nodded. 'Ah, I see. So your briefing . . .'

'Is largely missing.'

'Well, Edinburgh is an old city. We have old families who have held the influence here for hundreds of years. We're a small place, and those that are of status tend to know each other. We're also known for our learning.'

'Understood.'

'And darker things . . .'

'You mean Burke and Hare? That was a hundred years ago.'

'Long shadows,' said Sutherland. 'We might be known for our enlightenment, but this city is also a place of superstition. Now, with the war, and so many young men dying, we're seeing the rise of spiritualism again. That and mediumship. It's easy enough to shut down a street trader who professes to hear the messages of the dead, but harder when it's a significant citizen or his wife.'

'I'm not sure what you're saying, Mr Sutherland?'

'I'm saying, Mrs Stapleford, that there are folks in the city who not only believe in the supernatural. There are folks here who think they are magicians.'

Chapter Twenty-eight

Sutherland Shows he is not Dissimilar to Fitzroy

The lamp flickered obediently at this moment. The firelight cast streaks of shadow across the room and Sutherland's face. I wasn't having any of it.

'Next you'll be telling me that the city is haunted,' I said.

'Och, well, we do have our wee ghosties,' said Sutherland. 'It's an old city. But for the most part they don't bother anyone.'

'I suppose they drift around doing a little light haunting.'

'I think you may have misunderstood me, Mrs Stapleford. I did not say I believed in magic. I said there were more and more people in the city that did.'

'Because of the war?'

'That is part of it. But we Scots have always believed in the second sight. Edinburgh is a fertile ground for both charlatans and those who are desperate enough to believe.'

'But what has this to do with my investigation?'

'I was hoping you'd come to see this by yourself. But does it not strike you that the way in which Megan Luckett was killed was ritualistic?'

'So you know the details?'

'It was in the paper up here. The question that has always bothered me, and which I never got to ask—'

'Was how did McIvory know the details that were kept from everyone but the police?'

'Indeed. If the killing had happened here, then maybe I could understand it, but it happened in your neck of the woods hundreds of miles away.'

'Did you ever ask him?'

'Well, that's the thing with the well-connected of the city, it can be difficult to arrange an interview. Impossible even unless I could show direct relevance to our department, which I couldn't. I mentioned it to a contact in the police up here, but it will not surprise you to know that it never led to anything.'

'And now McIvory is dead. Does he have surviving family?'

'Aye, a widow, a son and a daughter, but you'll not get near them. That flimsy little private detective licence will only get you thrown in the local jail if you try.'

'This is a conundrum.'

'You don't seem too upset by it,' said Sutherland.

'If McIvory knew anything of the nature we suspect it seems unlikely he would tell his wife or daughter. His son perhaps.'

'The boy was a late addition to the family. He's only twelve years of age.'

'So I come back to the medical school,' I said. 'That is where I will begin my inquiries.'

'I would urge you, Mrs Stapleford, to take the greatest care.'

'That almost sounds like a threat, Mr Sutherland.'

'Och no, lass. I've no skin in this game. After the war perhaps I will have the time to look into some of the people there – or people who were there, but I have other priorities. Speaking of which I need to get you back to your hotel.'

'I don't understand. If you have a warning please give it to me in plain speaking.' I knew I was being short, but the events of the day were catching up on me.

'If I knew anything in particular I would tell you, but I have only suspicions that I do not feel would be helpful to your inquiries. Let us leave it at this: the medical school is full of important people you do not want to offend as they could hamper your investigation. On the whole we tend to keep a low profile here. I only venture my head above the parapet when necessary. We work quietly but efficiently. I hope you will manage the same.'

I almost said, *That wasn't so difficult, now was it?* But instead, I nodded and simply said, 'I understand.'

Sutherland appeared pleased and suggested we hail a cab on the High Street. I realised he intended to escort me back. I assured him I was more than capable of looking after myself. He insisted. Then on the journey back he peppered me with questions about being a female operative. I answered him as I would when questioned by any other department related to my own. That is to say truthfully, but with as little detail as I could manage. By the time we were back at the hotel it was nigh on eleven p.m., and I was ready to sleep.

'So how close are you to your partner?' asked Sutherland. 'I know you're married, but all that close-quarter working. Besides, Fitzroy has a reputation.'

I must have flinched slightly at the first mention of his name. 'We have never been and will never be romantic partners, for the very reasons you mention. We work closely and any such affections would be a distraction on a mission. We do have a camaraderie as most working partners do, but we do nothing that might cause us to value each other above any mission. And yes, I am aware of my partner's reputation. I can add that it is a well-earned reputation. I am generally aware of – of his situation. But he has always been clear that he wanted me as an equal skilled espionage partner.'

'Aye, from what you've said he has done you proud in that respect. Although I have not seen you in action.' We pulled up in front of the hotel. 'I can accept you and Fitzroy are not involved romantically. I wonder though, as you and he are so close, did he choose to train you as you are a kindred spirit?'

I frowned, puzzled. 'We both are absolutely loyal to King and Country.'

'I was thinking of more personal traits?'

'I think I am better tempered,' I said, forcing a smile. 'And we are perhaps akin in other ways. Although he is a master of modern languages and codes. I am not.'

'Och, I was trying to ask as politely as I could if there was any chance of my accompanying you upstairs to your chamber?'

'Good heavens!' I said. 'No, in that respect my partner and I do not share the same proclivities.'

'Och, well, fair enough. Have a good night, lass.' He opened the door for me to descend. I did so wondering what it was with male spies that they were always on the lookout for a new bed companion.

I stomped up the stairs to my room. When I opened the door Jack ran to meet me. I bent down to pet him. He looked happy and healthy. At least one of us was doing well.

Chapter Twenty-nine

Fitzroy is Much on my Mind

I awoke confused after a night of disconcerting dreams. Fitzroy featured frequently, oscillating between telling me he was having a great time and that he needed to be rescued. In the first sort he had a ridiculous long moustache, a smoking hat and a girl in a negligee on each arm. In the second he was covered in mud, and sinking into the mire. Somehow these dreams also featured a man, or possibly men, in dark hoods, who would appear skulking in the background carrying bloody body parts. When morning came I did not feel refreshed.

The lingering image of Fitzroy in a fez made me realise I had spared no thought for Bertram since I began this wild goose chase for Griffin. I went through to the bathroom and splashed my face with water. Then I sat down at the letter desk and wrote a decently long note to Bertram. It was no secret where I currently was, so I could get the hotel to post it for me later. I wrote using phrases we had agreed that meant I was working alone, but was in no danger. I told him how I was looking after a friend's dog, and listed some of Jack's exploits in an attempt to be amusing. I sent my love, and asked questions about the latest pieces he was working on for the newspapers that had recently hired him as a correspondent.

Then I turned back to work, and wrote to the medical school seeking an appointment with Dr Gibbons. I directed the letter to his secretary, and wrote under my guise as a private investigator. I had decided as I had so little time a direct and seemingly open approach was the best way to deal with the medical men, who I fully expected to be condescending to my sex. It was a notoriously male discipline, and many of them opined that no woman should ever join their ranks as women's brains were demonstrably smaller.

My choice to be an investigator I hoped would set them on the back foot. Generally I observe that people who find themselves confronted with an investigator (even a female one) or a policeman immediately feel ill at ease. Or was it simply that the people I knew were all hiding secrets?

I hoped the response did not come quickly for I had yet to decide whether I would use some aspect of the actual case or make up something entirely fictitious. I hoped inspiration would strike me.

Two days passed with no reply. On the second night I sat with a barely touched glass of brandy alone in my room, with the fire high, and Jack snuffling on the rug before me. I had much to think about.

Hans had become actually useful. He occupied Esmeralda, and provided a conspicuous escort at luncheon and dinner. After his misguided and alcohol-driven comments towards me, he now ensured he did not speak to me alone, and that when he did address me he was the model of gentlemanliness. This was a touch tiresome. Generally, when travelling with Fitzroy he would not pull out my chair when we dined, nor constantly be solicitous of my comfort, unless it was necessary for a role we were playing. And even if it were so, he would be grumpy with me in private, constantly enquiring why so many ladies were unfamiliar with the operations of a door handle. It always made me laugh. He respected me as an able human being, Hans was now acting as if I was as fragile a flower as Esmeralda. It should feel like part of an act, but I found it constantly irritating and I became much more acerbic. This had the effect of confusing Esmeralda, who grew so nonplussed I had to be increasingly agile not to be caught in a private tête-à-tête of womanly discussion. I could think of few things that did not involve physical pain that I would enjoy less.

Of all of us, Jack was probably the most content. His walking and feeding schedule was now firmly established with the hotel staff. He spent plenty of time lying in front of the fire, but had taken to giving long huffing sighs. It did not seem too ridiculous to think he was missing his master.

I had avoided thinking about Fitzroy, because there was nothing I could do to help him. My annoyance at his keeping me from the battlefield and careering off with another woman had long since faded. I knew too well that after the accident that had killed his mother, he was protective of any woman he truly cared for. I also knew there were few of us. This possible front-line dalliance he was on would be no more than that. At best he was indulging himself romantically. At worst he was trying to drive off the fear of death with a form of comforting relief. Or there might be nothing in it at all. Fitzroy was capable of admiring courageous women without feeling any need to possess them. His personal flirtations were always mutual decisions.

That I had spent any time thinking about the woman in the scarf had been merely a distraction. I knew, regardless of any green-scarf truce, he was in terrible danger. That he had even mentioned this possibility before he left meant that he was giving me a form of gentle preparation. My partner did not believe in fate – or if he did he had no trouble in giving his all to overcome it. He did not fear dying, but he was a skilled analyst, a brilliant strategist, an excellent tactician and a man who faced the truth head-on. I did my very best generally not to let him know I believed this. Sometimes it felt as if there was hardly space in a room for his ego, and I did not wish to enhance this. But it meant he did not exaggerate danger. I now understood that his fear came from the formidable German snipers, who lurked behind their own line, and sometimes ventured into no man's land. There were many plans and schemes one could concoct to survive in the most hostile of environments. The Crown trained its agents well. But avoiding the lens of a sniper, especially when it was liable to be a gentleman who before the war had been an expert in hunting, as most Germans are, is harder. You can do your best to leave no shadow, to show no outline against the horizon, but not always and not all the time. The very best marksmen will spend a day or more under camouflage to secure the prize of an officer. I had read the reports. For the first time Fitzroy had admitted to me there were things in this world he could not always overcome – and one was the marksman's scope. And he would know. In a moment of candour he had told me that early in his career he had trained as a sniper, in order for me to understand why he did not want me to train as such.

I went to bed and worried about him. I also dreamed of a cross Bertram, who was waiting at our dining table for me to serve him soup. I awoke as the grey of dawn crept under the hem of the blinds. I missed Bertram sorely, but I knew he was safe. Jack grumbled in his sleep. He had stayed by the fire, which was now out. I got out of bed, and taking the small blanket off the bottom of the bed I placed it gently over the sleeping dog. The whiffling stopped. With sorely cold nipped toes I hurried back under my covers, and dug down into the warmth. I slept fitfully until the maid arrived with my morning cup of tea and to take Jack down to the bellboy for his morning exercise.

I went downstairs to breakfast, and before Hans and Esmeralda had joined me a waiter brought me an envelope on a silver tray. Finally someone at the medical school had replied to me. I slit the envelope open with a clean knife. Dr Gibbons would see me today at three fifteen p.m. for fifteen minutes.

Chapter Thirty

Hans Plans a Surprise for Christmas

At this point I had yet to decide on my cover story. I was quite used to creating these for myself and Fitzroy during our missions. Or at least I had been before Colonel Morley and his army regimental style had arrived. We now had legend creators, wardrobe, and a whole host of others. Previously, Fitzroy had always dredged up someone from somewhere to do anything we could not. Neither of us were particularly skilled at forgery.

This gave me further pause for thought. As I bit into my toast, it occurred to me that I would have to put my limited forgery skills into practice if I didn't manage to get some petty cash somewhere. Hans hadn't stinted on the booking he had made for us, and I got the impression he had added Esmeralda's outgoings to our bill. He was not without means, but as not even a signed asset I suspected he would baulk at paying out the kind of bill we were racking up.

It quite made the golden yoke of my egg taste sour. Nevertheless it was not a problem to be solved today. If the worst happened and Jack and I made a run for it, no doubt the London office could reimburse the hotel later. I buttered another slice of toast. I was still worried about Jack. He was not his normal self. I had heard it said that dogs could often tell when their owners were in difficulties or ill, even when they were apart. It made me worry more about Fitzroy.

At this rate I was going to get indigestion.

Hans appeared, full of smiles and the jollity of the bright autumn morning, until he saw I was alone.

'Ah,' he said. He pulled up a chair. The waiter practically materialised on the spot like some kind of magician's trick, and Hans ordered himself a most hearty breakfast. After the waiter had left, he patted his waistcoat. 'I shall have to ensure I exercise the horses when I return home,' he said, 'or I fear I will grow fat.'

'You don't look to be in any danger of that,' I said truthfully. Hans was as slender as ever. Though goodness knew how. My poor Bertram could put on several pounds merely by looking at a slice of cake.

A waiter docked briefly at our table, and Hans accepted a coffee. Into which, being of European descent, he poured cream. I shuddered. 'Even I will not be able to retain my physique if we spend much longer in this hotel,' he said.

'I am sure Richenda keeps a good table,' I said, trying to avoid the issue of time.

'Oh, she does, and afternoon tea, and late suppers. I tend not to partake of such excess fare. Although she has reduced her intake since the accident. You should come and visit us.'

'I hope to,' I said. 'When work allows.'

'Will you be home for Christmas?'

'I really don't know,' I said. 'I would hope to be. You could always come to us.'

I said this without any real thought, and was somewhat taken aback when Hans jumped at the idea. 'Excellent. Just what Richenda needs. Some time away from home, but nowhere too challenging. Somewhere she is familiar with, and with people who care about her. Marvellous idea.'

'What's a marvellous idea?' said Esmeralda, who had finally emerged from her room.

'We were talking about our Christmas celebrations,' I said, watching to see if Hans blushed.

'Indeed, the hope is that Euphemia will open up her house to all her family, and we will have a most traditional Christmas. She has a lovely estate in the Fens. It is ever so pretty when it snows, and it usually does each December, doesn't it, Euphemia?'

'I have yet to work out how you are related,' said Esmeralda. 'I had been hoping to find an opportunity to ask without seeming to pry, but I have failed.' She gave a pretty little smile.

'It is no secret,' said Hans without a shadow of a blush, 'we are cousins on our mothers' side.'

Not by so much as a flicker of an eyelash did he betray the slightest discomfort when uttering this lie.

'I suppose Christmas is a time for family,' said Esmeralda, and gave a deep sigh. She lowered her eyes, and then looked up through her eyelashes at Hans. 'I will be all alone with my aunt. I am not even sure they celebrate Christmas that far to the north. They are strict about material things I hear. Believing more in the spiritual way of being, and cold porridge.' The sigh that followed this was sincere.

I could see from Hans's face that he felt sorry for her. I shook my head very slightly. Surely, he knew better than to suggest that the young widow join our Christmas party, which would include his wife and children!

But I was wrong. 'Perhaps I can prevail on Euphemia to include you in our celebrations. Her estate is more than large enough.'

Esmeralda regarded me with an expression glowing with hope. If I could have thrown daggers with my eyes at Hans I would have done so. But he merely deflected my glare with a flourish of his napkin.

'Indeed, I do not yet know what my plans may be,' I said as kindly as I could. I tested with my toe and found that Hans's shin was too far away for me to kick with any real force. I made my exit as soon as possible even though the omelette they brought Esmeralda was so light and fluffy that if I had been dining with Fitzroy I would have had no hesitation in ordering one for myself. He tended to eat so much when we were on a mission my appetite always looked birdlike in comparison.

I retired to my room. I found Jack huffling by the fire. He had been walked, but his food bowl was half full. I worried he was pining.

In the end I telephoned down to the front desk for someone to procure me a book on crimes in Edinburgh from the local bookstore. I was furnished with a rather salacious guide to the 'Dark Side of Edinburgh' that started with Burke and Hare and then focused on more contemporary cases. I had luncheon sent up and worked my way through the increasingly lurid descriptions of crimes. It quickly became clear that the book concentrated on crimes that involved either young women or men of business who ventured down dark lanes never to be seen again, although on one occasion a pair of boots was found, and the writer suggested that human combustion rather than mortal crime might have been the cause here.

I found myself smiling at the ridiculousness of it. It was clearly designed to give the reader delightful shivers by their fireside. Although, when considered rationally, there were no modern criminals who could in any way match up to their villainous nature or the sheer scale of their achievement.

Time ticked by and although entertained I was no closer to a cover story. However, I had the appointment, and the attention of the 'great' man for only fifteen minutes. I was sure I would think of something in time or failing that I would be able to play it by ear.

Chapter Thirty-one

The Great Medicine Man Himself

Edinburgh University's medical school was a large and imposing building, set out in a classical style. Descending from the carriage in front of the gates I felt small and unimportant. Here was a building designed to enhance the status of the art of medicine and the great minds that taught and studied here. There was a plethora of male statues, but then I had noted this was common in the city. London is the same, but the city is more spread out, so it is less obvious. I rather wished I had worn something purple and green with a touch of white. Except the suffragette colours always made me look like a mouldy cabbage, and with the war on it had been tactically agreed our protests would begin after it had ended. In the meantime a great deal of women were doing the work of the absent men. Surely this would be enough to send a message that women were capable and not the inferior sex.

Opposite the medical school stood a public house called Doctors. Men, I decided, with a very few exceptions, were the worst.

I strode under the dark stone arches and had gone no more than a few feet before I was accosted by a porter. The sight of a skirt clearly offended him. I explained my business and he walked me himself to the secretary of Dr Gibbons. This proved to be an older woman with iron-grey hair and a disapproving disposition. When I presented my letter she made a great show of asking me my business. I had intended to declare myself openly as a private detective, but her manner so annoyed me, I merely said it was a matter I wished to discuss with Dr Gibbons.

'I hope you understand the professor,' she said the word as if she were pronouncing capital letters, 'does not see patients at this time. If you wish to have a consultation there are procedures to go through.'

'I am not a patient,' I said.

'Then what are you?'

'Madam, I find your line of questioning intrusive. I have been kindly given fifteen minutes of the professor's time, and I would prefer to spend that in discussion with him, rather than with you outside his office.'

'If I had been on duty when your letter arrived I would not have entertained the possibility for a moment. Unfortunately I was not.'

'The appointment is made and I presume in the professor's diary?'

At this point she actually snorted. When she stood up I found myself checking for hooves under her skirt. She walked briskly across the room and opened a door. I followed her down a short, and rather drab corridor. She knocked on a wooden door, and I heard a soft man's voice bid us enter.

'Professor Gibbons,' she said, standing directly in front of me so I could not see into the room, 'I have your three-fifteen appointment. Mr Hardy made this while I was away. I have a female here, who claims the appointment is hers, but she has neither stated her business nor her name. I can be rid of her directly if you wish.'

I'm not quite as easy to be rid of as you might think, I thought, but did not say out loud. The professor's voice came again, too low for me to make out. I was about to plead my case when the woman turned and brushed rudely past me. If I had been less adept in hand-to-hand combat she would have struck me hard on the shoulder. As it was I twisted easily out of her way.

I could now see into the room. It was dimly lit with a shaded lamp on a large desk that stood on the other side of the room. The room was large, but it looked out on to a grey courtyard, and even the long windows could not draw much light from the Edinburgh gloom of gathering dusk. A contained small fire in a large hearth cast a weak amber glow over the rug in front of it. On the other three sides of the room bookshelves ran from floor to ceiling. I could make out the vague outline of other furniture, chairs, small tables and the like, scattered across the room in enough abundance to make me hesitate before walking in.

From behind the desk a man rose up in the shadows. 'Do forgive my secretary,' he said in a soft, low Edinburgh burr that was far from unattractive. 'She is most possessive of my time. And, I sometimes fear, of me. I am Professor James Gibbons. How may I assist you?'

I started forward into the gloom, and immediately banged my knee against a small table. The figure darted forward. 'Oh my dear lady,' he said with a gentle urgency, but still keeping his tone soft, 'you must forgive me. I shall ring for some more light to be brought. I am afraid I was so carried away with writing my recent observations of a case that I failed to see that the day was coming to a close.'

'I must apologise for my clumsiness. My eyes will accustom themselves in a moment. I quite see the appeal of the firelight on a drizzly day like today.' I reached out a hand. 'I am Lady Alice Stapleford.'

The professor flitted through the room and took my hand. It felt like a perfectly normal man's hand, so why I should suddenly feel my hackles rise I had no idea.

'Delighted, my lady. Let me lead you to a seat by the fire, and we can enjoy its amber warmth. Although I must warn you I do not do personal consultations here.'

'It is nothing like that,' I said. 'In fact you may find it rather extraordinary, but I am a lady private detective.'

'Goodness,' said Gibbons, handing me into a wing-backed chair. I felt a flood of relief when he let go of my hand. 'How interesting. I take it this is a direct result of the war, and the scarcity of men?'

'My profession?' I said, gathering my thoughts. My knee throbbed. It must have been a sturdy table.

'Well, I am thinking that as well as the lack of detectives, it is not unknown for men returning from war to become lost, either because they are confused or because they do not wish to return to their old lives. Indeed, I have seen some so injured they have begged their surgeons to not inform their relatives they have survived.' He paused and then added, 'Or worse.' He seemed to recollect himself, for he stood up straighter. 'Such dark times. Perhaps you would care for a little sherry to lighten the mood. Although I must confess I am completely in the dark about how I may be able to assist a lady detective.'

He walked over to the shelves, and I heard rather than saw him busy himself with a decanter and glasses. I had not responded in the affirmative, as I detest sherry, but I took the glass he returned with. 'You are very kind,' I said.

He gave another of his soft laughs. 'You perhaps thought as a medical man, and knowing intimately the size of women's brains, I might consider you too inferior to perform such a task.' He settled back in his own seat, and took a sip of sherry. 'I am currently engaged in writing a paper that suggests it is not the size or weight of the brain that matters, but its surface area.'

'Why, that would mean . . .'

'Indeed, that having a smaller brain does not mean inferior intelligence. In fact in some cases it might be quite the opposite.'

'Goodness,' I said, 'that would cause quite a commotion, wouldn't it?'

Gibbons gave another low chuckle. 'So you find me hard at work constructing my argument and completely unaware of the passage of time.'

'I am sorry I disturbed you,' I said, feeling uncomfortable.

'Not at all. It is always good to take a break from intense

concentration. And you provide, if you will let me say so, quite a lovely distraction.'

Although he had made no movement towards me I began to feel my skin crawl. It is not a sensation I have often experienced. It is rather like having ants roving all over your skin. I had felt it before once in a particularly unpleasant cellar where Fitzroy and I had been forced to spend the night. although on that occasion it had turned out to be fleas.

'You're too kind,' I said, feeling anything but this.

'So how can I assist?'

This must have been the third time he had asked me; I had to give an answer. 'I am investigating a case for a client, Professor,' I began.

'So I assumed,' said Gibbons. 'Although there is no need to call me Professor, we are yet to admit female students.'

'Indeed.' I gave a quick smile. 'And so far my researches have led me to the medical school here.' I paused, considering how to continue.

'I do hope there is no suggestion of any wrongdoing on the part of my students, or, dare I say, myself?' He rose before I could answer and fetched the sherry decanter, lifting my hand gently out of the way and refilling my glass. 'Doctor's orders. Edinburgh is a cold city for many a stranger. You must keep yourself well wrapped during your visit. How long are you residing here?'

'Until I have either found answers or concluded there are not answers here to be found.'

'Admirable,' said the professor, replacing the decanter. 'And what is the question you seek to answer?'

I found my thoughts stumbling, and decided to risk all. Rationally, I knew there was nothing amiss here, but my intuition was telling me something was very wrong. 'I have been hesitating to answer your reasonable question, Dr Gibbons, because I am unsure who may be involved in the matter, wittingly or unwittingly. I am looking into an old case. A young woman was murdered, Megan Griffin, née Luckett.'

The professor sat very upright in his seat at this. 'Surely this is an old story,' he said. 'I knew poor Megan's husband. We trained together. I have been fortunate enough to have something of a meteoric rise due to my specialism, but poor Griffin I believe was sent to jail.' He put up a quick hand, palm flat out towards me. 'Not, of course, that Griffin murdered his wife. No, he tracked down the miscreant who did, and took punishment into his own hands. I believe he was spared the noose due to his state of mind at the time. A colleague of mine argued he was insane at the time of the murder due to grief.'

'It is the man who he killed who is the focus of attention,' I said. 'David Bloom. I can find out very little about him.'

'Except, of course, that he applied to study here and was rejected,' said Gibbons.

'Exactly,' I said. Inwardly I breathed a sigh of relief; my wondering speculation had led Gibbons to assume I knew more than I did.

'You may also then know he was a friend of mine?'

'No, I did not,' I said, allowing myself to show my genuine surprise. 'I did not realise this case would be so close to your interests. I apologise for not alerting you to this in my request for an appointment.'

'Well, if you didn't know . . .' said the professor in his soft, slow voice, and gave me a shrug. 'It is all a long time ago. Did they hang Griffin in the end? Or does he still languish behind bars?'

'He has been freed,' I said. 'Hence my concern.'

'Gracious!' said Gibbons. 'I feel as if you may, my dear lady, be skirting around the garden path. I think you know a great deal more than I can tell you. Come, be fully open with me and I will do my best to assist you!' He gave me a smile of great charm and warmth. So why, despite the fire, I should suddenly feel as if a cold wind raked through the room made no sense at all. But I had to start somewhere.

'I would appreciate it if you could tell me why David Bloom was refused entry to the medical school.'

'Oh, that is easy, my dear. They really could not possibly have admitted him. A genius in his own way, but he fervently believed himself to be a vampire.'

At this moment the lamp on his desk behind us guttered and went out. It was with difficulty I suppressed a scream.

Chapter Thirty-two

Of Vampyres and Magick

'How deliciously melodramatic,' said Gibbons. He leaned over and patted my hand lightly. Then he got up and picked up a couple of candlesticks from the fireplace, placing them on a small table by us. He took a taper from the wall sconce and lit it from the fire. The wicks of the candles flared as he lit them. Then he snuffed out the taper with a deft flick of his wrist. 'I must remind Martha to ask the servitors to remember to keep my lamps topped up with oil. Alas, the fate of a university, always tied to a budget.' He sat back down. 'You must forgive my sense of humour. We doctors do often find levity in the darker side of life. Some of the things we see, you understand. Medicine is a fine art and it grows more powerful by the decade, but we are still a very long way from defeating the spectre of death.' He sighed. 'That monster comes when he wishes and often there is so little we can do to fight him off. Three score years and ten is but a blink of an eye to the universe, and yet some of our patients are allowed so much less.'

'The comment about a vampire then was your sense of humour,' I said allowing a little of the ire I felt into my voice.

'Oh, not at all, dear lady. He definitely believed this. Sadly, you do often find that with the finest minds come some of the strongest delusions. This isn't my area, but I have always wondered if the mind of a genius seeks an order in the universe that simply isn't available to the mortal mind. Then failing that they create their own answer to the nature of creation. Whereas the rest of us confine ourselves to our limited orbits and persuade ourselves of an artificial order that is fragile, but satisfyingly safe. Like dear Martha, who clutches my appointment book to her bosom as if she holds the keys to my knowledge and possibly, poor creature, my heart. It is nothing but a diary, and may be rewritten at any time by chance or fate. The truth is we spend our lives navigating the chaos of the universe, and that how our lives unfurl allows us some limited choice, but in the end we are mere mortals, and powerless in the face of eternity – or in Martha's case the hand of her temporary replacement!'

'A vampire?' I repeated, only half listening to his philosophical diatribe.

'Oh, he didn't go around biting the necks of young women, if that is what you are thinking. We were neighbours growing up, and I cannot tell you when the idea overtook him. We were also at the same school, which is how I knew he had a formidable brain. I do remember a time when we were still children, and he became very ill from drinking chicken blood. I now know he was lucky not to die. You see, he had developed the idea he was a vampire, but he was repulsed by the thought of drinking human blood. Although as I am sure you are aware in the Roman Catholic rite of transubstantiation all Catholics believe they do exactly that. On reflection it may even have been what gave him the idea. With these sorts of thing one can never know.'

'So you are suggesting he killed Megan Griffin in some kind of self-induced vampiric frenzy.'

'Oh no. I strongly doubt he ever harmed a hair on her head. For a man of such outlandish beliefs he was a most gentle soul. I once saw him as a grown man cry when he came across a dead chaffinch in the street.'

'Then you are of the belief that Griffin killed an innocent man, and Megan's killer roams free?'

'I am sorry to say that I am,' said Gibbons. 'And how are you drawn into this old affair?'

I had intended to say that I came from one of Bloom's relatives, but Gibbons had closed that avenue off to me. I changed tack. 'How did the medical school become aware of Bloom's fantasy?'

Gibbons hung his head. 'I think I will take another dram before I relate that sorry tale.' He reached for the decanter.

'You told them,' I said.

'Very astute, dear lady. I did and I do not regret doing so. I believe Bloom would never have knowingly harmed another. However, his fantasy permeated all areas of his life. After his experiments drinking animal blood he created an iron-rich potion with natural ingredients. As a doctor I know it would have done him no harm other than to possibly slow his digestive tract and cause occasional stomach pains. However he believed it compensated for not drinking blood.'

'I don't think I am following any of this,' I said.

'I know, dear lady. The twisted pathways of a sick mind are naturally difficult for those of a normal sanity to follow. Bloom believed he was a vampire. He believed he had found a concoction that prevented him from drinking blood. If it had been no more than this it would have been unnerving for patients to hear of his belief, and I would have felt it necessary to tell our professors should he have talked about his espoused identity. However, I am afraid it was far worse than that.'

'Please enlighten me,' I said politely. This all seemed far too tall a tale to me. I had begun to think that the charming and handsome Professor Gibbons had an unpleasant sense of humour, and that he was making me his dupe.

'Bloom believed that because he was a vampire, if he discovered the correct rite he would become immortal. He also believed he could read the minds of others, and on occasion was apt to announce that another individual present was thinking the most outlandish thoughts. In short he had detached himself too far from reality to be able to work with living patients. I did attempt to interest him in my own field, the study of the dead and the incurable. However, he was fixated on the thought that should he ever die, being a vampire he would be condemned to eternal damnation. Thus his only option was to seek immortality.'

'He sounds as if he should have been sent to an asylum!'

'Unless you were one of his intimates he would not talk about his "true" nature, nor speak of his ability to read minds. Without this outspokenness he appeared perfectly sane.'

'He wanted to study medicine because . . .'

'He wanted to understand how to defeat death. An answer all doctors seek, except that we seek this for our patients, not for ourselves.'

'But Griffin must have had a reason to think he was the killer? Did he know him?'

Gibbons shook his head. 'I do not think so. Although Griffin and I share a bond in that he had another of our cohort removed from the school. Nathaniel Warburton, an odd young man. Griffin caught him smuggling parts of a cadaver out of the school following an authorised dissection. I believe he has been in an institution for the insane for some time.'

'Are all medical students prone to these – unusual – behaviours?' I still could not make up my mind if Gibbons was telling me the truth or handing me a mouthful of lies.

He laughed at this, again in his gentle and controlled manner. 'As I said I believe we all have a rather unique sense of humour. If you consider we are a group of young men, who before this dreadful war began were the only ones to have seen both dead bodies and encountered the dying in any significant number before we were twenty-one. That and cutting up the body of another human being sets us apart from regular gentlemen. We see and experience life in its rawest forms. There is no pretence of universal order, the unfairness of one's lot or the inevitability that we all end up in a box in the ground at the end of our time. I hope that at its best it allows us to see that all men are equal; as we all live so must we all die.'

'But believing in vampires, stealing parts of the dead . . .'

'The latter is an old Edinburgh tradition. Have you heard of Burke—'

'And Hare? Yes,' I said. 'They were murderers, not corpse thieves.'

'You are certainly well read, my dear. However, I am afraid I have no more time to give you at this moment. I shall ask Martha to schedule another appointment if you wish. I fear we have not yet come to the heart of the matter for you. Do you wish to see me again?'

'Thank you for your time, sir,' I said. 'I need to think on our discussion. May I ask one final question? Who do you think killed Megan Griffin?'

'I think the police had the right of it. I believe Griffin did. Although he may never confess. There are things I could tell you about . . . but that is a discussion for another time. Would you allow me to give you a piece of advice, Lady Alice?'

'Of course.'

'Take care. Working with the police as I do, I see far more than I am generally permitted to speak about in public. Edinburgh has always been a city that attracts eccentrics: magicians, spiritualists, people who style themselves as practitioners of the dark arts. All founded in complete nonsense. However, lack of sense has never stopped men from committing evil. Megan Griffin was murdered in a ritualistic way, and thus in probability by a madman. If so he would be a madman clever enough to appear sane by the light of day. Through my connections I have heard of the new murder in London. The one I believe you to be so hesitant to admit to me that you are investigating. It is of the same manner. There is a madman on the loose who has killed at least two women between England and Scotland. If he should discover you are seeking him I would greatly fear for your welfare. I do not wish to impugn your intelligence, but in this case it would be better to turn over whatever you know to the police and let them investigate.'

'I doubt they are as open-minded about the ability of lady detectives as yourself,' I said.

'Then return and tell me. I shall ensure any evidence you have is put before them and considered seriously.'

'That is a kind offer,' I said.

He stood up and came to take me gently by the elbow to escort me out. 'Then we shall talk more. I shall get Martha to send a new appointment to you. Now, allow me to see you into a cab. I would feel most anxious should you walk home in the gloaming by yourself.'

When we emerged out on to the street the lamps had been lit. Beside me Professor Gibbons looked every inch the gentleman. A light rain had begun to fall. He hailed me a cab and handed me in, giving me the most charming smile. The cabbie doffed his hat to him, and promised to take care of me. He stepped away as the cab moved off, and gave me a small bow. Every inch of him spoke of respectfulness and integrity. I sat back in my seat. My shoulders slumped, and I realised my whole body ached with the tension I had been carrying. Was this merely the result of being ill prepared and verbally fencing with a man of possibly superior intelligence or was it something more?

Chapter Thirty-three

An Old Acquaintance Appears Quite Unexpectedly

I committed the hideous sin of abstaining from high tea, and instead spent some time luxuriating in my bath. I had much to think over. Both Sutherland and Gibbons had warned me about Edinburgh being an old city of dark secrets. I sensed they were both proud of their city, and not above frightening Englishwomen with their ghost stories. Sutherland would be happy to see me return down south out of his area of control, and Gibbons? He was more complicated. I still could not rule out that he had been amusing himself at my expense. I had worked as a nurse, and I met doctors who valued nurses. But I had never met a medical man who believed women to be the equal of men in intelligence, and certainly no gentleman I knew other than Fitzroy, if he could be counted a gentleman, would agree to that preposterous idea.

After my bath I decided I would go down to the lounge and see if the latest editions of the newspapers were available. I could have rung for them to be brought to my room, but I was beginning to dislike these four walls. My thinking had become stuck, and a change of scenery, no matter how small, and a nice cup of tea, might send my thoughts in a different direction.

I ensured Jack had all his needs attended to, and gave him a good petting before I left. He gave me a solitary lick on the hand, and went back to his huffling sighs. Normally, I would be grateful I did not have to redo my hair or rearrange my clothing after his often-rigorous attention, but currently I would have been very happy to see a hearty display of affection from this sad, small dog. I felt as if I was failing him in some way, and thus also failing Fitzroy, who I knew prized his dog above most people he knew.

I found a quiet table by a window. The ends of the day saw increasing rain, and the wet pavements outside were black mirrors returning the brightness of the street lamps with melancholy, distorted effect. I had barely ordered myself a cup of tea, having explained repeatedly to the disbelieving waiting staff that I did not require scones and jam, when I heard a little shriek of joy. Followed by the sound of Esmeralda's voice crying, 'There she is! We must tell her.'

I turned in my seat to see a glowing Esmeralda accompanied by a smug Hans hurry across the room. Both were dressed ready for dinner.

'Oh, my dear Mrs Stapleford!' cried Esmeralda, 'this darling man took me to speak to my husband!' Hans pulled out a seat for her, and she sat down. I glanced up at him with a raised eyebrow. He avoided my gaze. 'Edwin is happy! Or as happy as he can be without me. He has his little sister with him. She died when he was twelve in some kind of accident, and now they are reunited. He says she is as close to an angel as it is possible for the mortal-born to be. He told me to no longer fret over him. He told me to live my life as I wished. He told me to live! I cannot go to Aunty Morag's now. I see it. I must return to the metropolis. Perhaps I shall become a nurse to help other ill soldiers.'

I looked directly at Hans. 'A séance?'

'Oh no, Madam Arcana said it is a communication. A meeting of minds across the plains. She explained everything so very clearly. I have not half her eloquence, but it was clear she was no charlatan. I am so very happy!' Then she burst into tears and ran from the room. Hans blushed faintly.

'What did you do?' I asked sternly. Inside, I was telling myself that Madam Arcana was a common enough stage name.

'I thought it might bring her some comfort.' He hailed a passing waiter and asked for coffee. 'You look very nice, Euphemia. Meeting someone?'

'No, I have merely bathed and warmed myself after being exposed to this terrible Scottish weather.'

All artifice fell from Hans's handsome face. 'It is rather dreadful, isn't it? You see why I was looking for an indoor engagement.'

'You appear to have rather more than you bargained for. It seems your new friend not only thinks she is coming to White Orchards for Christmas, but has now decided to renege on living with her lonely spinster aunt.'

'Aunt by marriage only,' said Hans. He had the grace to look slightly shamefaced. 'And I have not named your estate in her presence.'

'I feel certain she would be able to uncover it. I am not using a pseudonym.'

'I was surprised at that,' said Hans. 'Hence my decision to adopt one.'

'And you have papers to support your new name?' I said.

Hans frowned.

'Goodness, man, we are at war. We have hostile foreign agents among us. If you were discovered to be using a false name you could be arrested.'

'But you are here!'

'This mission was to prove your worth. I do not have written authorisation for you. Besides, the head agent here would like nothing better than to catch me at fault.'

'Making enemies already?'

I was exasperated enough with Hans that I barely restrained myself from pulling a face at him. Instead I gathered my things and prepared to make a dignified exit. I had only half risen when a middle-aged woman with an enormous turban descended on us. To my astonishment she embraced me, kissing me on both cheeks.

'I do hope that you are going to look after your distressed

friend,' Madam Arcana said to Hans. 'Did she not leave the room crying some few minutes since?'

Hans and I exchanged guilty looks. We had both completely forgotten about Esmeralda as our discussion became more heated.

'I think Euphemia . . .'

'No. No, Mr Miller. Euphemia and I have much catching up to do. We are old friends. Now run along and try to repair some of the damage you've caused.'

Madam Arcana took a seat at my table, adjusted her turban and turned her attention to me. 'You still look pale, dear. I heard about your last mission. I was sorry to hear you were injured.' She turned her head on one side. 'I think seeing you now it was somewhat more serious than I was told. You lost—'

'Only Fitzroy and the doctors know,' I said, biting my lip.

Madam Arcana reached a heavily bejewelled hand across the table to pat me. 'Probably for the best, dear. I never think that sharing something that would hurt someone else is a good choice. One should only share such things when it helps not hurts. Sometimes there is nothing more one can do other than move on. Speaking of which, where is dear Eric?'

'I don't know,' I said. To my horror tears sprung into my eyes. I looked up and blinked rapidly. One cannot cry while looking up. I have no idea why, but it is a good trick to know.

A waiter provided a distraction for me to recover myself by bringing a tea tray to our table that was brimming with cream cakes. Madam Arcana regarded them with the same degree of intensity that a shark might regard a plump baby dolphin. 'The séance tonight was most exhausting,' she said, licking her lips. 'Those kinds of ones always make me so hungry. You must excuse me for a few moments.' Then she fell upon the food with a barely restrained savagery. Before she had finished Hans had returned.

'I have arranged to have lavender water sent to her room. She is resting now. Despite the emotional display, she seems easier in her mind.'

Madam Arcana delicately wiped her mouth with her napkin. Before her lay a puddle of cream and a few crumbs. 'Much better,' she said. 'They should bring some more hot tea over soon. Shall I say three cups?'

'Euphemia?'

'Madam Arcana belongs to the same group as myself and which you may be joining.'

Hans's eyes widened and his jaw slackened. 'You mean she's a . . .'

'Someone who communes with the spirits for the rich and poor alike. I have been summoned by kings, by queens and by numerous foreign royalty. I travel widely and I see all.'

'But it's a trick, isn't it?' said Hans.

I am not certain what would have happened next if the tea had not appeared. An expression crossed Madam's face that was so intense and unpleasant that if she had been capable of casting a spell Hans would have either been turned into a frog or inside out. Or perhaps more likely she would have struck him on the head with her reticule. This was a large item, and should it have contained her crystal ball, it could have done him serious injury. He seemed to realise this for as the tea was being poured he attempted an apology.

'I meant no offence, but so many people have lost loved ones in this war, and are seeking comfort . . .'

'That they are fair play for charlatans?'

'We have heard that there are many people capitalising on the nation's grief,' I said. 'It is easier for someone who is not suffering to believe that those who seek out such comfort are fools.'

'I suppose so,' said Madam. 'Is it what you think, Euphemia?'

'I would never suggest that you trick people, Madam. I believe your work is conducted for the good of all.'

'Very diplomatic, my dear,' she said, spooning sugar into my tea without asking. 'I will own that the connections to the other world are more difficult than usual to understand.' Hans looked surprised. 'Normally there are only so many people attempting to take the telephone line,' continued Madam, 'but this war is rather jamming up the channels.'

'So you told Esmeralda . . .'

'What her husband would have wanted her to hear. That she should move on with her life, and that where he is now he is beyond pain and suffering. She can be grateful for that.'

'But did he actually speak to you?' pressed Hans.

'I said what he wanted me to say,' said Madam Arcana with quiet conviction. She turned to me. 'So I take it Eric is off on a little adventure?'

I nodded.

'One that is out of the ordinary?' she asked.

'He has not been gone long enough for me to have any real concern. Nor do I believe anyone back at the office is worried about him.'

'But?'

'But before he left he was concerned he would not return. He made arrangements.'

'Well,' said Madam Arcana, 'it makes sense in our line of business to keep our arrangements up to date.'

'I don't mean he was afraid,' I said. 'I am uncertain if he is capable of feeling fear.' I gave a small smile. 'But he was wary this time. He is an expert at measuring risk, and he knew he was putting himself in serious danger. Danger that he could not personally remove.'

'You mean he had to surrender himself to fate to some degree?' said Madam.

I nodded.

'I can see he would have hated that,' she said. 'But we all do that all the time, my dear. I have never felt that Eric would have a short life. Although you are wrong in saying he rarely feels fear, he is often afraid for you.'

'He said that?'

'No, he would not be so disloyal,' said Madam Arcana. 'I only mention it because it is a handicap you would do well to be aware of in future missions.'

'So you believe there will be future ones?'

'I feel a strong degree of confidence. Although we are always in the hands of combined fate.'

'Combined fate?' I asked. I was aware Hans was watching us both closely.

'It's a very interesting idea being proposed at the Theosophical Society here in Edinburgh. In fact it is my main reason for visiting the city. In layman's terms it refers to the idea that the actions of others, if there are enough, can affect what otherwise would be a predetermined fate. As you can imagine, regardless of the normal open-mindedness of the members, such a challenge to the innate Calvinism of the Scots is causing quite the debate. The meetings are spread across this week, and already the fractiousness has been most entertaining.'

'Who are the members of this society?'

'Interested people,' said Madam Arcana. 'Spiritualists, mediums, magicians, the second-sighted – the usual groups.'

'Do you believe any of this?' Hans asked me suddenly.

'I have experienced things I cannot explain,' I said. 'But I would account my experiences among the kind that suggest there is life beyond this one.'

'It is perfectly correct to have doubts about magicians,' said Madam. 'Some of them may be perfectly harmless, but anyone who wants, let alone believes that they should have, power over the natural order is someone to beware of to my mind.'

'Madam, you may be able to help me with a problem I am currently investigating,' I said. 'What do you know of ritual killings?'

Madam Arcana regarded me with acute interest. Hans, seeing I was in earnest, dropped his teacup in surprise. Tea splashed all over his perfectly fitting suit, and his face was a picture of dismay. 'I must take this off at once,' he said, leaping to his feet, and for a moment I thought he meant what he said. He stopped at removing his jacket, and hurried away bearing it before him like an injured animal.

'Handsome men are always so limited,' said Madam Arcana.

'Thank goodness Eric has red hair. He might dye it, but it's most definitely not acceptable in men. It's really all that saved him.'

'I sometimes wish Fitzroy was a little limited,' I said. 'His presence can be – overwhelming.'

Madam Arcana put her hand on my arm. 'You miss him, don't you?'

Chapter Thirty-four

A Light Discussion on Ritual Murder

Madam and I retired to my suite of rooms while Hans went off to change. Jack, who generally hates all women except myself, got up at Madam's entrance and waddled up to her wagging his tail. She let him lick her hand and patted him on the head. He then returned to the fireside.

'Poor thing is missing his master, isn't he?' she said.

'I fear so.'

'It must indeed have been serious for Eric not to take his dog with him.'

'Across enemy lines,' I said.

'Ah, so it would have been the snipers that concerned him. He would know all too well of their far-reaching abilities and the difficulties in evading them. No wonder he tried to prepare you. He does worry about you so very much, my dear. If you can help him with that it would make his chances of survival higher in the future.'

'How exactly would you suggest I do that?' I said, stung.

'Why, demonstrate to him that you would survive without him.'

'I train constantly.'

'Don't be obtuse,' said Madam Arcana, 'you know what I mean.'

Fortunately before things could become any more awkward Hans returned. Madam Arcana gave me a look that suggested this conversation wasn't over, but changed topic when Hans appeared.

'I believe your first wife would appreciate it if you were kinder to your second,' she said as Hans seated himself. 'She is aware of your proclivities, but seems to think that despite them you can still make your wife a decent husband.' She made a humpfing sort of noise at the end that suggested she might not agree with Hans's late wife.

Hans turned puce. He struggled to speak for a few moments, before saying, 'Madam, you know nothing about my circumstances. You are impertinent. Do not foist your parlour tricks on me.'

Madam Arcana tilted her head on one side. 'She says I am to remind you about the pearl earrings.'

Hans shot to his feet and exited the room.

'Ah, now we can speak freely.'

'Pearl earrings?' I asked.

'I have no idea,' said Madam Arcana. 'I merely repeat what I am told.'

'Hmm, by earthly agencies or others?'

Madam Arcana gave me a tight little smile. 'If it does the job. I believe Morley will be in agreement that Hans will be a useful asset. The problem will be in bringing him to heel. Handsome and charming men are so very difficult to control.'

'Are you familiar with what brought Griffin to Fitzroy's side?'

'I read a file around the time it happened. I suspect it will have been either redacted or updated – or possibly both – by now. He killed the man who killed his wife?'

I told her about the recent murder and Griffin's arrest.

'Oh dear, that would be unfortunate,' she said. 'I have found it rather comforting that you and Eric have had a medical man to hand. I imagine Griffin would be distraught at having killed the wrong man.'

'My conversation with him on the matter was cut short by his arrest. However, I believe I have convinced them to release him, and am awaiting word. But it means there is still a murderer at large.'

'Tell me about the original murder.'

I told her all the details I knew. 'I see why you are considering some kind of ritual killing. Although I cannot bring to mind anything I might have read that would suggest killing a woman in such a way. No, the crime speaks to more of a hatred of women.'

'I have met with Professor Gibbons . . .'

'The corpse man?'

'Anatomy professor at the Edinburgh School of Medicine. He was in the same cohort as Griffin. He told me some very odd things about Bloom, the man Griffin killed.' I related the information as simply and clearly as I could.

'Sounds like tommyrot,' said Madam Arcana. 'I don't believe a word of it. He's telling you stories. The question is why.'

'Is it not true that some people suffer from sick minds?'

'Of course it is. We will see many of them after this war. The horrors those young men are seeing! And one of the main casualties of war for them will be religion. It is hard to believe in God when your companions are dying in droves all around you.'

'You mean why would God let such a thing happen?'

'Exactly. Although the answer as ever is man is doing it to man.' She gave a sigh. 'Sometimes I think we are a miserable species that does not deserve the gift of life.' She gave herself a little shake. 'Although, yes, I agree with you that some ail in their minds without any apparent external cause, but what Gibbons told you sounds more like a fairy story than reality.'

'How am I to argue? Against a man of status in the city my thoughts and actions count for little – as far as he is aware.'

'I have always thought some men become doctors because they enjoy the power they have over their patients. Not that they would necessarily harm anyone, but rather there are those who enjoy being more knowledgeable and being the dominant and powerful partner in a relationship. If you think about it the relationship between a doctor and patient is akin to that of priest and supplicant.'

'So I may be right in thinking he was merely playing a cruel joke?'

'Which means he is either a very arrogant man or he wanted to confuse your investigation. Regardless, I would suggest you do not return to visit him alone. If you take Hans with you he will be forced to either backtrack on what he said, deny it, or possibly even tell the truth.'

'I was warned not to visit him alone,' I said.

'But you ignored the warning because you thought you knew better?'

I shook my head. 'Because I didn't like the man who gave it.'

'Goodness, if I didn't take messages from people I didn't like I would be out of business within a week. Just because someone is dead it doesn't make them a good or redeemed individual. In fact, quite the opposite sometimes!' She laughed and I did too. Although I was unsure how serious she was being. Mostly, I wanted to stop thinking dark thoughts. It had been a long time since I had shared genuine amusement with anyone.

'So what can I do to help?' she asked.

'You could check for me if Fitzroy is on the other side? Or perhaps Griffin's late wife might have a message?'

'Oh, another séance? Perhaps with the cross young man and his mistress-to-be? I think that could be interesting. However I am rather tired tonight. But yes, I can certainly do that.'

'I didn't mean—' I was interrupted by a smart rap on the door, followed by the entrance of Hans and a rather heavy-eyed Esmeralda.

'Here, this is the medium. She is known to Euphemia,' said Hans in a cross voice. He was now dressed, quite splendidly, for dinner.

'Good evening again, my dear,' said Madam Arcana to Esmeralda. 'Euphemia and I were just setting about arranging a private little séance. We do so hope you will join us.'

Chapter Thirty-five

Jack Attack

Esmeralda's arrival put an end to any serious conversation. Madam Arcana declined joining us for dinner, so it was left to Hans and me to deal with Esmeralda's raptures over her experience, and what she hoped for in her next encounter with the spirit world. Hans was wise enough not to directly contradict her, but it was clear to me he thought it a lot of nonsense. I excused myself before coffee, pleading a headache. I went to bed early as I felt I could do with the rest, but sleep eluded me.

I tossed and turned for what felt like hours. Madam Arcana was a wily woman. I had met her before, and she was expert at reading people. But there were times when she said something that did indeed turn out to be prophetic. She had worked for the department for a long time, and I got the impression she had known Fitzroy since he was a boy. At one time I even wondered if she could be his mother. She certainly knew his name, and that he kept it as a closely guarded secret from as many people as possible. He was known to use aliases even in what otherwise might be considered his private life. But then since I had become his partner I had realised that outside of the missions his life was limited to affairs of the heart, and building, with incredible secrecy, his property portfolio.

What troubled me now was that she had referred to Esmeralda as Hans's future mistress. His intentions were clear for anyone with a modicum of training to realise. But her referring to it openly had made it seem more of a certainty. This had reminded me of Hans's comment that when he had first known me I would have interfered with his intentions. I came to the conclusion in the early hours of the morning that he was right.

I knew no wrong of the young woman. She was grieving. Hans was playing on her loneliness and impending exile with an old woman she didn't know. He had paid her enough attention to convince her to delay her trip north and to join us in Edinburgh. He had yet to reveal he was married.

Hans could be incredibly charming, and he was undeniably handsome. He had married my husband's sister for her money, which he had needed at the time to inject into his business. However, he had been open from the start. He had lost a beloved first wife, and his marriage to Richenda was a marriage of convenience. Most of the time it worked well. But . . . he took mistresses. I had turned a blind eye, as had his wife, but now I wondered what became of these women when he tired of them.

Esmeralda was a widow, without close family. Would Hans's intentions ruin her in the eyes of the world? How discreet would he be? Would he cast her adrift when he was bored, not caring what happened to her? Had he done this before?

Why had I not warned her? I had once been young and without a guardian. I had been fortunate in my attachments and friends. They had protected me – even Fitzroy had warned unsuitable suitors away from me.

Fitzroy was nothing like Hans. He had numerous affairs, but they were well managed. Generally he preferred married women, whose reputations would not be damaged. But I knew for all his wildness he had a sense of honour when it came to his *belles amies*. Hans did not. I had not expected this.

I also realised, shortly before breakfast, that I would not be warning Esmeralda. I had too much to achieve. Griffin's freedom, if not his life. My continued undercover work as an agent of the Crown, and my intention to make best use of Hans as an asset.

I was dealing with greater priorities than the virtue of one young war widow. I could not afford to stir up the matter. Even as I acknowledged this I felt rather nauseous. I had overcome my strict Christian upbringing long ago. I knew how to kill and I had killed. But somehow not coming to the rescue of this young woman seemed worse.

I had breakfast brought to my room, and determined to turn my mind to matters I could affect today. It was early enough that I decided I would take Jack for his walk myself. I still worried the animal was pining hard and might begin to ail.

The air was filled with the scent of petrichor. The pavements retained enough of their moisture to make them a little slippery under my feet. I walked the short way to Princes Street Gardens, and descended stairs steep enough to slow Jack, with his odd gait. We eventually gained the lawns below. The gardens dip down, but one side is close to Princes Street, and this seemed to be the most popular side. I decided to stay close to this side. I wanted the security of people around me, not because I feared attack, but because I wanted to be reminded of the normality of the public's life. This was, after all, what the agents of the Crown conspired to make continue.

The lack of young men was all too evident. I saw a few in uniform, walking briskly, and some older men who sat on the park benches feeding the pigeons. I remembered how Bertram liked to refer to them as piegons, and it made me smile. My husband likes to think of himself as a gourmet.

Lower down the gardens I again saw nannies steering prams and airing their charges despite the dampness of the day. There were no children running alongside them, so I presumed that they must be at their lessons.

My mood was low, and the day seemed oppressive. Jack, of course, cared nothing for all this. I had let him off his lead, and he was running through piles of fallen leaves. I suspected he wanted to encounter a squirrel and give chase. As I now knew he had little chance of catching one I let him be. At least one of us would be cheerful.

I mused on my conversation with Gibbons. I was still undecided about the man. My intuition told me that something was very wrong with either my appointment yesterday or with the man himself, but I could not put my finger on it. I needed to have a clear plan when the next appointment came through. He was fiercely intelligent, and I knew I had told him more than I had originally intended. I did not think I had let anything too important slip, but I should prepare better. The question was how? I wanted to know more about Griffin's cohort – particularly Bloom, Warburton and even Griffin himself. I acknowledged to myself the longer this investigation had gone on the more doubtful of Griffin I had become.

He could not possibly have killed the woman found at the railway station. He had confessed to killing Bloom, but had he killed the right man? He had not been able to tell me why he had decided on Bloom as the killer. Gibbons had stressed the man was against physical violence. How might I discover the truth of that? Who else might have known these men and be available to consult?

I had to admit this was not the work I had been trained to. It was more in Rory's line. I only wished I could trust him to uncover the truth. I frowned heavily, and a man who had raised his hand to doff his hat to me turned quickly on to another path. I followed him with my eyes, and to my astonishment saw Willoughby. At least here was something I could do. Even if it took a full-on tackle in public sight I would have my man!

Now Jack may know some commands, but Fitzroy has never seen fit to explain them to me. However, I knew that above squirrels or even swans Jack prized shoes. I had seen more than one tussle between him and Griffin. And Fitzroy, who had handmade shoes, was forever complaining that he had to remember to keep them out of Jack's reach.

'Shoe,' I said to Jack. The little dog stopped what he was doing and regarded me with his head on one side. 'Yes, shoe.' I pointed at Willoughby. 'You can have that shoe. Shoe!'

Jack's tongue protruded from his mouth as he effectively gaped at me. 'Yes, you can have it.'

Never let it be said that little things, like a man's foot still being inside a shoe, will keep a good English bull terrier down. Understanding gleamed in his eyes and he was off, haring towards Willoughby like a dog possessed.

Willoughby was determinedly not looking in my direction, and had quickened his pace. Yet another sign that he was not adept at following people. Trying to pretend your innocence in such situations, as Willoughby was doing, is akin to a child covering their eyes in the hope they will not be seen!

In this case it was Jack Willoughby did not see. Willoughby tried to hurry past the end of the path and they met at the bottom by the fountain. Willoughby went down as a man only will when he is hit by a small thunderbolt of a dog. But almost at once he was on his feet again. He was obviously very fit. He did his best to fend off Jack, raising his arms and backing away as fast as he could. That he didn't turn and run suggested to me that he thought Jack was some kind of attack animal. A belief I felt certain Griffin would have shared.

'No! Down! Back! Help!' cried Willoughby, his arms and legs going in all directions as he attempted to both block Jack and make his escape.

Of course he was not expecting Jack to go for his shoes. In a confused and desperate attempt to save himself, Willoughby raised his leg high, attempted to protect his groin and fell backwards over the side of the fountain.

It was deep enough that for a moment I feared for him. His legs stuck up in the air, and his torso and head were down in the water. Now he was in the well of the fountain his legs were several feet higher up in the air. Jack jumped like a mad thing and eventually managed to attach himself to the lower part of one of Willoughby's appendages. I was still hurrying over, but Jack's actions may well have saved the man's life. The pain and weight of the dog on his leg caused him to shift in the water, twist, and although he sank further his head and shoulders broke the surface. Jack, still determined, landed in his lap.

I reached them and hauled out the wet dog. Jack gave me a look that said he felt betrayed, as I was removing him from the shoes. But when I set him down he carried on to a deliciously large pile of leaves that promised hidden delights. I stood above Willoughby seemingly asking him if he was injured. I held out my umbrella as an aid to help him get out. In reality I dug the point of my umbrella (for who goes anywhere in Scotland without one?) into the edge of his neck.

'If you have a desire to continue your existence you will get up very slowly, and you will stay here. If you move I shall either stab you with my umbrella, which has a blade concealed in the point, or I will send the dog to take you down once more. Only next time it will be discovered you have seriously, if not terminally, hurt yourself. Do you understand me?'

Of course, my umbrella was merely one I had borrowed from the hotel lobby, and Jack was far more likely to continue digging for squirrels than accede to a command to bring the man down again. But Willoughby didn't know either of these things. My mother has always been proud of making a duke cry when she was a young girl merely by her tone of voice and her words. It is solely on occasions like this that I attempt to imitate her.

Still lying on the ground Willoughby, or whoever he was, raised his hands in a surrendering motion.

'Do not be obvious,' I hissed, and dug the point of the umbrella into him, pinching a small section of his neck against the side of the fountain bowl. This would not do more than cause a bruise, but it would hurt like anything.

I do not enjoy causing pain, but I was fearful he might be signalling another, who might come to his aid. Instead he emitted a small squeak and dropped his hands to his sides. I saw his eyes shine with tears of pain. I am not that old myself, but he looked more like a boy in distress.

'Who the devil are you and what do you want with me?' I demanded. 'Why are you following me?'

'I'm not,' squeaked Willoughby. 'I'm following the man who is following you.'

'What?'

'Please remove your umbrella, Euphemia! I work for Fitzroy too.'

Chapter Thirty-six

A Secret Shared

We found a hotel on Princes Street that would give us tea, and allow the muddied Jack to lie at my feet and accept a man who looked as if he had been half drowned in a fountain. At my direction they sat us in an alcove where I could both see the layout of the room, the exits and where when I allocated Willoughby his seat it would be difficult for him to get past me.

To be fair, he had come meekly from the gardens to the hotel. He had had more than one chance to attempt an escape as the first two hotels took one look at Jack's muddy paws and declined to accept us. Needless to say it had been the most expensive hotel that had accepted us. I made use of this by getting them to remove Willoughby's coat to clean and brush it while we had our tea.

The bill here was going to make a large dent in the money I had been carrying. I could only hope that either the London or Edinburgh office was in the process of sending me funds. Either that or I would have to convince Hans to pay all our hotel bills. Honestly, since arriving in this wretched city it felt as if I had accomplished nothing but being overwhelmed with problems.

Willoughby sat opposite me, sipping a cup of tea and looking forlorn. The bruise on his neck was blooming quickly, and looked nasty. I felt a pang of guilt.

'Explain,' I said when he had finished one cup of tea.

'I am one of Fitzroy's junior trainees,' he said. 'I obtained an injury on the battlefield that precludes me from returning to my unit. Morley asked Fitzroy if he had anything for me. I think he thought as I had been a spotter Fitzroy would be best placed to use my skills – you know he went out with the first wave? The veterans and . . .'

I nodded. 'I don't think we should discuss his career so openly. This is a quiet place but from what you have said I see you have knowledge of him and our commanding officer. This makes you either one of the department or an enemy agent.'

'Oh,' said Willoughby. 'I'm not awfully good at this. I'm much better out in the countryside. Grew up there, you see.'

I gave him what I hoped was a steely-eyed look.

'Have you got something in your eye, Euphemia? I have a clean handkerchief if you need it.'

'No, I do not,' I snapped. 'If Fitzroy sent you, why did he do so?'

'My task was merely to follow you and ensure I knew where you were.'

'Spying on me,' I said grumpily. All spies are fair game, but I didn't like it. 'Why?'

'Honestly, I don't think he knew what to do with me. We had done a little bit of urban observation, but then he was called up for – you know what. He'd been training me in between doing other things. He's been monumentally busy. I rather felt I was wasting his time. It's just, as you know, we have fewer men than usual.'

'So this was another training exercise? Did he think I wouldn't spot you?' My indignation must have shown, as Willoughby leaned forward and spoke hurriedly.

'No, not at all. He was certain you would. It was all about when. He told me to say that I'm "Dormouse". I don't know why he chose such a code name, but that you would understand.'

I felt a smile tug at the end of my lips, but I suppressed it. 'He had his reasons.'

'I think he thought that when you did catch on to me I might be of some use. You know, running small errands and the like. I also have to check in with his man at the office to let him know where you are.'

'His man?'

'Oh, yes, I remember,' said Willoughby. 'I wasn't meant to talk about that. Forget I said anything.'

'Now wait a minute . . .'

'But the thing is, it's just as well I was here. I mean that chap who's tailing you, he looks what I would call a right piece of work.'

I wanted to say nonsense, no one is following me. I would have seen them. But I knew I had been preoccupied. I was also in unknown territory. There are times when one had to swallow one's pride and be open-minded.

'Describe him,' I said.

'Around thirty, I should think. He runs his fingers through his hair, so it's always sticking out in all directions. Brown. Brown hair. Sort of normal muddy-brown.'

'Height?'

'Average-ish. Maybe five foot nine? Terribly thin though. Like he hasn't had a decent meal in ages.'

'A tramp? Or someone disguised as a tramp?'

The dormouse shook his head. 'That's the thing. His clothes are those of a gentleman. They're well kept even if the man within them isn't. I caught sight of one his hands once. Really long and dirty fingernails. Almost like claws. Can't imagine how he holds his cutlery.'

'Do you know where he abides?'

'No, he's too good for that. I've managed to tail him both down to the old part of town, and also over to the New Town. He seems to come and go between them. He definitely followed you that night you went up to the Royal Mile. It was touch and go whether I interceded before you went down that close. But once you moved into the shadows he moved off. Another time I thought I had him cornered in one of those big squares, but the wind got in my eye. I can't have turned away from him for more than a few seconds, but he'd melted into thin air. Whoever he is, he knows the city very well.'

'If he is this good how did you manage to follow him?'

'The first time it was a complete accident. I was watching you and I saw him. When you went back to the hotel I thought I'd check him out. I followed him into the old town, but he stopped suddenly on a street corner and turned around. I had to dive behind one of those old water pumps. When I re-emerged, he'd gone. I ran to the corner and looked in all directions. Not a sign of him. I even paid a couple of street urchins to tell me he where he went.' He sighed. 'They lied.'

'But after that you saw him again?'

'Only because he was following you. If I tried to follow him he always got away. He's odd. It's as if he spends a lot of time lost in thought. Then every now and then it's as if he wakes up and realises I'm there – and then poof! He vanishes. Probably one of this city's famed magicians.' He gave a short, not bark, more of a yap, of laughter. Jack lifted his head, but I quickly passed him a bit of shortbread and he settled straight back down to eat it.

'So he's good enough that when he follows someone – like me – he is able not to be seen. But if he doesn't know he has to conceal himself, like when you are following both of us, he can be lost enough in his thoughts not to notice for a while. But he will eventually, and then you lose him?'

'Sounds about right,' said Willoughby the dormouse. I was going to have to come up with a shorter nom de guerre.

'Would you mind if I called you Barney?' I said. 'The way you keep opening your eyes so wide, I think you're more of an owl than a mouse.'

'No, that's fine. What should I call you?'

'As you have started with Euphemia we shall continue with that. It is the name I am using at the hotel where I am staying. Should I have to introduce you to my companions there . . .'

'Barnabas Willoughby isn't my real name. I'm related to – well, I'm not allowed to say.'

'Fine, I'll use that.'

'Who am I to you?'

'You'll have to be a friend of a friend. Hans Muller, who is with me at the hotel, knows me too well. Are you any good at mathematics?'

'I was a bit of a whizz at school. Might have gone on to study it if it hadn't been for the war.'

'Right, you are a friend of my friend Mary, who teaches maths at one of the female-only colleges in Oxford. We only know each other slightly, but as we are in a strange country, when you saw me you reintroduced yourself.'

'Strange country?'

'Scotland.'

'It is a bit of an oddity, isn't it?' said Barney. He had relaxed enough now that he reached for a piece of shortbread as he spoke. 'A lot of the time I didn't have that much I could do, so I read up on the place.'

'Then we must talk further. You should come to luncheon at the hotel early this afternoon.'

'Two o'clock,' suggested Barney.

'Yes, and if you run into anyone I know then you're a mathematician friend of Mary. We can say you've been doing book-keeping and working on the logistics of supply chains for the army since you've been invalided out. I take it that works?'

'Oh yes, I probably could do that sort of thing. It doesn't sound too hard. They put me out in the field because they're so short of younger fit men.'

I nodded to him and rose, leaving him to pay the bill. The waiter returned with his coat, which I noted was of good quality. I doubted he would have trouble paying the bill.

Two thoughts occupied me as I returned to the hotel. The actions of my follower did not suggest he was a trained agent. They sounded more like the actions of an intelligent man, who got lost in his thoughts. Could the odd hair be a wig? Gibbons was about the right height. I had not observed if he was thin. The lighting had been too poor. However, I thought I would have known if he was as emaciated as the man Barney described. So who the devil was he?

The second thought, less troubling, but more bewildering, was that Barney said he had been invalided out, but also described himself as a fit younger man. What was it about him that had prevented him from being re-enlisted? Was it the powerful relative he hinted at, or was it something else, and if so what?

Chapter Thirty-seven

Luncheon with Barney

Poor Jack more or less collapsed in front of the fire in my room. I changed out of my damp clothes and rang for the maid to run me a bath. While I waited I sat in my robe by the fire attempting to arrange my jumble of thoughts into some kind of order. I was not successful.

However, although this was my second bath in a few hours, I found it most relaxing and refreshing. I had slept so very badly that the warmth and smell of rose oil helped rejuvenate me. If I had felt more on top of things I might have allowed myself a pre-prandial nap. Instead I spent the time writing up my notes, and continuing to fail to understand what was going on. I was almost certain Barney was on the side of the angels, but I wasn't yet prepared to let my guard down. If he proved to be working with this odd fellow who was tailing me then I was in serious trouble. I had never seen Hans fight, and perhaps he would surprise me with expert knowledge of German swordsmanship. Or it would turn out in his youth he had learned the art of pugilism because he had been teased about his German parentage. But I suspected at the end of the day Hans was a lover and not a fighter. I supposed I should be glad he hadn't turned out to be a poet. I should have to get Fitzroy to arrange some basic self-defence lessons for him. Goodness knows, I didn't have the skill or the restraint not to damage him should I attempt to teach him myself.

Luncheon was memorable largely for the Dover sole, the unusual water-ice pudding and the information Barney was able to impart.

'It might style itself the Athens of the North,' he told me between mouthfuls of filet mignon, which he was clearly enjoying, 'it might have a good medical school, but an awful lot of the prominent people here seemed to be a bit barmy. It's as if the city attracts them.'

'What do you mean?' I asked.

'Have you heard of Arthur Conan Doyle?

'The man who wrote Sherlock Holmes?'

'He trained as doctor here in Edinburgh before he became a writer. He's even meant to have based Sherlock on one of his professors.'

'And he was mad?'

'No. Not that. I see why . . . anyway, the thing is Doyle is really enthusiastic about his secret clubs. He set up the Crime Club.'

'And that meets in Edinburgh?'

'Again no, but if you'll let me continue, with respect of course, I sometimes take a country mile when I'm speaking, but it all adds up to a clear picture in the end.'

'That's not how we work.'

Barney cast his eyes down and looked rather shamefaced. The elegant gentleman I had met in the London park had been a disguise. But rather a good one.

'The major has explained that to me on more than one occasion.'

'I should imagine he has. We don't often have the luxury of exchanging information over a quiet luncheon.'

Barney wasn't listening. 'He was quite – er – forceful.' He looked up, wide-eyed. 'Is he like that with everyone? Even you?'

'He can be blunt, and he has a tendency to shout when he's annoyed. You have to learn how to deal with all types of personality in this job.'

'I don't think I'm going to be doing the same as you,' said Barney, delicately cutting up his steak. He seemed to regard it as a thing of beauty to be savoured. 'The people part might not be my strong point. I think I'm not meant to do much more than follow and observe. I mean the reason I was invalided out . . .' He trailed off. Then picked up his glass and took a long drink of water.

'Oh, I don't know. I'm rather impressed with the character you presented to me in the park originally.'

'My cousin. He's easy to copy. He's so proper. And he's very charismatic.'

'I noticed, but I thought that was you?'

Barney speared a piece of steak. 'Oh no, I'm more of a bumbler, especially now. The war, you know. Dreadful.' He shook his head and popped the steak into his mouth.

'Were you at the front?' I asked, getting as close as I felt I could to asking why he had been discharged.

'Hmm,' he said, nodding and chewing. He swallowed. 'Very nasty. Can't talk about it to a lady. Not allowed.'

'Well, I'm—'

'No, you see when I came back I wanted to tell everyone. I thought if they knew what was happening they'd make it stop. It's inhumane what's happening. Men say it's hell come down to earth, and it is.' He gestured around him. 'Anyone living in this world has no idea. No idea of what the truth really is. How we are no more than walking mounds of meat. How the best of us can be gone in an instant. Or worse, how the best of us can become beasts moaning and dying in their own filth. Getting caught by a sniper is a blessing. Most of the men I saw in hospital had been eaten alive, as if the war was some great shark, still living but knowing they would never be real men again. Whole men. Knowing that they had been kept alive for nothing, because there was nothing they could do anymore but live with the pain and the madness. Knowing that when their loved ones saw them carved open and still living, with missing eyes or ears or noses, with wounds that would never heal, with broken spirits, knowing that they couldn't do that to their families, longing for that last bullet, wishing someone would—'

Barney was getting louder and louder. I reached over and touched him gently on the wrist. 'I know a little of what you are saying. I've worked as a nurse with men who have come back from the front.'

Barney's eyes lost their glazed look and refocused on me. 'God bless you then, ma'am. If war has done anything it has shown the female to be superior to the male. You console the inconsolable. We men simply continue to butcher each other.'

'You do need to be careful speaking about the war,' I said as tactfully as I could.

'I know,' said Barney, his voice now lower and calmer. 'The major warned me. He said the general public can't understand, and the politicians don't want them to understand.'

'No,' I said. 'Fitzroy and I often think that what we do is about the prevention of war, or at least about helping it cease. But this war is becoming bigger and bigger. I fear for all of us. I have to do what I can.'

'I like the idea I could help stop the war,' said Barney. 'I know I have to support the King. Duty and all that. But I do wish he and the Kaiser would sit down and talk. Understand what they are doing.'

'I think we should leave politics and the like aside,' I said. 'We have a role and that's what we should do. Although I admit all this is all one man's life, and little to do with the war. But then if we're not prepared to work to see justice for a man, what is the point of anything.'

'Principles. Morality,' said Barney. 'Duty. They crumble for a lot of men at the front. It's too much. So many things become meaningless in the faces of the dying.'

I was beginning to think that Barney had quite a poetic streak. He clearly had a talent for imitation, which would be useful, but he seemed fragile in other ways. I needed to treat him carefully.

'You were telling me about Doyle's secret clubs?'

'He's involved in the Ghost Club too. The members investigate spiritualism and the like. He's very keen on that kind of stuff. And mesmerism too. Apparently, the Edinburgh medical school used it long after the others had gone on to ether. It's a way to make your mind control another's.'

'I've heard about it. Fitzroy was reading up on it and he told me a little. I can't say I understood how it worked.'

Barney shook his head. 'From what I was reading it seemed to have a basis in science, but even the doctors didn't fully understand it. But imagine being able to speak to someone in such a way that they no longer feel pain? Or so it slows how much they bleed? That is a skill I would dearly like to learn.'

I headed him off before he returned to his war memories. 'So what is the Edinburgh connection?'

'More secret clubs than there are stars in the sky. Doyle belongs to a lot of them. There's the Theosophical Society, Golden Dawn . . . and well, they're not precisely secret anymore. More of a widely known secret. They have stated aims but if you're not actually a member you won't ever be sure what is going on.'

'I have a connection who is in the Theosophical Society. What is this Golden Dawn?'

Barney polished his last piece of steak around the plate with his fork to mop up the last of the *jus*. 'Well, it's the Hermetic Order of the Golden Dawn. Founded at the end of the last century by three men to study the occult, metaphysics and the paranormal. It all went into rather a spin a few years ago when this chap Crowley started making a fuss of things. Have you heard of him?'

I shook my head.

'Believed he was a magician, did a lot of rites, and sex orgies. Caused a bit of a hoo-ha because he mixed in high society. All sorts of nonsense about him believing himself divine, controlling people's minds and whatnot. The Golden Dawn rather fragmented for a time. The people involved being divided between those thinking him capable of actual magic and those who thought he was a charlatan bringing their order into disrepute. He ended up setting himself up as a sort of religious guru. Odd sort of chap from what I've read.'

'Is he in Edinburgh?'

'Oh no,' said Barney. 'Do we have time for a sweet?'

I assented.

'Right, no. The original Golden Dawn and the loyal true are still around apparently. I suspect I could dig up someone for you to talk to if I looked in the right places. Do you want me to try?'

'I really want to know if there have been any ritual killings in the city,' I said. 'Particularly ones involving rites that include cutting women up.'

Barney shook his head. 'Not their sort of thing, but I suppose they might know if anyone else was doing it.'

'You seem to be taking this very calmly,' I said.

'Oh, I don't believe in any of it,' said Barney. 'The dead are gone. And as for magic, or whatever you want to think of it as, if it existed it would have either have been used by someone to stop the war, or to win the war. The reality of what mankind does to itself is worse than any fairy tales.' He looked suddenly so glum, I summoned the waiter immediately so we could speak of sweets, which seemed to cheer him.

Chapter Thirty-eight

I am Followed Again

I returned to my room to find a letter waiting for me. It was from Bertram, who said he was missing me quite desperately.

> *I don't wish to appear selfish, my darling, but is it too much to hope I might see a little of my own wife? You seem to have been taking on longer and longer missions. You were hardly back from your last adventure when* that man *called you down to London again. I am all for supporting the Crown, and the war effort – do take a look at my latest piece in* The Times, *I feel I have hit the mood of the time exactly. Asking questions people don't want me to ask and all that. But honestly, I thought that F had said you would be largely doing analysis during the war, and that could very well be done from White Orchards. Isn't that why he set you up a remote operation station here? I fear the more time you spend in London the more likely it will be he will draw you into some madcap scheme abroad. He's so very reckless of his own life, I fear in time he will be so with yours as well. I know his type. He is a man who lives for excitement, and although you've done some amazing things in the service of the Crown I don't think you are of the same cut. I know you enjoy being at home with me in White Orchards, in our own little world. Regular meals, the turn of the seasons, the growth of life in our farms, and the local people to whom we owe a duty as landholders. Christmas will be upon us shortly. I hope you will be home well in time to make our plans. Mrs T has already started on the mincemeat, and the Christmas cakes and puddings were made some time ago. I stirred in some wishes for you.*

When you were last at home you were pale, and worn. That man places too much on your shoulders. You need to come home. Even the troops at the front get time away from the war. You need to let F know your limits. Or I will write to him if you want.

I do miss you, but I fear for you too. You work too hard, and unlike others may believe I know the war will not be over by Christmas. This is a long haul, a horror of attrition. And I need to discuss with you what we do about the mills and how we support the families of the men who have left their work to go to war. I do not want to employ children as Richard did, but it is complicated. Many of the families rely on the children's wages, so I cannot simply ban them from the mills. I need someone with a clever brain like yours to work out what I should do next.

There are so many reasons for you to come home.

He went on to tell me about various happenings with mutual acquaintances, that there was still no news of my dear friend Merry's husband and to lament the death of a cow of which he had been particularly fond. Needless to say I had no idea which animal he was talking about. But the letter produced the desired aim in that I felt desperately guilty after reading it.

I had also told Bertram I was in no danger. Now, Barney had confirmed I was being followed, not by him, but someone else, I wasn't entirely sure this was true any longer. I hadn't wanted to dwell on it with Barney because firstly I was incredibly annoyed that he had spotted someone I had not, and secondly I knew I was liable to be safe in the hotel.

The only candidates I had on my list of suspects for who might be following me were Professor Gibbons and Nathaniel Warburton. Gibbons repulsed me. I could not explain why. He was the epitome of a gentleman, charming, courteous and learned. There was nothing in his voice or his behaviour that warranted my dislike. The lighting conditions under which I had seen him were dim, but I was reasonably sure he was not particularly thin. Also from the way he moved, and from the musculature I had felt in his arm when he escorted me, he did not display any of the aspects of a man used to combat. But then overwhelming a normal young woman of this era did not require skill or strength. The suffragettes might be keen on training women in hand-to-hand combat, but the ordinary woman was as physically able in a fight as a wet lettuce. It was one of the advantages I had should Gibbons turn out to be my follower.

I hadn't the faintest idea what Nathaniel Warburton looked like, nor where he might be or what interest he might have in myself. He was merely another name connected to the case.

Jack gave a particularly loud snort in his sleep and expelled air from the other end. It was bad enough to make me leave the room.

I took to the corridor for a moment. It was empty. At least no one was hovering outside my room, but again the hackles rose on my neck and I felt like I was being watched. It was a straight corridor. How on earth could someone watch me without my seeing? I looked up and down, and there suddenly was a quick sparkle of light at the far end. I ran towards it, but by the time I got there I saw the lift on this floor was already descending. I went for the stairs that were adjacent. However, running down a main staircase in a long skirt, while trying not to attract the attention of hotel staff and other guests, is hard to do.

I settled for a hurrying motion. I gave myself a slight frown as if I was late for an engagement and had at this moment remembered it. A late engagement within the hotel that was, for I had no coat.

I did my best to project this character, but it was not enough to stop one bellboy stopping me and asking if he could be of assistance. I reeled off my lie, and continued on. The lift was old, and descended slowly. I was fit. Despite the interception I arrived ahead of it. I planted myself in the centre of the lobby, so that there was no way he or she could pass me unseen and awaited the culprit.

The door of the lift opened and there stood Esmeralda.

She looked a little surprised to see me, or perhaps it was the expression on my face. 'You!' I said. 'What do you want?'

Now, she definitely looked alarmed. She had stepped out of the lift, but at my tone took a pace backwards. 'Is something wrong, Euphemia? Were you looking for me?'

I almost said something sarcastic about it being entirely the other way round, but I hesitated. Although Esmeralda had attached herself to us with alarming ease, and I had always had it at the back of my mind that she might have an ulterior motive, she seemed, or did a remarkably good impression of being, not that bright. This, to the extent I would never have considered her as an asset.

I took a step forward. 'I am sorry to surprise you,' I said. 'I had quite expected someone else to be in the lift. Someone I was most eager to speak with. What are you about this rainy afternoon?'

Esmeralda came forward cautiously, like a dog that was unsure if it was about to be given a treat or kicked. She looked behind herself in the lift.

'I am the only one in here. No one else has got on or off since I left our floor. I feel certain I would have seen them.'

I had no idea how to answer such a statement. 'I must be mistaken. Come, let us walk together. Where are you going?'

Esmeralda came forward slowly. 'I had thought to take some air, but the rain continues. I thought if I could not walk then perhaps looking outside through the larger windows of the downstairs coffee room would give less of a sensation of being shut up in this place.'

'An excellent idea,' I said. 'Let us have some afternoon tea. I am sure they would serve us some. In general I have found the staff to be most accommodating.'

'Yes, I suppose they are,' she said in a lower voice. 'But recently one of them asked me about payment for my rooms and I did not know what to say.'

I took her arm and led her through the lobby to a sheltered table. I chose a table where large ferns obscured the viewpoint. I was thinking that if she was a spy this would unsettle her, but sitting down I realised that of course it also blocked my view and unsettled me. I was definitely not on top form.

My guest arranged herself prettily. 'I know it is not the done thing to speak about such things, but I believe I have may have formed an erroneous impression.'

Tea and cream cakes of the kind that Bertram would have adored arrived. 'And what was that?' I asked. With alarm I saw tears quivering on the end of her eyelashes. If only Fitzroy was here to say something stupidly charming and divert the impending bursting of an emotional dam! I had always found his flirting with the opposite sex during missions annoying, but now when his skills could be of use he had to be away!

'Well, you see Mr Miller invited me on such a short acquaintance that I think now I should not have accepted.'

'So he offered to pay your bill?'

Esmeralda shook her head. 'Not in so many words, but I should have realised that such a gentleman would never enter into an arrangement that could be read by others as – not precisely correct.'

'Aah. You are having doubts about him?' I felt some of the tension in my shoulders release.

'Well, no, it was simply that I mentioned my encounter with the management, and he said . . . he said . . .'

I thrust a napkin at her. 'What did he say?'

'He said he could never pay my bill as it would shred my reputation.' A sob escaped. I pushed a cake towards her on a little plate. It was quite the best of them, and it gave me a pang to see it go. She took the cake and, to my dismay, began to mush it about with her fork. 'He was quite affronted that that is what I thought he meant when he invited me to Edinburgh.'

'I see,' I said, not understanding what Hans was up to, but thinking he was being a cad.

Esmeralda looked up at me with wide, teary eyes. 'It seemed so like a dream. We met, we fell in love in a matter of moments, and a new life was opening before me. You see, when you have known the horrors of war, as I have . . .'

At this point I almost choked on my tea, but she continued, far too wrapped up in her story to notice anything as insignificant as my impending demise.

'You know you have to live life in the present. Grab what little happiness you can – as long as you act with propriety, of course. I thought that was what Frank was doing. After all his wife died. Like myself, he is no stranger to sudden loss.'

His first, I thought, his second is very much alive. But I didn't think this was the right time to mention it. We only had two napkins between us, and clearly Esmeralda did not carry handkerchiefs.

'So you were hoping Hans – I mean Frank, would propose?'

'Why else would I have agreed to come with you to Edinburgh?'

I took a breath. There had been a time when I, my mother and my younger brother had been left destitute. I had sought out a position as a servant, and my mother had taken to giving piano lessons. While our life before had never been full of riches it had been a massive step down in my mother's eyes. But we had done it because we needed to survive. Clearly, if this whole narrative Esmeralda was weaving was true, then she too had been left in a terrible position. I tried to feel sympathy. I knew how frightening it could be to be able to depend on no one but yourself. However, her total and utter lack of backbone was startling. Were females generally as weak and helpless as this? Were my mother and I, and any of the suffragettes I had known, peculiarities of our sex? Aberrations, as the papers had designated those women who pursued the vote.

But then Hans's first wife had been, by all accounts, a gentle creature. Perhaps those were the kind of women he sought out?

The real question here was could anyone act as foolishly, naïvely and pathetically as Esmeralda claimed to have done? Wasn't it more likely she was running some kind of subterfuge? There were female enemy agents, and I knew they were as able as their male counterparts. Could she be one? But if so how had she found me? Surely whatever was going on with Griffin was no more than a mild domestic issue as far as the rest of the world might be concerned?

I had no choice but to reserve my opinion. I sat with Esmeralda for a while, and talked with her about her family, and her dead husband. Her descriptions of both remained consistent, and there were no obvious gaps in her story. I consoled her and told her I would talk to Frank. I added, slightly maliciously, that I knew he would be more than able to pay her hotel bill, being of reasonable fortune.

The truth was I knew I was in for a tussle getting the department to pay my and Hans's bills. There was no way they would consider paying for what would be thought Hans's bit on the side. As far as I could see Esmeralda presented no operational use.

Unless of course she was a foreign spy, or even something to do with the killer of Griffin's wife? My decision to help Griffin was not secure. I had had to deal with Rory, and whoever he employed in his office. I could not rule out that an interested party might have heard what I intended. Could this young woman be an agent not of a foreign power, but of Rory McLeod's investigation department, the true killer, or even someone trying to get leverage over Fitzroy? The latter happened frequently, and he always confounded them. I did wish he was here.

Despite everything, and perhaps because of the degree of what my little brother would have called 'wetness', I could not accept Esmeralda at face value.

It was only after I escorted her upstairs to change for dinner, and was lamenting so many wasted hours consoling her and listening to her story, that I realised that she had never once asked why I called her 'Frank' Hans. It was almost as if she knew he was German.

There was something not right about the woman.

And there had been that flash of light in the corridor.

Chapter Thirty-nine

Barney Comes to Dinner

My evening dress was more snug than I would have liked. It felt for the first time too open in the chest area. The problem with conducting a clandestine and subtle operation, especially one based in a hotel, is that most of your meetings were liable to revolve around food. The one thing the British public will always do, even if the war forces their portions to become smaller, is stop for luncheon, tea, dinner and even breakfast. We are a nation who live life as much by our stomachs as the clock. Thus sitting and talking over a meal is rarely remarked on by anyone.

I had got used to eating more when I was in Fitzroy's company, but then, and to be fair, even when I was at home, I trained constantly. The last week or so had been one of comparative lethargy, and it was beginning to show in my measurements. Perhaps it was just as well I had let Esmeralda destroy that cake. As far as I saw she never even took a bite.

It also made me wish I had a maid with me to help me rearrange my person more suitably. At home I had Bertram, who had surprisingly deft fingers, or one of the housemaids. Fitzroy's present to me on becoming an agent had been a buttonhook as used by ladies of ill repute to do themselves up. It had actually been useful, but as time had gone on we had devised costumes and disguises that allowed me the freedom of movement necessary should I need to lay out an opponent. For the past week I had been wearing proper dresses, with proper underthings. No wonder I had become so grumpy. I resolved to be pleasant to Esmeralda over dinner.

I was on my way down when I encountered Hans. I linked arms with him in a friendly fashion, as a cousin might, and keeping my voice low told him of Esmeralda's worries. 'Did you offer to pay her bill?' I asked.

'I suppose she might have thought I implied I would,' said Hans. 'But she told me her husband had left her well provided for financially. It was that she was without any direct relatives except for his aged aunt. It never occurred to me it might be a difficulty. I did pick quite a good hotel, but I never imagined it was beyond her means.'

'So why should she plead poverty to me?'

Hans looked down at me from his superior height and gave me a tight little smile. He was looking even more handsome than usual if that is possible. His blond hair shone in the gaslight the hotel preferred. 'My dear Euphemia, has it occurred to you that perhaps our Esmeralda had been out to catch a new husband, and may not have been entirely honest about her affairs? From what you tell me now, the sob story she has woven for you does not fit wholly with the young adventurous woman she presented to me. The young woman who positively jumped at the idea of a small adventure before her incarceration in the Highlands?'

'Is that why you refused to pay her bill?'

'Money. Money. It all becomes so tawdry,' said Hans.

'Money is only unimportant to those who do have it,' I said.

Hans gave a sigh. 'If the girl is without funds then I will of course pay her bill. I demurred the other night because it felt like extortion, and it feels even more so like one today. Besides, it's always awkward hiding these sorts of transactions from Richenda.'

'She takes an interest in the house accounts?' I said, surprised.

'Hmm, she does since marrying me and a certain little incident I feel no need to enlarge on.'

He gave me a most direct look. I felt the blood rush into my cheeks. Hans looked away, and ahead. 'It is most inconvenient. However, I can arrange to move some finances around to pay for the girl if I must. I rather thought your department would be footing the bill for you and me. Tell me at least, Euphemia, that I am not expected to pay for your stay as well? If Richenda does discover the transactions she will be convinced I have started a harem. She might turn a blind eye to the occasional piece of misbehaviour on my part, but paying for several suites of hotel rooms! Goodness knows what she might think.'

We arrived at our table, and Hans pulled out a chair for me. I wished I had the chance to go and bathe. I had had a quick tidy-up, but now after talking about the purchases required for having a mistress, for what else could he have meant, I felt dirty. I could feel a relief that I had become a sort of honourable male, for him to tell me such things, rather than a potential mistress, but at the same time the more I knew about the way gentlemen conducted their affairs the more I felt dismayed and disappointed in the sex that was meant to protect me. Then there was Fitzroy and his exploits. Although in general I knew he followed his own kind of code, and sought not to take advantage of the vulnerable. 'I'd much rather women took advantage of me than I them,' he had told me one night over supper, his eyes sparkling like a naughty schoolboy's.

A waiter wafted open my starched napkin with a snap. I wondered if that was the difference between Hans and Fitzroy, and why I never felt as shocked by his behaviour. Fitzroy made no secret of his adoration of female companionship in all its forms. Hans, well I sometimes wondered if he liked women at all. He seemed much more interested in the conquest than in a love affair as such. But then I knew by many standards Hans was a very amateur philanderer.

'May I ask what you are thinking, dear cousin?' Hans's voice dragged me from my thoughts. I saw Esmeralda had now joined us.

'I was thinking about you, dear cousin,' I said.

'What you will buy him for Christmas, no doubt,' broke in Esmeralda. 'I always try to spend my time getting exactly the right present.'

'But I thought you had so few to buy for?' said Hans.

Esmeralda heaved a big sigh. 'I was thinking of the past and our family Christmases. My parents. My two brothers and I.'

'Brothers?' asked the insensitive Hans, who I tried to kick under the table and missed.

'George and Charlie,' said Esmeralda. 'Gallipoli.' She dabbed her handkerchief to her eyes.

'And your parents?' continued Hans like some unstoppable steam train.

'My mother of a broken heart, and my father, well, they said he almost certainly didn't see the tram coming.'

I felt a sudden bubble of laughter within me. It was not merely Hans's shocked face, but the series of catastrophes were coming so thick and fast it felt like a Victorian melodrama. I suppressed an urge to ask if she had had a kitten as a child and what woe had befallen that.

I also felt an absolute cad. But this couldn't all be true, could it? Hans now showed an expression somewhere between disbelief and acute embarrassment. To someone not privy to the conversation it would look as if he was having severe gastrointestinal problems.

'Evening ladies and gents,' said a cheerful voice. I looked up to see Barney in somewhat worn evening dress. A waiter with a most disapproving expression was bringing across another place setting. 'I hope you don't mind my inviting myself like this, but I found myself in the area earlier than I intended. I could have asked for a separate table, but that would have looked rude.' We all gaped at him. 'Barnabas Willoughby,' he said. 'I'm joining you for the session with Madam Arcana tonight.'

'Of course,' said Hans, the first to recover, 'then you must join us. We all insist. Don't we, Euphemia?'

'Of course, and what good timing, Mr Willoughby! We have yet to order our first course.'

'Oh, don't worry,' said Barney. 'I'll pay my own way. I don't wish to impose.'

Now it was Hans's turn to blush. 'Good heavens, you mustn't think of it, man. You are our guest.'

This resulted in a bit of a gentlemanly spat between them that was resolved by Barney ordering some rather expensive wine for the table. I foresaw that despite his best intentions this too would make it on to our bill. I really had to ask Fitzroy how he worked his expenses. We always ate in the very best of places when it was possible during a mission.

Esmeralda seemed to perk up a fair bit with Barney's arrival. He was clothing himself in his cousin's persona again. I had seen the real, and very young, Barney, but at the table now he was all his cousin. He passed easily for an older man, slightly too self-assured, but with a gallantry that made its own excuses. He let slip he had been at the front, and Esmeralda bombarded him for details, which to his credit he did not supply, but instead gave out the normal platitudes of soldiers returning home, who never want their loved ones to know what they have endured.

At a suitable pause in the conversation I managed to draw Barney aside to ask if he had been following me today. He shook his head. 'Was I meant to? I hurried off to my digs and had to round up this rather sorry affair.' He pulled at his lapel. 'Why, has someone been following you again?'

'I'm not sure,' I said, and told him about the flash of light.

'You think it was a mirror being edged round a corner, don't you?'

I nodded.

'I'm sorry to say if there was someone spying on you it wasn't me. Couldn't it have been a ray of sunlight bouncing off something?'

I raised an eyebrow.

'I see your point,' he said, and then Esmeralda asked him about his background, and Barney gave her his complete attention as he wove more and more elaborate lies.

Chapter Forty

A Shocking Séance

Madam Arcana awaited us in the séance room. The hotel had repurposed a downstairs room of good size for us. The ordinary drapes were augmented by black throws, and the furniture had been largely removed and replaced with a large round table. Two lanterns glowed in the far corners, and a thick single candle burned in a stand in the centre of the table. The light level was low, but our eyes quickly adjusted, and with only a little fumbling (Esmeralda) we took our seats around the table. There was an odd scent in the room, a cross between rose and cedar. It took me a while to spot the faint glowing ember of an incense burner on a console table at the back.

As well as the door through which we entered I remarked a further door to the left that presumably led into what was the rest of the suite. The layout differed from that of my own suite, which along with the dark and the odd scent I found disorientating. I put my hands on the table, and closed my eyes to centre myself.

'I see you are eager to start, Euphemia,' said Madam Arcana.

I merely smiled, and left it to Esmeralda and Barney to express their enthusiasm.

'I have asked the hotel staff to ensure we are not disturbed. Can I please also ask that all present give their full attention and focus to the proceedings regardless of personal opinion. Mr Miller?'

'Of course.' Hans's voice sounded deep and rich in the dark. He was carefully modulating it.

'Mr Willoughby?'

'Keen as mustard, ma'am.'

'Ladies?' I made assenting noises along with Esmeralda.

'Well then, can we all place our hands on the table, little fingers touching please. Have no fear, there are no tricks here tonight. This table will stay firmly in place. I will call the spirits and if they wish they will speak through me directly to you. I cannot guarantee who will come nor what they will divulge. I am merely the messenger.

'Now, ladies and gentlemen, close your eyes and concentrate on who you would speak with. If there is no one you wish to contact please simply retain a calm composure. Think of your favourite colour. Or a favourite food. We are creating a welcoming atmosphere for the spirits to join us. Doubt, anger or any negative emotion can give them pause, so the calmer we can be the more likely they will come. Good. Good. I feel we are approaching the threshold.

'I ask you now to open your eyes and focus upon the candle flame. When the first spirit appears it will blow out. Do not be startled. There is nothing to fear here. Concentrate on the flame. Concentrate. Will those who have gone before join us?

'Is there anybody there who would speak to anyone here?'

I couldn't help but hold my breath. Madam Arcana, whether or not she had any actual ability, was a consummate performer.

'Is there anybody there who would speak to anyone here?'

Then again in a lower register. 'Is there anybody there who would—'

The candle flame went out. It was not snuffed. There was no smoke. It was gone. The lanterns at the back of the room also dimmed further. If this was a trick it was a clever one. I heard Esmeralda give a barely contained squeak.

'Hello, lad,' said a deep voice. It was barely recognisable as Madam Arcana's. 'The others wanted me to drop in and say you did a damn good job. Not your fault, son. You did as much as any man might be expected to do. Rest easy now.'

'What's it like there?' asked Barney in a trembling voice. 'How are you?'

'How are we? Not being shelled or shot at anymore. It's bloody paradise. Lots of us coming in. Old friends reunited. Not a bad place. Missing our loved ones. But we'll see them one day. Even old Colonel's here.'

Then the voice changed to that of a woman, young by the sound of her sweet voice. 'Oh *Liebling*, not again.'

It changed again to a male voice. 'Tell your mother I am happy she remarried,' said my father. 'Do be careful, dearest.'

I had had messages from Madam Arcana before, and more convincing ones, but I decided to accept this at face value. So far the rational side of me thought there was nothing Madam could not have got from departmental sources. The soldier was clearly meant to be someone Barney had served with, and the *Liebling* was Hans's late wife despairing of his adulteries – another sure bet. I had hoped for something more.

Another man's voice: 'I'm sorry we didn't get it done properly, Es. Would have made it back if I could. Don't go to London. Not safe. Don't go to London. Not safe.'

The voice was cut off suddenly by a woman shouting, 'He didn't do it. He didn't do it.'

Madam Arcana's voice came through. 'Calm down, my dear. You're tearing at my throat. You need to speak slowly.' There was a pause. 'Oh dear, now she's gone. Sometimes they are too emotional. I'm getting a vague warning about – what – an ape? A threatening age? Who? Ah, no. It's gone now.'

'Is that it?' asked Hans. He sounded displeased.

'No, I feel the presence of one more . . . I think . . .'

Suddenly there was a bang in the room next door. We all jumped. A man's voice called, 'My turn. My turn.'

It sounded horribly like Fitzroy. I felt tears spring to my eyes. 'Oh no,' I whispered. 'Not him.'

The air in the room changed somehow, and the candle flame flared. I blinked in the flare of light. Fitzroy's face hung in the air inches from my own.

I screamed.

He kissed me on the cheek. His touch was warm.

Madam Arcana stood and drew back the blinds. The door from the suite was open, and Fitzroy was there leaning across the table, a lit taper in his hand.

Esmeralda scrambled backwards and out of her chair. 'Who the devil are you, sir?' she demanded.

Fitzroy took a step back and bowed. 'Why, I am Euphemia's husband, Bertram. Delighted to meet you, ma'am.' His eyes twinkled as they met mine. 'So good to see you again, my dear wife.'

'Bertram,' I said from between gritted teeth, 'I need a word in private!'

Chapter Forty-one

In which I Want to Slap Fitzroy Harder than Ever

Fitzroy and I stepped through to the other room, and closed the door behind us. He immediately threw himself down into a chair, roaring with laughter and hugging his stomach. 'Oh, oh, that hurts. I don't think I've laughed so much for months. Oh, stop looking at me like that, Alice. You should know by now even your most poisonous looks will not pierce my insensitive hide. Oh, ouch, ouch. Laughing this much hurts.'

'Fitzroy, stand up!'

'Why?'

'So I can slap you!'

Fitzroy ceased laughing, but continued to grin. 'Then I most certainly shan't. Goodness, I never thought to hear you scream again. But you still have it. Loud enough to—'

'Waken the dead,' I interrupted. 'This séance was important to the people here. Or some of them. Besides, you made me think for a moment you were dead.' And then to my horror I burst into tears. Fitzroy rose and manoeuvred me into a chair, and from somewhere produced a glass of brandy while I got myself back under control. I finally lifted my head to see him regarding me with caution. 'Don't do that, Alice. You don't cry. I hate it when you cry. It's unnerving. A man never knows what to do when a friend cries.'

'Jack's fine,' I said.

Fitzroy's face lit up. 'You brought him with you?'

'He's in my room.'

'Well, let's go back there. Face the rabble outside and off to bed.'

'You can't,' I said. 'Hans and Barney know exactly who you are. As does Arcana.'

'What? Oh, no. Don't fret. It's just that I'm a bit prone to nightmares since I've come back. Thought you could wake me and stop me screaming the place down. I'll sleep at your feet like a dog.'

'That's where Jack sleeps. You can sleep on the hearthrug.'

'What a way for a dear husband to be greeted,' he said. 'Let's keep it up for the sake of the girl, and I also don't want Sutherland knowing I'm up here. He's never set eyes on me so . . .'

'Fine, right. Let's go. I could do with a lie-down.'

'Has it been too much? This Griffin thing? I can help now. I'm back. For good, I hope.'

'Let's deal with everyone next door and then we can talk,' I said.

When we finally made it to my room, Jack went mad with excitement. Fitzroy threw all dignity to the winds and rolled around on the floor with his dog. I couldn't tell which one was happier to see the other. While he was doing this I told him the rough outline of what had happened in his absence. It was either that or join in playing with Jack, and doing that in skirts would have been most difficult.

Eventually man and dog lay down together by the fire. Fitzroy propped himself up on one elbow and regarded me sitting on the edge of the bed. 'I'd draw up a chair and join you, but I must smell decidedly doggy by now. I take it this rather pleasant suite comes with a bathroom.'

I pointed to the adjoining door.

'Excellent, no expense spared. Who is paying by the way? Have you convinced Hans to cough up?'

'I assumed the department. I was going to wire for expenses.'

'Ah,' said Fitzroy. 'They don't tend to do expenses.'

'But how do you manage? You've paid our hotel bills before when we've been . . .' I trailed off. 'You've paid,' I said as the penny finally dropped.

Fitzroy didn't meet my gaze. 'It's sort of expected that we manage our own financial affairs on missions. You found my note, didn't you? In the flat?'

'Telling me you're disgustingly rich?'

'That's the one. I am, you know.'

'So you often tell me. How very embarrassing. I will have to get Bertram to wire me funds.'

Fitzroy bounced to his feet. 'You will do no such thing. I'm Bertram, remember. If you think Sutherland isn't keeping an eye on you, you're mistaken. I'll sort it out.'

'I don't want you to pay!'

'Is this some kind of female independence objection because I don't understand the difference between either Bertram or me paying?'

'He's my husband.'

'And I'm a Crown official.'

I bit my lip. I wasn't going to win with him in this mood. Fitzroy went over to the wardrobe, and saw his clothes had been hung up by the maid. Opening a drawer, he took out an elegant pair of silk pyjamas. 'Look, I'm going to have a bath and have a think over what you've told me. Griffin will be with us tomorrow or the day after. They're sending him up by rail like a parcel.' He chuckled to himself and then promptly locked himself in my bathroom. For the next half-hour I was treated to a selection of opera, *Tosca*, I think. The walls were slightly muffling, but not enough to stop the strength of Fitzroy's annoyingly pleasant baritone. Was there nothing the man could not do? I took the opportunity to change into a nightdress and robe. There comes a point at the end of a long and wearying day when a woman really cannot stand the tightness of the clothing current fashions demand – even a lady such as myself.

Eventually he came out of the bathroom, dried, dressed in his nightwear and with a ruddy red skin. Clouds on steam bled into the room. 'Water warm enough, was it?' I said tetchily.

'I am still cold from being at the front! That cold gets into your bones.'

'I thought you were going to a code-breaking unit, not the actual front?'

Fitzroy sat down in a chair by the fireside, and Jack immediately jumped on his lap. The red light from the fire danced across his face, and I realised how very worn he was. No wonder I had mistaken his visage at the table for an unearthly apparition. There were lines around his eyes that I had not noticed before, and his cheeks were slightly more hollow. But what I read from him mostly was sadness. Sitting there he seemed smaller somehow. Jack sat up and licked his face. Fitzroy pushed his muzzle away. 'I'm already washed, you silly dog.'

Jack continued to nuzzle at him as if sensing his master was out of sorts. He hadn't replied to my question so after a long pause I asked, 'You seem lost in your thoughts.'

'Hmm,' said my partner, fondling his dog's ears. 'Sorry, saw some things it will take me a long time to forget. I did see the code-breakers, but then I got sidelined into an IToc project. It's a way of eavesdropping using remote listening sets. They put them behind the lines in prisoner cages for officers. Needed my help with some of that. We got some useful information, but it led to another bit of slaughter. The chiefs seemed to think it was worth it. Seeing the carnage I am inclined to disagree. Not that anyone cares what I think about trench warfare. Not my department, thank God. Those poor, poor buggers.' He shook his head and gazed into the fire. 'Bodies everywhere. Unconscionable injuries inflicted by both sides, and men who are there one minute and gone in a cloud of blood the next. I suppose those are the lucky ones.' He looked up at me. 'Sorry, I shouldn't be telling you this. Not meant to share it with the people back home. The things that are being done in the name of this country . . .'

'Shall I ring for some brandy?' I asked, and did so before he could answer. 'I do know something of what you speak. At the hospital. I didn't work on the ward with the most serious injuries, but you couldn't avoid seeing them. I still think about them. How some of them will ever live with what happened to them.'

Fitzroy passed his hand across his face. 'I'm sorry you had to see that, Alice. There are some things you can never unsee. God, don't I know it.'

Fortunately the brandy arrived at this point. I poured him a large glass.

'This is only likely to make me more maudlin,' he said, taking a large gulp. 'But I suppose it might help me sleep. I haven't had a full night's sleep since I went out there.'

'No wonder you look so tired.'

'Are you really going to make me sleep on the floor?'

'There's a chaise longue,' I said, 'and I will donate blankets and pillows. Unless you need to take the bed, and I can sleep there.'

'Couldn't do that! Too much of a gentleman.' He swallowed some more brandy. 'I have been thinking about what you said, in between the waking nightmares.' He smiled, so I wasn't sure if he was serious. 'I think it's liable Sutherland has someone following you. Keeping an eye out – not for you, but to see what you're up to. Goodness knows even spies on the same side spy on each other. Whole bloody thing can go round in circles like a damn carousel.'

'I like carousels,' I said. 'But I would be happier thinking that it was one of his men than that Esmeralda was some kind of plant or enemy agent.'

'You still have a feeling there is something off about her?'

I nodded.

'Yes, well I trust your intuition – although I must say she seems a bit of a wet dishcloth to me. Kind of weepy, clinging female Muller goes for.'

'Richenda!'

'Yes, well his current wife might be the opposite, but I bet the first was the clinging vine type. I expect he misses the feeling of being needed, or being someone's saviour. Men with fragile egos or small equipment often behave like that.'

'Small?' I found myself blushing hotly.

Fitzroy, with his unnerving timing, looked up at that moment.

'Considering Hans's equipment makes you blush? I suppose he is handsome. Bad lot in many ways though.'

'I have no desire to think of any man's equipment but Bertram's,' I said. My skin felt hot enough to burst into flames.

Fitzroy seemed to mull over several thoughts, and although I deplored our risqué conversation I could see more of the old Fitzroy and all his mischief returning. It was, if uncomfortable, better than a sad Fitzroy. 'Well, I'm Bertram at the moment.'

'How did you get Madam Arcana to go along with your little surprise?' I said, attempting to change the subject. 'I thought she would be all for being professional.'

Fitzroy shrugged. 'We go back a long way. She owes me so many favours. Besides, there was no one of import there. You're right that she didn't like it.'

'Why did you do it?'

'Sheer devilry.'

'Oh, I know that was part of it,' I said severely. 'But it was more than that, wasn't it?'

'I was interested in the reactions of the others. Young Barney in particular. He's a fragile soul, as you suspected. I need to establish his limits.'

'Dying of a heart attack being one of them?'

Fitzroy shook his head. 'No, he's A-one fit. In the body. Hand me over some pillows and blankets will you. I'm going to settle down and do some thinking about your problem. I think there are still pieces of the puzzle missing.'

'Are they letting Griffin go free?'

Fitzroy was rolling himself up in the bed coverings I had given him. 'Hmm, yes. Like I said, I believe he is being sent up under escort, like a parcel. I wonder if they will tie a label to his collar. But no, he's not free from suspicion.'

'I . . .'

'Tomorrow, Alice. I really need to sleep.'

Within moments I heard his breathing slow and deepen. I found the night colder than usual. Not only had I lost some blankets, but

Jack had managed to curl up in the blankets with him. I missed the little dog's warmth.

I slept fitfully because I was cold, and the night only became colder when the fire dimmed. It was still dark when I came fully awake. Someone was shouting. Jack was barking. Sleepily I realised it was Fitzroy. 'What's wrong?' I asked, not wanting to leave the warmth of my bed.

He didn't answer except to continue speaking loudly, except his words were slurred and they didn't all sound as if they were English.

I got up and turned on the gas lamp by the door. Fitzroy was lying on his back, eyes wide open, but clearly seeing nothing. Jack was jumping and barking. I ssshed the dog, and went closer. Fitzroy gestured wildly with his arms, but his eyes were still blank. He began to fling himself about as if trying to dodge something.

I knew children had night terrors. My brother Joe had had them after my father died, but I had never seen them strike a grown man. I knelt down by his side, near to his head, and out of the way of his thrashing arms. 'Eric,' I said quietly. 'It's all right. I'm here. Alice. You're safe with me.'

He muttered something incoherent, but at least lower in volume.

'You're dreaming,' I said. 'None of this is happening now.'

Then suddenly he sat up and grabbed me in his arms, swinging me round in front of him. 'Alice, you can't be here. It's not safe. I can't protect you.' The last words were almost a wail.

I struggled to get my arms free, and gently stroked his face. 'We're safe,' I said, still speaking softly. 'We're completely safe. You got us to safety.'

At that some recognition did seem to come into his eyes. 'I did?' he said. 'How?'

'You took me away from it all. We're safe here. The war is far away.'

He looked at me then. Really looked at me. 'Thank God you're safe,' he said. He released me and slumped back down. In a moment his breathing went back to a deep, slow pattern and he was clearly asleep. Jack tilted his head, and then cautiously climbed back on the chaise longue. I went back to my now cold bed, and tried to sleep. I saw dawn's light creep between the drapes before I finally fell asleep.

Chapter Forty-two

Finally Proof, but not What I Wanted to See

When I awoke Fitzroy was gone. The pillows and blankets had been put back on to my bed, and if it wasn't for his clothes in the wardrobe it would have been as if he had never been there. There was no sign of Jack either.

I went through to the bathroom, and ran a warm bath in the hope of ridding myself of both the actual chill I felt in my body and the one I had in my spirit. I had seen Fitzroy in many moods. Admittedly a lot of them negative, but I had never seen him so scared. As I sank into the warm water I realised it reminded me of the first time my father had made a mistake in my lessons. It was that tipping point when you realise someone is fallible. I knew Fitzroy was very far from perfect, but I hadn't considered how much I took him for granted and how reassured I generally was by his overbrimming confidence. He made mistakes like anyone, but yet he always got himself, and sometimes myself, out of trouble. This last week or so I had been content to work alone. Although I still found Griffin's situation a complete conundrum, and I had been annoyed by many of the people I had needed to approach.

I had been hoping for Fitzroy's return because I wanted him safe, but also, I now realised, because I assumed everything would get easier now he was back. Previously I had insisted how capable I was, but I found it much easier to work with him as a partner. I wanted his support, and his experience. However, returning from the front it seemed as if he needed me more than I needed him. It was an uncomfortable feeling, but I was resolved to do all I could to aid him. It was only fair. I was unnerved though. A world without an overconfident Fitzroy seemed a much more frightening place.

Despite my bath I was still up early enough to get down for a late breakfast. The waiter led me to our usual table where I found Hans gingerly cutting up an omelette. The reason for his hesitancy was revealed the moment he lifted his head. The shadow under his eye was only just beginning to form, but his cheek was red and swollen. He had been punched in the face, and by someone who had chosen not to punch him on the nose. Which was odd. It was more effective, and more stunning, to punch someone on the nose.

'Good morning,' I said. 'What has happened?'

'I had an argument with a door,' said Hans. He gave me a weak smile. 'As you see the door won.'

'It looks painful. Shall I ask the waiter for some steak to put on it?'

'I did when it happened. And I shall ask for an ice pack when I retire to my room after breakfast. I am afraid I will not be in a position to help you today. My head is remarkably sore.'

'Oh dear,' I said. 'I am sorry to hear that. May I ask if Esmeralda is aware of your situation? I did expect to find her at breakfast. I know she is not an early riser.'

'I believe she has gone somewhere with Fitzroy,' said Hans. 'I thought you might know his intentions.'

'Hardly ever,' I said with a bright smile. I accepted coffee from the waiter and placed an order for a large breakfast. Hans winced again.

'I take it the muscles around the jaw are also swelling?'

Hans nodded. His cheek was continuing to puff up, and clearly eating was becoming more and more painful.

I ate my breakfast in what I hoped was considerate silence. Hans made the occasional grunt of pain. He was still sipping his coffee by the time I had finished. I rose and said, 'You know, Hans, that door must have had some liking for you. It would have been easier to hit your nose and ruin your handsome visage.'

Hans looked up at me, horrified. I left him staring at me and went to see if Fitzroy had returned to our room.

He had not. Nor had he left any messages. I was loath to strike out on my own until I had had a chance to talk matters through further with him. I felt like a child holding a jigsaw box full of puzzle pieces from which I knew some were missing. I needed Fitzroy to help me find them.

Strangely, this didn't annoy me as much as it usually would. Fitzroy had, whether or not voluntarily, showed me he was vulnerable. It had done nothing to help my confidence in how the war was progressing but it had made me feel a lot closer to my partner.

I decided to jot down everything I knew about this very odd case. Hopefully Griffin would arrive today, wrapped up in brown paper and string – a lovely image, and I would be able to question him. This, I hoped, would fill in the parts that were missing for me.

I was under no illusion about his release. This case was as important as ever. Rory McLeod had let him go because legally he had no right to hold him further. In his particular department that might not have counted for much, but Rory was a moral man, and as I had extinguished his only reason for keeping Griffin in jail he had let him go. If nothing else Rory respected the rules. We would never have worked as a married couple. I was far more comfortable bending the rules with Bertram, and in my work often ignoring them, as Fitzroy usually did. He was very much a take-action-now-and-ask-for-permission-later spy. So far that hadn't ever gone terribly wrong.

I did wonder why on earth he had punched Hans in the face. That he hadn't smashed Hans's nose, and ruined his exemplary looks, suggested he thought I was correct that Hans would make a good asset. It also suggested that whatever transgression he thought Hans had made, it was not serious. Indeed, Fitzroy was quite in the habit of punching people, generally junior agents who erred. Most of them actually seemed to prefer it to being put on report – or so he claimed.

I looked down at my notebook, it was more full of doodles and swirls than any real information.

David Bloom might or might not have killed Megan.

Griffin had killed Bloom believing he had killed Megan.

When Griffin was at medical school he got another student dismissed – Nathaniel Warburton.

Warburton tried on at least one occasion to remove parts of cadavers from the school – to do what with them?

Warburton, Griffin and Gibbons had all been at medical school together.

Gibbons was now a specialist in anatomy, promoted to professor at a young age, and often helpful to the local police in investigations. (What kind?)

Griffin disliked Gibbons.

I disliked Gibbons. He made my skin crawl. But was outwardly a highly skilled medical man and perfect gentleman.

Gibbons told me that Bloom believed himself to be a vampire. Gibbons had known this from when they were children, and blocked his entry to medical school. However, he claimed that Bloom was a very gentle man, who abhorred violence.

Did Griffin kill the wrong man?

What would happen if he had? And should we cover it up if he had?

What if Griffin was the killer?

Griffin had an old picture of a young woman, not his wife, in his shoe. (Only I knew this.)

All of them came from Edinburgh.

Edinburgh is in the grip of an esoteric mania, as well as the spiritualism that is sweeping the country.

Did Griffin kill his wife?

Jack hates Griffin.

Someone is following me. Willoughby, who was following me on Fitzroy's instructions, noticed him. I did not.

I sat back and rubbed my hand across my forehead. What had I not included? What had I missed? The pieces I had did not add up. As if in answer to my prayers there was a knock on my door.

''Cuse me ma'am. Telephone call for you. Will you follow me?'

It says something for my state of mind that I didn't even ask who it was, I was so desperate for information.

I entered a little kiosk put aside for such purposes and picked up the machine. 'Yes,' I said.

'Hello, darling,' said Fitzroy's voice. 'Sorry to leave before you woke. I wanted to get a good start on the day. I hoped you didn't miss your hubby too much at breakfast.'

This was his way of telling me the line was not safe. 'No, Bertram dearest. I managed without you. Especially as it meant that for once I got some marmalade.'

Fitzroy gave an embarrassed laugh quite in Bertram's manner. It was uncanny. 'Well, dear, I wanted to let you know that Frank's companion is with me. I fear we must dissuade him from marrying her. It is not that I find her largely cabbage-brained, but rather she is undoubtedly a fortune hunter. I believe she has misrepresented herself badly, but that her intention was only to find someone to keep a roof over her head.'

'So cunning, but harmless?'

'I also have information about the doctor you were interested in, Dr Nathaniel?'

'Oh yes, I had some reservations.'

'Quite right, me dear. The man was attending an institution for some time, but has now gone out on his own. One has to wonder why he left the institution?'

'He was working there?'

'Yes, dear. You could say he was well bedded in. Apparently, he spends a lot of his time walking now. You may run into him in the city.'

'A casual encounter might be more useful than a formal appointment,' I said. 'I do not yet know if I wish to engage him.'

'Don't be too headstrong, my dear. Remember your reputation and keep to public places when you are meeting gentlemen.'

'Of course, my love. I am always careful of my reputation as you would wish.'

'Speaking of which, I understand, from speaking to your uncle, that you remain concerned that I asked another lady to host my last charity benefit. I meant to say that it was a difficult event, with many annoying patrons, but what most decided me was that she was already in the area, and knew most of the – er – combatants. It was not a situation I would have wished on you. Am I forgiven?'

'Always,' I said. 'How was Uncle?'

'I believe he is sending you a little present via our nephew. I am not sure you will like it, but it will help you untangling your knitting.'

'I should be grateful then, for I am still deeply entwined with the skeins. I was hoping for your help.'

'I shall be back for dinner tonight. I will be delighted to help in any way I can.'

'Frank seemed a little unwell this morning?'

'I would not let Frank concern you in the slightest. I must go, my darling. I love you. Take care of your dear self and I will see you in a few hours. Contain yourself until then. Adventures await, but let us do these side by side. Do you understand?'

'Yes, I do. I love you too.'

There was a slight intake of breath on the other end.

'I have to go.'

The line went quiet.

I hoped the abrupt end to the conversation was due to Esmeralda or some other person, and not to any danger. Certainly, Fitzroy had not used a code word to indicate he was in danger. Although he had couched the whole discussion in veiled metaphor. If I read him right, Warburton had been in an asylum, and only recently released. Uncle had to be Morley, and our nephew was Willoughby. I went back to my room, and waited for Willoughby to arrive.

I did not have to wait long. Willoughby was at my door within an hour.

'I got dragged out to Sutherland's office,' he said. 'We had a cable. It told me to go and buy this morning's *Times*. Now why they couldn't have . . . anyway. I have the paper.' He took it from under his arm and flourished it at me. 'The only other part of the message was fifteen. Shall we look?'

I was so eager to see what had caused the two departments to actually interact I knelt on the floor and spread the paper out in front of me.

On the page was a new story about the girl killed at the railway station. They had managed to identify her. The name meant nothing to me, but they had also got a photograph of her, presumably from her family. Under it in large black type it said: **Misfortune dogs maid, who died as her mistress did at the hands of a maniac**. The headline was the most damning of all.

'Oh no,' I whispered. 'Oh, no, no, no.'

MURDERED MEGAN GRIFFIN'S MAID FOUND DEAD AND MUTILATED AT RAILWAY STATION.

Chapter Forty-three

Suspicions Harden

'Something wrong?' asked Barney. 'Not what you expected to read?'

I sat back on my heels in a most unladylike way. Barney looked faintly embarrassed. 'Can I help you up?'

I moved my skirts, modestly, to get them out of the way and jumped up. 'Not necessary,' I said, looking at Barney's surprised face. 'I am an agent, not a shrinking flower.'

'I never meant to suggest—'

I put up a hand to stop him. 'I apologise. I am out of sorts. This is damning. But I don't – can't believe what this implies.'

'I don't know a lot about it,' said Barney cautiously, 'but this seems more like a case for the police.'

'Yes and no,' I said. 'An agreement was made with the department on certain aspects, and it would not be good, whatever the truth, for that to become public knowledge.'

'You mean Mr Griffin and whether or not he's a killer?'

'You are better informed than I realised.'

Barney shook his head. 'I got told some things. How the set-up is, and all that, but not the ins and outs.' He tapped the side of his head. 'Mind you, I'm sharp. I watch. I work things out.'

'Well, I wish you could work this one out,' I said, flopping into a chair. 'Have you managed to get me someone to talk to in the esoteric circles in this city?'

'Still working on it. There are possibilities, and most of them would be happy to talk. It is as much a case of finding people. This lot are always in and out of their clubs, each other's houses and various eating establishments. For people into esoteric considerations they seem to be socially extremely active.'

I was only half listening. 'Do your best, Barney. I suspect I am going to need a miracle to solve this.'

'I will try my hardest to find you one, ma'am.'

I smiled. 'You seem quite chipper today.'

Barney shuffled his feet, and avoided my eyeline. 'I appreciated being in on the séance.'

'You enjoyed Fitzroy's sense of humour?'

'Er – not sure what I should say about a commanding officer. It certainly gave me a shock. No, the part before. It was good to hear from the lads that they didn't blame me. I mean I knew, or I hoped, they would know I had done my best, but there's nothing like hearing it from the horse's mouth as it were.' His eyes looked a little bright. 'They were grand men the lot of them.'

'I am sure they were,' I said, carefully avoiding seeing the tears in his eyes. 'I am glad Madam Arcana could give you some comfort.'

'We'll be able to help, won't we, ma'am? Help stop this bloody war. I mean we will be able to make a difference doing what we do?'

'Yes, Barney, you will still be able to make a difference. Almost certainly you will be able to achieve more than you could do as a single man at the front. Our work is sometimes subtle, but it is effective. This issue with Griffin is more about consolidating our assets. Once it is done, one way or another, we will get back to the heart of things.'

'One way or another?'

'I think you know exactly what I mean, Barney.'

He frowned, but nodded. Without another word left. I watched the newest convert to Madam Arcana's abilities leave.

It was less than a quarter of an hour later, and I had been staring out of the window with thoughts circling endlessly in my head, when there was a knock on the door. I got up immediately and went to open it. 'That was quick work,' I said, expecting to see Barney, except it was a bellboy standing there.

'I have a message for you, madam,' he said.

I held out my hand.

'Sorry, miss, it's a words message.' I must have looked confused because he added, 'I've got to say it. It ain't written down.'

'You had better come in,' I said and stood away from the door.

The boy came in. He must have been new to the job as he looked around him tentatively as if he had never seen such a room. I noticed his uniform was a bit loose. Clearly he was someone who had been newly hired.

'So?' I said.

The boy closed his eyes and began to recite, 'Message for Lady Alice Stapleford, Dr Gibbons would be grateful if you could attend him at your earliest convivence at the Surgeons' Hall. He suggests that it would be safer for you not to mention this message to anyone else.' He opened his eyes. 'That is all, ma'am.' He held out his hand hopefully. I placed a shilling in it. His eyes popped open.

'Thank you, ma'am,' he said, and then before I could ask him a single question he bolted from the room, presumably either to spend his riches or display them to his peers. At least I had ensured that he would remember me and the message.

I was extremely suspicious that Dr Gibbons didn't want me to tell anyone where I was going. However, as I knew I had been followed it might be better to heed his advice. After all, although he didn't know it, I was hardly a helpless woman.

I changed my costume. I still looked perfectly respectable. I doubted anyone would realise how I differed from the norm. I left Fitzroy a note that said, in our code, *Back shortly out following a lead*. Then I went downstairs, out of the lobby, and asked the doorman to summon me a cab.

As soon as I stepped out of the door I was assailed by typical Edinburgh driving rain. I could hardly see my hand in front of my face. Fortunately the doorman got me a cab almost immediately, and was able to hand me in out of the wet. I had barely mentioned the direction before we were off.

I sat back in the cab, and relaxed for a moment. It was a good time to clear my mind. I didn't know what I was walking into. I could have taken Hans with me, but from his reaction to being punched by Fitzroy I didn't think he had ever been in a fight in his life. I did not need an extra back to watch. I might have taken Barney, but he must still be about hopping from café to café trying to find another possible lead.

Far earlier than I imagined the cab stopped. The rain was blinding. The cabbie, a most thoughtful man, held up an umbrella as I stepped out. In front of me stood two large metal doors, which opened rather like some kind of sepulchral gate on to a paved area that led directly towards what could only be described as a large tomb-like building. The door to this opened a moment after the gates clanged shut behind me. There, standing in the doorway wearing a charming smile, was Dr Gibbons. He held out his hands to me. 'Come in! Come in! The weather is terrible. I have so much to tell you.'

I was only too glad to get in out of the weather now I no longer had the shelter of the cabbie's umbrella. I hurried forward and gave what I hoped was a suitably demure smile.

I didn't see the man tucked behind the door. I felt him throw his arm around me, and place a hand over my mouth. I had dealt with such encounters many times before, and reacted instinctively to throw this man over my shoulder. Only as I dropped my weight to twist and throw I suddenly found myself feeling very drowsy.

The hand over my mouth . . . I was being drugged . . . blackness.

Chapter Forty-four

All Tied Up

I came to strapped to a table. A white light glared down from above me. It was hard to see anything beyond the glare. My coat, hat and shoes had been removed. I had lost my hatpin. However although the leather straps were tight across my torso, my feet and my arms, my head had not been bound in place. I lifted it slightly to squint around. Immediately, everything became slightly blurry and I felt seasick. I put my head back down at once, and took some deep breaths.

It must have been chloroform. I couldn't have been out for long if I was still feeling the effects. I twitched various muscles to see if anything had been done to me: a cut, a scratch, heaven forbid some kind of minor operation. Then I stopped and listened. I could hear no one, so I decided to test my bonds. I took several deep breaths in and out, and by expanding and contracting my ribcage I managed to loosen the straps enough that I could breathe more easily. This gave me hope. Wherever I was these straps were old, and given time I could work them apart. Although it might take rather a lot of time. I carried on testing my restraints and found that the one around my left wrist was also looser. Unfortunately, I carried my knife in my right sleeve. Fitzroy had been telling me for a long time that I should carry knives on both sides. It was only fair that I should tell him he was right later.

I focused on the here and now. I focused on loosening the belts. I tried to think about anything other than the fact I was bound to an operating table. If I even let my thoughts slide for a moment then

I saw that poor woman, on the mortuary table of the police station. The woman I now knew to have been Griffin's family maid, and of whom he had kept a photograph long after his wife's death.

If only I had brought Jack with me. With his love of chewing leather he would have made quick work of these ties. I tried to think of reasons Fitzroy would have to follow me here, but I couldn't even be certain I remained at Surgeons' Hall. I could have been moved elsewhere while asleep. Not far, certainly. Was there any chance Jack could follow my scent? But it had been raining. Unless I cast my salvation to the whims of fate, it was clear I would have to save myself.

I carried on working at the strap, tensing and releasing muscles, twisting and turning my limbs. It hurt, and I would have burns, even through my clothing, but these minor inconveniences were far better than being caught helpless like a fly in a spider's web.

I was achieving considerable success when I sensed that something had changed. I froze and strained my hearing. Faintly I became aware of breathing, a strange, wet sort of sound as if the person had too much saliva in their mouth. It both repulsed and frightened me. I stayed still. The sound came closer, but whoever it was stayed within the dark. I did not speak. I knew that asking who was there, asking for help, or saying anything would display a vulnerability I had no intention of showing. Instead, I did my best to lie there in dignified silence. However, being bound and splayed upon an operating table it was hard to do.

'You are certain she is awake?' said the voice of Dr Gibbons. 'She is very quiet. You haven't hurt her, have you?'

There was a grunt from the darkness.

'Very well,' said Gibbons, and stepped into the light. He looked down at me. 'I am terribly sorry, my dear. That looks frightfully uncomfortable.' He lowered his voice, 'Don't be afraid.' Then he stood up once more. 'What have I told you about these wretched straps.' He bent lower.

'They are a little uncomfortable,' I said, deliberately pitching my voice low and calm.

'Indeed, and yet still too loose.' I managed not to utter a squeak of dismay as Gibbons bent over me once more and tightened all the straps. All the progress I had made was gone in a moment.

'Can I take it you did not mention to anyone where you were going?' asked Gibbons.

'I left a message for my husband.'

'Ah, yes, Bertram. I looked you up. He has a weak heart, does he not? I imagine you would not have wanted to alarm him. You perhaps told him you were meeting a friend. Nothing else.'

'I have other friends at the hotel, who are not troubled by any disability.'

'Ah, yes, a strange group of people. Obviously, I have read the hotel registry. It is remarkably easy to bribe badly paid staff to supplement their income.'

'The bellboy,' I said.

'Ah, no. He is the nephew of one of my servants. A bright lad. Always happy to earn an extra shilling. Of course, I told him it was for a jape. But to return to your travelling group. It has taken me some time to understand, but I believe you travelled together to Edinburgh for the spiritual benefits of the city. You have already led them to one séance with Madam Arcana. You presented yourself to me as a private detective, but I suspect you to be a charlatan, a parasite, feeding off the grief of the bereaved. Really, I will be doing the world a favour by hastening your exit. For such an attractive and intelligent woman, you have considerably disappointed me.'

I could see how he had come to this conclusion. Barney, fresh from the battlefields; both Hans and Esmeralda had suffered at least one bereavement. I did not know where he was getting his information – possibly words overheard by the hotel staff, but it made a good case. I decided not to deny it at present.

Although I was now completely at his mercy, I felt calmer. I had found my villain, and when he finally came into the light I would see his henchman. I felt huge relief that Griffin was not part of this. If anything happened to me it would prove Griffin was not guilty.

That was a small consolation, but I still had hope I would escape.

'You do not deny my accusation?' said Gibbons.

'I see no need to explain myself to you,' I said.

'Interesting,' said Gibbons. 'Although of immoral character, you are not as afraid as other women have been in your situation. Perhaps you are of an optimistic disposition and still hope to be rescued?'

'Other women,' I said. If he had thrown a bucket of iced water over me I could not have felt more chilled.

'Oh yes. I have needed many. Up and down the country. I need variety, and I am so often called upon to speak at various institutions. You see, the solution to my enigma still eludes me, and so I must continue my research.'

'Solution?' I asked.

The other man emerged from the shadows. He was tall, and thin to the point of emaciation. At first I thought he suffered from a harelip, but then I saw the scar on his cheek, and the small hole that remained at the centre of it. Whatever had happened to him had been done through violence. His hair was dark and matted. He didn't look at me, but held out an operating tunic to Gibbons who stepped into it.

'This is my friend, Nathaniel,' said Gibbons. 'He has suffered much, and of course is looking for healing. My work will in time be able to help him.'

'He is the one who stole from the cadavers at the medical school,' I said.

'Yes, he did do so, and John Griffin had him dismissed for it.' He sighed. 'He was sent to an institution, and you can see what happened to him. Griffin cost him everything. You must know Griffin is a simple-minded individual. He lives very much in the mundane world of flesh and order. We could never have explained our research to him. He would not have had the imagination to appreciate it. Still, his exposure of Nathaniel put us back years. It is only fitting that we will be able to lay our most famous escapades at his door.'

'Does that include me?' I asked. 'I am curious to know how you will blame my butchered body on a man who is currently residing in another country. You Scots do like to think of Scotland as being distinct from England, do you not?'

Instead of answering he swung one of the lights out into what I saw now was a small auditorium. It must have been used for anatomy displays in the earliest days of the medical school. Rows of seats rose up all around rather like some kind of Roman coliseum. Only instead of lions and victims, there were Gibbons and I.

But this was not what shocked me. There sitting three rows above me was Griffin. His eyes were closed, and he was leaning back in his seat.

'Griffin!' I exclaimed involuntarily.

'So you are lovers,' said Gibbons. He rubbed his hands together. 'This becomes better and better. Nathaniel, would you be so good as to wake our guest.'

Chapter Forty-five

The Knives Come Out

Nathaniel strode up the stairs with an odd loping gait. He produced a bottle of smelling salts that he held under Griffin's nose. Griffin started awake. As he moved I realised he too was bound. Not to his chair, but his hands were tied behind him, and I expected they had also tied his feet. He started awake and his eyes met mine. 'Euphemia!' he cried. 'Not you!'

'So you are on first-name terms,' said Gibbons. 'How sweet. I always regretted that Griffin was unable to see us slaughter his wife. There was the issue of revenge for Nathaniel, but there was the smallest chance that as a medical man he might have understood what we were attempting to achieve.'

Griffin swore loudly at Gibbons, and in language I had never heard him use before rained down curses on Gibbons's head. I was proud of both his ire, and also his creative and imaginative use of language. However, Nathaniel cut him short by stuffing a handkerchief in his mouth.

'Thank you,' said Gibbons. 'So unnecessary. Now Mrs Stapleford, I will need to remove items of your clothing.'

Behind him I saw Griffin struggling with his bonds, his eyes desperate. 'But have no fear, I am looking upon your form as a doctor, and of course as a high priest. A zelator, as you may not know, is the highest form of magician on this plane of existence. So again, be assured that your physical form is of no interest to me in its earthly sense.'

'You believe yourself capable of magic? You're insane.'

'You'll forgive me if I don't wash my hands.' He was now in the gown. Nathaniel came back down the stairs carrying a small leather case. 'Ah, my knives. Actually they are scalpels, but I have consecrated them. A neat idea, do you not think, my dear? No one looks for ritual instruments of murder among the tools of an eminent surgeon. Especially one who has been so helpful to the police.'

Slowly things were beginning to connect in my mind. I could also see the unattended Griffin was continuing to struggle hard. 'So the previous professor, the man you replaced, and who wrote about the murder of Griffin's wife?'

'My predecessor in the order. He wrote of my actions as a warning. A warning I was not to try to take his place or he would reveal all. Writing that article was one of the last things he did.'

'Are all the students in the medical school would-be magicians?'

'Hardly,' said Gibbons. He opened the case that Nathaniel held out to him and hovered his fingers above the knives as he considered his choice. 'Only the very best of the anatomists understand the quest. The others, they seek to hold back death in the ordinary ways of things, and so they fail and will always fail.'

'You are trying to achieve immortality?' I asked.

Gibbons picked up a scalpel and moved towards me. He hovered the blade above me. 'What, no scream? You can scream if you wish. There is no one else within earshot, and I do so want to replicate the experience of Griffin's wife for her husband there.'

'Immortality,' I demanded. 'Is this all about saving your own skin?'

My comment struck home. 'It is about raising humanity to the next level!' said Gibbons. His handsome face was suffused red with sudden anger.

'By mutilating women?'

'By uncovering the source of life all women carry within them. Isolating the power that was kept from men since the beginning of time.'

'You want men to be able to give birth?' I said, almost laughing with hysteria.

At this he leaned over me and slashed twice across my waist and abdomen. At this point I almost cried out. Griffin did, uttering as much of a howl as his makeshift gag allowed.

I felt nothing, but I knew that slices from the sharpest knives might not be felt at once.

'Remarkable fortitude,' said Gibbons. He handed the scalpel back to Nathaniel. Then he peeled off the layers of clothes he had sliced through, revealing my upper and lower abdomen. I immediately felt the heat leaving my body. When he turned away, I managed to raise my head and see there was no sign of blood. This was either a coincidence or he was a remarkably precise surgeon.

'And a well-toned stomach too. It will take some time and effort to cut through such a mass of muscle. Unusual in a woman. Never mind, we have plenty of time. Of course, it will be the more painful for you, my dear. I'm afraid I cannot give you a sedative. I cannot risk anything damaging the essence.'

'You gave me chloroform,' I said.

'Ah, yes, but the influence of that is gone now. Your purity is important to me.'

'I'm a married woman. An adulterer according to you. Hardly pure.'

'But you have not yet spent your essence on creating a child.'

'I was pregnant,' I said, 'but I lost the baby.'

'What,' said Gibbons. 'You were pregnant? Think carefully how you answer me. It will not save you, but your death will be longer and more painful if you lie.'

'You can check with Griffin. He knows,' I said. I had no interest in a painful death but every moment I kept him talking might bring help, and as yet he had not noticed that I had begun once again to very slowly loosen the strap on my right wrist.

'Ask him,' said Gibbons. Nathaniel ran up the steps and removed the gag from Griffin, who immediately coughed and choked.

'You bastard, Gibbons. You bastard. You don't know who you have there. If you hurt her the wrath of God will fall on your neck. She has more powerful friends than you can imagine.'

Nathaniel slapped him hard to stop him talking. 'Just answer the question!'

'Powerful friends?' Gibbons asked me. 'Really? And yet you do not threaten me with them. But your lover does?'

There was the sound of another slap. 'Tell him!'

'Yes, she has been pregnant.'

'Damn it,' said Gibbons. 'She's no use to me.' He tore off his gown. 'You have squandered your life-giving essence, Mrs Stapleford, and lost an opportunity to be of use to change the very essence of human nature. You are a great disappointment to me.'

'I'll try to live with that,' I said. The strap over my right wrist was becoming looser. I needed only a little more time. Time and a significant degree of luck.

Gibbons straightened his tie. 'Oh no, my dear, you won't be living with it. You'll be dying with it. You are of no use to me, but Nathaniel is most out of practice. He can rehearse our next investigation on you.'

'Your friend from the insane asylum?' I said, and it took all my willpower not to let my voice shake.

'You even knew that. I see I was wise to remove you from the equation. It will be blamed on your lover, Griffin. In case you were wondering.'

'Griffin isn't my lover, and I am not a detective or a spiritualist leader. I came here with a team to investigate Megan Griffin's death.'

'And yet you are no detective?'

'I work for the government. As does John Griffin now. How else do you think he escaped the noose when you framed him for his wife's murder.'

'I blamed it on a sentimental judge. Nathaniel, go and ask Griffin if they work for the government. No need to be gentle.'

Nathaniel repeated the process of ungagging Griffin, but this time he punched him in the head. It was a vicious blow, but Griffin knew enough to move his head with the impact, and I hoped Nathaniel, with his skeletal frame, would not be able to deliver much force. Griffin confirmed that we worked for the government, and were investigating his wife's death.

Gibbons gestured to Nathaniel to re-gag him. Gibbons had now donned a coat, and was pulling on leather gloves. 'I suspect you are the brains of the pair,' he said, looming over me. 'I assume it was the death of Griffin's maid that opened everything up again. A shame and an opportunity. Her organ is proving most interesting. I was giving a talk in London. I had no intention . . . but I always carry my knives.'

'Did you think she had seen you kill Megan?' I asked.

'Clever,' said Gibbons. 'I thought it unlikely but when we met on the train – myself stumbling into a third-class carriage as I had barely made the train – her eyes betrayed recognition. I really had no choice but to kill her, so I thought I might as well make use of her. I had my medical bag with me. It was easy enough. I drugged her enough to accompany me to first class, and of course no one there would disturb us.'

'It was pure chance you met her again?'

'Fate. I had heard Griffin was at large in London once more, so copying the old procedure exactly I hoped to lay the blame on him.'

'Did Bloom help you kill Megan?'

'Oh yes, sobbing all the time like a child. But he wanted to ascend to a higher level in our society, so it was required. Did Griffin tell you we fed her liver to his dog? Kept the animal busy.'

I retched. 'You are disgusting,' I said. 'And you will be found. Whatever happens to me my colleagues will find you, and if you have harmed Griffin or me, your death will not be easy. We don't have to play by police rules.'

'Such threats are beneath you,' said Gibbons. 'But I consider myself warned. I think I shall go away for a little while. Nathaniel, attend to the lady and then kill Griffin. Ensure you clean up after yourself. This theatre is rarely used, but care is essential. Griffin's must look like a suicide.'

Gibbons picked up his hat from beyond the shadows, and placed it on his head. 'Such a pity,' he said, looking down at me, 'I would have enjoyed hearing you scream.'

I didn't beg him to stay. What would have been the point? Nathaniel made his way down from Griffin. He trod hard enough to make each step creak. He moved closer and closer to me, the light increasing his shadow into stick-thin giant. He looked down at me, and said in his wet, lisping voice, 'I like that you're pretty. I like my specimens to be good.'

'What happened to your face?'

'A fight. A man with a knife in the asylum. But when we find the essence I will be restored. The essence of life will be able to cure anything.'

'This essence is in all women?' I asked, pulling harder at my strap. It had yet to yield.

Nathaniel nodded. 'All the ones who have yet to give birth. We thought we might be able to steal it through sexual congress, but all we did was give the women our strength.'

'So this is science?'

'Ha,' said Nathaniel, 'this is magic and science. The laws of the universe unlocked.'

'Will you use magic on me?' Almost there.

'No point. You are useless to us. Spoiled. I must begin or we risk being found. I must obey the professor, and practise well. I shall need to take my time. I must remove the organ intact.'

He went to the table and I heard him rummage through metallic objects. He was choosing his scalpel. I heard Griffin moan through his gag. He was trying to shout for help. I wondered he could not break his bonds, or perhaps he was trying to. The situation must be almost horrifically overwhelming for him.

It wasn't too good for me either.

Nathaniel came back. He held up his scalpel so it glinted in the light. Then he bent to do his work. As he did so I pulled my arm free, and plunged my knife into his neck.

Despite the limitation of my movement I was able to bury it to the hilt. This was some justice for all the women this monster had cut up before. I thought of them as I pushed the knife deep into his skin, twisting it, before he tore himself away. He pulled out the knife, but it was no use. My aim had been true, and his life blood gushed out over the theatre floor, falling first like pattering rain and then like the killing deluge it was. It did not take long for him to fall lifeless to the floor.

Chapter Forty-six

An Ending

Griffin and I were in a cab racing to the railway station.

'Are you certain you can do this?' I asked Griffin. The man was ashen. Sitting next to him, I could feel he was shaking ever so slightly. He needed warmth, but I had his coat to disguise my torn clothing.

'I will help you catch him,' said Griffin, 'if it is the last thing I do.' His teeth chattered as he spoke.

I put a hand over his. 'Do not believe all he said. Whatever else the man was he was a sadist, and clearly wanted to distress you.'

'And her,' said Griffin.

'You had a picture of the maid in your shoe,' I said to distract him. I needed his help stopping Gibbons. The station was too large for me to ensure I caught him on my own. That is if he had gone there, but after I had freed myself, which had taken far too long, I freed Griffin and we decided if he wanted to escape pursuit a train was his best bet.

'I should have known I could keep nothing safe around spies.'

'Indeed, it was silly of you to think so.'

'When Megan began being afraid of everything our maid would often sit with her. She went above her normal duties to be of service to us. So one day when Megan's mother had come to town, and had taken her out, I took the maid on an outing. Just to say thank you for all she had done. It was a good day for both of us away from the worry. One of those street photographers snapped our picture, and I bought one for both of us. It was no more than a breath of happiness in what had become a stressful situation.'

'So you weren't . . .?'

'No, I never thought of her like that. Besides, she had a beau, Mathew. They were saving to be married. I wonder if they ever did get married. I don't think I could ever face Mathew. It's all—'

'No,' I said sternly. 'None of this is your fault. Gibbons is a madman.'

The cab stopped. I turned the door handle without waiting for any help. 'And we must stop him before he harms more women.'

Griffin gave me a grim-faced nod, and we stepped out into a day that had become incongruously sunny. We ran down the steps into the station. Our haste cleared a path for us. As we emerged into the station the sunshine streamed through the glass roof casting wide shafts of light across the platforms and the waiting trains. Standing in the centre of one of these beams, scanning the scene around him like a captain on his ship, stood Fitzroy. I didn't hesitate; I ran over to him.

His face registered relief as soon as he saw me, and his habitual frown vanished. He caught my hands as I came up to him.

'Thank goodness. What happened? Griffin is gone,' he said. Then he registered the coat I was wearing. Before he spoke I answered.

'Yes, this is Griffin's coat. He is a little way behind me. He is shaken by what we have seen, but he is coping.'

'What is this?' he said sharply, turning my bloodstained right wrist.

'Not mine,' I said. 'But time is important. Gibbons was the killer and he is here, we believe, trying to flee.'

'For both women?'

'Yes, countless others and almost myself.'

A shutter came down over Fitzroy's face. His eyes hardened to flint. 'I have Barnabas with me.'

He was interrupted by Griffin catching up with us. He was panting, pale and sweating. 'He's on platform six. He didn't see me.'

Fitzroy took off his hat, turned it over it in his hands and replaced it. Much in the manner of a gentleman thinking about this next move. But I knew it was a signal to Barney to join us.

'Can you manage a four-man hunt?' Fitzroy said to Griffin. 'Alice says you have suffered.'

'No more than she has,' said Griffin. 'I remember the pattern.' He paused. 'I want this man dead.'

'We must attempt to capture him,' said Fitzroy. 'But he will hang. There is no doubt.'

Griffin nodded. Barney arrived, red-faced from running. 'Four-man hunt,' he said to Barney, and designated our quarters to us. We moved off as one. I am not generally fantastical in these situations, but it seemed to me as we walked on we did so more than purposefully, we did so in an almost animal-like way – like wolves going on a hunt. All of us were determined to catch this prey.

In a public place it is important not to put the public at risk. We may work for the Crown, but ultimately the aim of the Crown is to preserve the peace and safety of its citizens. We knew where Gibbons was. We were walking rather than running. I had forgotten myself and run to Fitzroy, but by catching my hands he had made us look like a couple reunited.

Now, our job was to approach Gibbons from all directions, the edges of the platform allowing, and trap him in the centre of our group. We needed to mingle with the crowd and not draw attention to ourselves. Gibbons should be surrounded before he knew it. The hope was then he would come with us without physical resistance. For all I knew Fitzroy had a gun under his coat. However, he would be loath to even display it in a public place. The problem was while no train stood at six, as soon as one arrived, getting Gibbons off a train, even a stationary one, became much more of a problem. It would be much more of a public scene. I wondered if Fitzroy had asked for assistance from Sutherland in his search for Griffin and me. My path took me by the departure board. I could spare no more than a glance, but I saw that a train was due into platform six in three minutes. My experience of Scottish trains told me it was liable to be on time if not early.

I quickened my pace. Fitzroy, who was on my diagonal, flickered a look at me and sped up. I could only hope the others would do so. Except it was Fitzroy and I who were partnered on the square, and would be the first to notice each other's movements. Griffin and Barney should check us less frequently, but they were both less skilled. Fitzroy and I had taken the dominant line.

All these thoughts were passing through my head at speed. I caught sight of Gibbons standing by the platform. He had a small valise in his hand. Turned out as impeccably as ever, he was shuffling from foot to foot, and he kept glancing around. I lowered my head, and pulled up the collar of Griffin's coat. I went faster. Fitzroy must have spotted Gibbons too. He gave us the signal to switch to a semicircle formation. We did so, and closed in on our prey.

At the last minute Gibbons looked over and met my eyes. He scanned the platform, and we were so close there was no possibility he would not spot our formation. I darted forward before he could act. From the tunnel we heard the sound of a train whistle. Gibbons turned, looked at me. Then abandoning his valise he leaped down on to the track and ran for the next platform. The train emerged from the tunnel. Braking for the platform, it still had significant speed and weight. Could I make it? I had to try. I couldn't let him get away. I lurched forward, but I was pulled roughly back by an arm around my waist. 'Let him go,' said Fitzroy 'It's cleaner this way. We keep it in the shadows.'

'Gibbons,' called Fitzroy. The man, still running, turned to look behind and tripped. He went down. He was up again like a flash, but it was enough.

The train ploughed into him.

Gibbons was gone.

Behind us, I heard a beast-like howl. It was Barney.

Epilogue

After we had returned to the hotel, having left the police to deal with a terrible accident, Griffin gave poor Barney a sedative powder. Fitzroy arranged for a room for the two of them, and took me off to ours, where he insisted I took a bath, and then lay down for a rest. Of course because we were professionals I gave him a brief report of what had happened. I heard him leave the room while I was in the bath.

I was awoken later to singing in the bathroom. Fitzroy appeared in the doorway, washed and dressed. 'I have a private table for us for dinner.'

I sat up sleepily and observed that the floor appeared to be a riot of feathers.

'What on earth is that mess on the hearthrug?' I asked.

'The remains of Esmeralda's hat,' said Fitzroy. 'I thought Jack deserved a treat too. Now, Barney and Griffin will join us. Get dressed. I'll see you downstairs in fifteen minutes.'

Most women could not ready themselves and dress for dinner in such time, but I had practice, and my hair was still shorter than most women's.

'Very nice,' said Fitzroy appreciatively when I joined the others. Over dinner, he explained he had looked up the register for doctors of Griffin's year, and contacted a peer who had been able to tell him about Nathaniel Warburton.

'I never knew doctors had a register,' I said.

'No reason you should,' he said. 'When I arrived back at the hotel and there was no sign of you or Griffin, I was not immediately concerned. I read your note, but I was uncomfortable at the lack of detail. It seemed unlike you. When I checked with the station that Griffin's train had arrived, and we had no sign of him, I took Barney with me to search for you both. It was not a good lead, but it was the best I had. I consigned Esmeralda to Hans's care, having explained in front of her what she was. I left them to it. I imagine one way or another they will sort out their situation. There was no way I was bringing Hans with me. He is not at all trained. I am sorry I had to bring you, Willoughby. If I had suspected what might occur . . .'

'I am deeply embarrassed,' said Barney. 'I have no memory of what happened after the train . . . it's why I was invalided out.' He looked at me. 'I become useless under situations of high stress. Catatonic is the word the doctors used.'

'I have been at the front,' said Fitzroy. 'There is no shame after what you endured.'

Then he raised a glass. 'To a job well done, and an evil man removed from society.'

We all drank gladly.

Later when we retired to our room I broached the subject of going home for Christmas.

'Of course you must,' said Fitzroy. 'What's more the rest of us are coming too.'

'The rest of us?!'

Jack gave a happy little woof of agreement.

We hope you have enjoyed reading *A Death of a Dead Man*.

For further information about Caroline Dunford's Euphemia Martins mysteries and to find out all about Caroline's latest Word War II series, featuring Euphemia's perceptive daughter Hope Stapleford, as well as to read exclusive extracts from Fitzroy's private diary visit: caroline-dunford.squarespace.com.

And if you'd like to receive the Euphemia and Hope monthly newsletter please email carolinedunfordauthor@gmail.com with your request.